Praise for t

Boots Un...

Jodi Thomas

"A masterful storyteller."
—Catherine Anderson, *New York Times* bestselling author

"Exactly the kind of heart-wrenching, emotional story one has come to expect from Jodi Thomas."
—Debbie Macomber, #1 *New York Times* bestselling author

Jo Goodman

"Goodman's elegant and wryly written style ensures . . . a perfect treat for readers who enjoy smart, sensual love stories."
—*Booklist*

"Goodman knows how to turn up the heat."
—*Publishers Weekly*

Kaki Warner

"She is a fine talent."
—*RT Book Reviews*

"Without a doubt, Kaki Warner is a writer to watch. . . . She's definitely an addition to my must-buy authors list."
—*All About Romance*

Alison Kent

"Alison Kent delivers up sizzles and thrills."
—Tess Gerritsen, *New York Times* bestselling author

"One of my writing idols—consistently awesome, always on my auto buy list!"
—Lauren Dane, *USA Today* bestselling author

Boots Under Her Bed

JODI THOMAS

JO GOODMAN

KAKI WARNER

ALISON KENT

BERKLEY BOOKS, NEW YORK

THE BERKLEY PUBLISHING GROUP
Published by the Penguin Group
Penguin Group (USA) LLC
375 Hudson Street, New York, New York 10014

USA • Canada • UK • Ireland • Australia • New Zealand • India • South Africa • China

penguin.com

A Penguin Random House Company

BOOTS UNDER HER BED

A Berkley Book / published by arrangement with the authors

For information, address: The Berkley Publishing Group,
a division of Penguin Group (USA) LLC,
375 Hudson Street, New York, New York 10014.

ISBN: 978-0-425-26784-4

PUBLISHING HISTORY
Berkley mass-market edition / January 2014

PRINTED IN THE UNITED STATES OF AMERICA

10 9 8 7 6 5 4 3 2 1

Cover art: Guy by Claudio Marinesco; metal sign on
wood © caesart / Shutterstock; background © frescomovie / Shutterstock;
background © Paul B. Moore / Shutterstock; buckle by Shutterstock.
Cover design by George Long.
Interior text design by Kelly Lipovich.

Contents

CRAZY CALLIE

Jodi Thomas

Chapter 1

January 27, 1882

THE wind howled through the dusty streets of Shallow Creek like a pack of hungry coyotes running free. A full moon hung amid wispy gray clouds promising rain, but no one in town seemed to notice.

Callie Anne Cramer pulled her buckboard behind a row of seedy saloons and began her shopping. She had one hour until dawn . . . until her stepfather noticed her disappearance . . . and she planned to change her future by then.

"This is the dumbest idea you've come up with," Lindsey Baxter, Callie's only friend, whined. "I thought when you went away to school in Iowa to study to be a horse doctor was dumb, but this beats that plan."

Callie Anne's glare missed its mark in the darkness. "I had no choice then—it was the only place where I could get the education I needed—and I have no choice now, so stop complaining and help me search. You're the only one I can trust."

"Lucky me," Lindsey answered in a scratchy whisper. She might be Callie Anne's age, but her voice had the low roughness of an aging smoker. It somehow matched her dark hair and gray eyes. "I could have been sleeping, but instead I'm trolling the alley of every bar in town looking for a husband for my only friend. Makes sense. Nice night to be out husband hunting."

Callie Anne fought down panic. "This is my last option. Howard has made sure I don't have the money to run and he's spread enough rumors about me that no one would believe me sane. So start looking for the love of my life. Find a tall one if you can. I don't want to look down at my husband for the rest of my life. Or until he gets smart and runs."

"You want me to smell him? I'm guessing if he doesn't smell like a horse, you're not interested. Too bad you couldn't marry one of those animals you love so much. Your stepfather says you sleep more in the barn than you do in the house."

Callie laughed. "The company's better in the barn."

The first man they passed was throwing up; the second smelled so bad she didn't want to get close enough to talk to him. The third, a cowhand, from the look of his clothes, was slumped over, passed out against the outhouse wall. He looked promising, but when she swung the lantern by his head, she saw that he had to be twice her age, maybe more.

"The pickings are pretty poor tonight," Lindsey whispered. "Maybe we should try another plan or lower our standards."

"All I'm asking is he's single, breathing, and taller than

me. Don't think I can go much lower. And I may not have another night. Howard's been making threats, bragging that he'll have me gone off my land before spring."

The buckboard rattled past a wooden porch at the back of the biggest bar in town.

"What you doing, Crazy Callie?" Plain Edna called as she walked out the Watering Hole Saloon's back door. She leaned over the railing, a thin cigar hanging off her red lip as she stared in open curiosity. The tattered feather she wore in her hair drooped over one eye, giving her a pirate's gawk. "That our old-maid schoolteacher, Miss Lindsey Baxter, with you? If she's looking for her pa, he left hours ago, sober enough to walk."

Callie didn't defend her sanity or her friend's state of marriage. It would have been no use. "We're looking for a husband for me. Anyone will do, as long as he's drunk enough to marry me. I can't stop to talk tonight, Edna. I only got an hour or so before dawn. Lindsey's riding along to help me shop."

Plain Edna laughed. "You won't find a fit husband out here. Besides, what would you do with a man if you had one? You've spent most of the time since your bosom filled out trying to avoid marriage." Plain Edna blew a ghost white ring of smoke. "Now, why would you be in an all-fired hurry tonight?"

Another barmaid joined her rouged-up friend on break. Callie didn't know the new working girl's name, but she'd seen her in town. Everyone in Shallow Creek knew one another if only by sight.

The new girl had long red hair nature hadn't provided, and a dress that looked like it was made from string doilies. When she leaned over the rail, her wares showed creamy white in the moonlight. In daylight, on the main street, neither of the soiled doves would have spoken to Callie, but here among the garbage and the drunks, all seemed equal. Callie's stepfather had sent her often enough to collect drunk ranch hands that she knew the curve of the alley.

"Howdy, ladies," Red shouted. "What you doing out here this late?"

Callie didn't want to talk to any strangers. She and Lindsey had gone to school with Plain Edna so they trusted her, but this girl might spread stories. Callie had learned the hard way how much damage gossip could do. Talking got her into this mess in the first place. Too much talking and not enough acting.

The redhead tossed her cigarette in the alley and went back in as if bored.

Plain Edna moved down the steps and stood close to the wagon. "Tell me how I can help. You ain't got much time. Red's probably in there telling Quentin McCaffree you're out here right now." She pulled her shawl around her, making her look almost presentable.

"I have to get married or my stepfather is going to send me off to the asylum in Austin. I saw the paperwork on his desk when I went over to help Mamie clean the main house." Callie fought back tears. Howard Thornville had been trying to marry her off since her mother died six years before. He wanted her hitched, not to a man who'd stay, but to someone who'd take her away.

Plain Edna snorted as she walked along with the wagon. "Didn't you try getting married once? I heard tell you got all the way to the church, and when Thornville went to walk you down the aisle, you'd cut your dress into tiny squares." She laughed loud with her mouth open. "That was about the time folks started thinking you crazy. Ever'one I meet swears they saw you heading home in your drawers."

Callie shrugged. At the time it seemed the only thing that would stop the wedding her stepfather had arranged.

She'd only been fifteen and her mother had died that winter. The husband-to-be was a middle-aged peddler who'd been paid a hundred dollars to take her with him. When Callie asked where they were going, he'd said simply, "Never you mind, girl. You're going with me. That's all you need to know."

That had been the final insult. She'd done the only thing she could think of while locked in the preacher's tiny office. She'd cut up the dress her stepfather paid twenty dollars for into tiny squares.

A year later he tried to get her to marry the neighbor's half-wit son. She was sixteen by then, and the groom was too shy to talk to her. Both parents agreed to give the newlyweds a worthless strip of land between the two ranches. The kid was a likable enough boy when he wasn't nervous, but he had the strange habit of trying to set fire to everything. She objected to the wedding when she smelled her hair burning. Her stepfather said she'd have to marry him anyway, since all young couples have their problems.

Callie didn't say another word, but that night, at their engagement party, she took him behind the barn and told him she was a witch born at midnight and destined to wash in blood. She swore, if he told anyone, she'd make his tongue swell to the size of a horse's tongue and his ankles snap like twigs.

The next morning, he refused to marry her and offered no reason. In fact, word was, he didn't open his mouth for three weeks.

Thornville gave up for a few years, resigned to the probability of being stuck with her. When she asked to go to Iowa to study veterinary medicine, he gladly paid the tuition and board, thinking she'd find someone up there and never come back. Then for two years, while she was there, he refused to send extra money for her to come home for a visit.

When she finally returned and started treating every hurt animal in the county, he left her alone in the little house on the edge of the ranch.

Then the stories started about how she talked to squirrels and practiced witchcraft with the blood of some of her patients. Thornville didn't like having a crazy stepdaughter, but as long as she left him alone to run the ranch, he decided to ignore her. She'd stay at her little cottage in the woods, and he'd live in the big ranch house.

At about the time Callie turned twenty, a widow, Charlotte Van Buren, moved to town and Callie's stepfather took up courting. Charlotte wouldn't consider being his wife as long as he had the crazy daughter running around. So Howard took up the cause to get rid of his too-tall, too-crazy stepdaughter and all her animals.

He brought several prospective husbands around, but Callie quickly told them all that she was already engaged to a lumberjack who wouldn't be too happy when he returned to discover someone pestering her.

When one cowboy repeated her story to her stepfather, Thornville told the whole town she'd moved another step up the ladder of crazy, which got rid of the husband prospects faster than an invisible fiancé.

The widow backed Howard up with stories of finding Callie talking to a stray dog as if he might answer. There were even whispers in town about how Callie danced in the moonlight with birds. By the time Callie turned twenty-one, everyone but Lindsey Baxter shook their heads when she passed. The little schoolteacher hung on to their friendship.

"Climb down and lie next to that one." Lindsey, beside her, broke into Callie's thoughts. "See if he's tall enough."

"He's not," she answered, fighting down panic.

"Last month, Thornville turned reckless from pining

after Mrs. Charlotte," Callie Anne whispered as they moved on down the alley.

"It seemed the widow demanded that I be gone before she'd let him close enough to see if they were suited for one another. Bottled-up longing got the better of him the last snowy morning. He dropped by my place to check on a horse one of his men had brought over half-dead. Howard found me in the barn feeding my animals, and in a rage, he hit me with a shovel. He said it was an accident but I tumbled out of the loft faster than a falling star."

Plain Edna shook her head. "I've been hit like that, by accident, you know, and it hurts just the same."

"You should have gone to the sheriff," Lindsey chimed in.

Callie shook her head. "It would have been my word against his. No one would believe me. When Howard looked down and saw I was only bruised, he decided to tell everyone I'd tried to commit suicide. He went right to town and sorrowfully admitted he could no longer handle me even though he couldn't have loved me more if I were his own."

"Thornville wants you gone," Plain Edna said. "Suicide or insane, either one would make the ranch his. Since he'd been married to your mother for two years, then put up with you for six more, he told everyone in the bar straight-out that he figured he deserved all the ranch, including the little cottage at the far corner."

Callie didn't argue. "I know, and most folks agree with him. He's built the ranch up since he's been there. I'll give him that."

"That doesn't matter," Lindsey added, patting Callie's hand. "It's legally yours, Callie."

"There's one." Plain Edna ran ahead of them in the alley. "He's young, not more than seventeen or eighteen. This is his first big drunk and he turned mean and loud until Quentin knocked some sense in him with a chair." She giggled with excitement. "Serve the kid right to wake up married to you, Callie."

Lindsey climbed out of the wagon. "Edna, this isn't funny. We're serious here. Callie's running out of time. Do you think this one's tall enough?"

Plain Edna shook her head. "Everyone's tall to me."

"Never mind, ladies," Callie said. "He's not the right one."

Callie Anne put her mind to the task at hand. Maybe everyone was right about her; a thought did seem to wander down one pig trail after another in her brain. Maybe she was crazy for loving animals more than people, but in her life she'd been hurt far more by people.

For once she had to do something right, and tricking a kid into marriage wasn't right. She was running out of time. Her grandparents' and parents' graves were on that ranch, and she wouldn't give it up without a fight. She couldn't leave and she couldn't stay with her stepfather. If he forced her to go, then half, maybe more, of her patients in her barn would be put down, or, worse, Thornville would simply let them starve.

"Over there is one!" Plain Edna yelled. "He passed out a few hours ago, and Quentin brought him out here to sleep it off. He's been drinking for three days."

Callie climbed down from the wagon and held the lantern high. The man sleeping facedown in the dirt was long and lean, with clothes that looked store-bought. She grabbed his hair so the light could shine on a dirty face in need of a shave. "What's wrong with him?"

Edna shrugged. "Hear tell he's a lawyer. They're usually the noisiest drunks in the world, but this fellow just sat and drank. Didn't even want any company to help him drown his sorrows."

Other than the dirt, Callie looked for what else might

be wrong with him. He looked to be in his twenties and had curly hair as dark as coal.

Edna laughed. "I'm guessing he'll marry you. I heard he came all the way from Virginia to marry Dorothy Trimble and she ain't half as pretty as you, Callie Anne, even if she is in her right mind."

"But Dorothy married last year." Callie stared down at the man, feeling sorry for him. Dorothy could never pass geology in school because she thought the center of the world was circling her feet. "In church last Sunday, I noticed Dorothy's baby must be due soon."

"I know. Too bad this fellow didn't know that before he got on the train," Edna said. "Seems they met when her daddy sent her back east to visit relatives and they been writing for three years. She must have forgot to add the fact she married in her letters."

"It was so sad," Lindsey chimed in. "One of my students told me about him. Lovers never to be united even after he traveled halfway across the country. Dorothy must have been his world for him to come here, and she tossed him out like he was nothing when he came knocking. The neighbors for half a block heard her yelling at him."

The barmaid agreed with a sigh. "He said she told him he was no more than a paper man to her, not real flesh and blood. He said she tossed his letters at him and told him to go away."

Lindsey patted the drunk's back. "Many a man has been driven to drink by a hard-hearted woman."

"I'll take him." Callie made up her mind. "Help me get him in the wagon."

All three women lifted the stranger into the wagon bed, only banging his head twice against the tailgate. Callie figured she'd patch him up if need be. After all, doctoring a man couldn't be that different from patching up a horse.

Quentin, the saloon's bartender, stepped out onto the back porch to tell Edna they were closing.

When he asked what the ladies were doing, Lindsey said simply, "We're picking up Callie Anne's groom and heading for the church. You want to come along as a witness?"

To everyone's surprise, Quentin pulled off his apron and hopped on the back of the wagon. "Why not," he said, never taking his eyes off Lindsey. "It'll probably be the only wedding I ever see."

"How about you coming along?" Callie Anne asked Edna to be polite.

Plain Edna shook her head. "No, it wouldn't do to have me along, but thanks for asking."

Callie Anne smiled and waved good-bye. It didn't seem so very long ago when she and Edna and Lindsey had played together. Now Edna wouldn't allow herself to be seen with them for fear of hurting their reputations, or what little they had left. Everyone thought Callie was crazy and Lindsey dressed and acted like the old-maid schoolteacher she'd become. It seemed to Callie that knowing Edna wouldn't hurt them.

The only one who remained the same was Quentin. He'd grown up next door to Lindsey and seemed to think of himself as her personal guardian though he never talked to her.

Callie Anne smiled. Somehow, Quentin must think Lindsey was in danger tonight for he was coming along to the wedding.

Chapter 2

A COLD dawn broke on the horizon when Callie Anne turned the buckboard toward the preacher's house. She knew she was about to step through a door that might close behind her. There was no going back, but marrying a stranger had to be better than being afraid to sleep at night. In the best of times, Howard Thornville couldn't be considered much of a father, and this wasn't the best of times. He'd sweet-talked her newly widowed mother into marrying him and then never wasted another kind word on her.

Quentin, Lindsey's silent guardian, jumped out of the wagon and tied off the reins while Callie climbed into the back. She shook the drunk as hard as she could, wishing she'd asked Edna his name.

After a few slaps, he came around and jerked free of her long enough to throw up. She didn't miss the fact that he was polite enough to turn away, then wiped his mouth on a white handkerchief before he faced her.

"I'm sorry, miss," he mumbled.

She handed him a canteen. "What's your name?"

"Morgan," he answered before taking a long drink.

She couldn't see much, just a silhouette, but he looked normal enough. "You want to get married?"

Her words sobered him.

She hurried on. "I'm Callie Anne Cramer. I own a ranch a few miles from here. I read in a law book that my step-father can have me committed for being insane and take over my place, but if I'm married, my husband would have to sign the papers 'cause he'd be the next of kin."

"I'm sorry, miss." The drunk sounded like he meant it. "I'm not licensed to practice law in Texas." He dug long fingers through his midnight hair. "However, it would be my educated guess that you are correct. If you have no other relatives, of course."

"I don't need a lawyer. I need a relative. A husband, to be exact." She swallowed hard. "A husband who'll swear not to have me committed or try to kill me. That's all I'm asking, mister."

He raised an eyebrow. "Are you crazy?"

"It's a strong possibility." She'd been told it so much she couldn't flat-out deny it. "But if you'll marry me and stay around long enough for me to sell half my cattle this spring, I'll give you the money from the sale for your service and we'll call it even."

She couldn't tell if he was thinking about her offer or about to pass out so she added, "It's not like you got a better offer." She could see well enough in the dawn light to tell his clothes were not fancy and his shoes were worn. If he'd had any money left, Quentin would have put him in one of the rooms upstairs when he passed out and not in the alley.

"The money will be enough to get you a fresh start anywhere you want to go." If he said no, she saw only one option left. She'd have to run and, if she did, Thornville would win. He'd have the ranch.

While Morgan thought her offer over, Quentin helped Lindsey down from the wagon. The bartender always showed a gentle touch with the little schoolteacher, like she was breakable.

Her one friend stood beside Callie Anne as she always had. Miss Lindsey Baxter might not be two years out of her teens, but she straightened as if she were a witness on the stand. "I'm her friend, Mr. Morgan, and, though she does do a few strange things from time to time, she's not insane. I've never known her to give her word and not keep it."

Morgan looked like he was trying to focus.

"I'd ask nothing from you, mister, except to stand as my husband and help me get the cattle to market. The marriage has to be real. I'm not asking for you to lie. It would need to stand up in court if my stepfather decides to fight." She jumped from the wagon bed and waited for him to follow. He was too big to drag in to the preacher, and she'd said all she could to convince him.

Slowly, like a man lowering into quicksand, he slid from the wagon and stood; he was almost a head taller than her.

Quentin moved toward him to offer help, but Morgan held up his hand and faced Callie Anne.

"I'll marry you," Morgan said with only a hint of a slur. "Only don't say anything about it being a bargain. As far as everyone in this town knows I married you for love, and you are the woman who loves me back."

She tried to get a good look at the man. He sounded strange, talking of love and all, but he did seem to be sobering some. He had his own reasons, and she'd not pry. "Fair enough, we marry for love." She shook his hand and added, "But you got to swear you won't put me in the nuthouse or hit me."

"I swear."

"And the ranch is mine when you leave. All mine, like my real father meant it to be. You'll lay no claim to it."

"I swear. When this is over I can think of nothing that would make me stay here. When our marriage is finished, I'll never step foot in this state again, and Shallow Creek can dry up and blow away."

She waited while he washed up at the preacher's well. Quentin and Lindsey moved on to wake the old man and his wife. Callie hadn't seen the retired preacher since he'd said the words over her mother's grave. He was a good man, who helped out with hurry-up weddings and sudden burials. The only other thing she remembered about the man was that his wife never stopped talking. Most of the time she didn't seem to need an audience, she just rattled on. Callie Anne had no doubt that, by noon, everyone in town would know about her dawn wedding.

Morgan's eyes were still red when he returned from the well. He wasn't a man people would think of as handsome, but she thought he had strong solid features beneath his week-old beard.

"I'm ready," he said as he offered her his arm.

"You sure?" The weight of what she was about to do settled over her as she felt the strength in his arm.

"Why not?" He smiled, with no humor reaching his eyes. "I've got nowhere else to go, lady, and nothing else to do. The road I thought I was following ended, so any path seems preferable to standing still."

They walked to the front door, where Lindsey and Quentin waited as if they were part of the wedding procession.

Preacher Winters greeted them warmly and showed them into his dusty parlor. Spiderwebs hung in the corners like fragile lace over faded furniture.

While his wife rushed around getting everything

ready, Winters asked them to fill out the paperwork. Her groom's hand shook slightly as he took the pen, but his writing was bold.

The preacher's wife hurried Callie and Lindsey off to the hallway, explaining that they had to wait until the music started before coming back in. Callie looked down at her jeans and oversized shirt. She wasn't even marrying in a dress. Even the drunk groom looked better than she did.

Callie forced herself not to look at him. She might be ruining his life, but he didn't seem to care one way or the other.

"The man has a dead look in his eyes," Lindsey whispered. "You know, like he's about to step in front of a herd of running horses and doesn't even care. Maybe we should go back and look through the pickings again now that it's light."

"No. He'll do." He was tall and not scary to look at. That was enough. She wasn't planning to spend the rest of her life with him, just a few months. As the piano clanked, Callie pulled Lindsey along. "The sooner we get this over with the better."

Lindsey smoothed her hand over Callie Anne's unruly blond curls and smiled. "I wish you happiness and love," she whispered. "It's about time some came your way."

"I'll settle for peace," Callie Anne answered. "I don't believe I was meant to be loved." She wouldn't think of him as anything more than her one chance. This stranger would never matter more to her than that.

Yet, when she stepped next to her new husband, she fought back the urge to run. This was the last option. Her last chance.

When she turned slightly and saw Morgan standing at attention beside her, she couldn't help but wonder if this wasn't his last chance also.

Chapter 3

LUKE Morgan tried hard to focus. For three days he'd drunk enough to keep reality at bay, but he knew this wasn't a dream. Not that it mattered all that much. He'd take a dream over the reality of his life.

Tiny shards of sunlight blinked through the lace curtains of the little room he stood in. His eyes and throat burned as he fought down the urge to vomit again. Concentrating on the thin slices of morning light, Luke remembered the shafts of light that would sparkle into the tunnels when he walked out of the mine after work. If he were lucky and nothing went wrong, he'd finish his shift underground and be up in time to see the sunset. For a few moments there would be light in the world, but for three years he'd felt like he lived in darkness. Mining all day and studying as late into the night as he could, with his only day off spent sleeping to catch up so he could work the next six days and study every night.

The past three years had passed like one long nightmare.

The same never-ending schedule, the same meals, the same darkness. The only thing that kept him going was a letter from Texas now and then, from a girl he'd met once. She was waiting for him to become a lawyer and come get her. She'd promised they would both start their life together, and all the work and study and loneliness would be worth it.

Only she hadn't waited. The last year the letters had grown short, notes really, and far between. He should have known not to come.

Luke glanced over his shoulder at the tall woman standing in the foyer looking like she was waiting for sentencing. Her hair curled around her head like a halo. She was far too pretty to be marrying a drunk she'd picked up in an alley, but judging from her tattered clothes she must be on hard times.

He remembered how Dorothy Trimble had called him a paper man. Maybe he could be some help to this woman. Maybe he could prove Dorothy wrong, and she'd wish she had waited for him.

The room started spinning as the worst piano playing he'd ever heard filled the air. Luke closed his eyes and swore he'd be the man Miss Sunshine needed or he'd die trying.

He wasn't a paper man. He deserved to have someone tell him she loved him. It might be the only way the darkness wouldn't swallow him whole.

Chapter 4

TO Callie's surprise when the preacher asked for a ring, Morgan pulled one from his pocket and slipped it on her finger. It was a delicate weave of thin gold and silver bands. She knew, without asking him, that he'd had it made for another. She promised herself she'd give it back to him when he left.

They both said what Preacher Winters told them to say. Lindsey cried softly and Quentin shuffled behind them. Everyone seemed to take a long breath when Mrs. Winters played the final march and they could leave the parlor.

Lindsey paid the preacher with the bill Callie had given her without anyone else noticing. When her gaze met that of her best friend, Callie knew Lindsey still wasn't sold on this wild idea of marrying, but as always, she'd stood beside her friend. "Thank you," Callie whispered to Lindsey as she took Mr. Morgan's arm.

A moment later she saw her new husband clearly when

they walked from the house into the sun's light. He was a little on the thin side, with his clothes hanging on his frame as if he'd bought a suit one size too big. Dark whiskers spiked across a hard jawline, and his hair had been cut far too short by a barber with little skill. Just as she'd suspected, he wasn't handsome.

She thought of turning away; nothing about the man was interesting. If she'd seen him on the street, she wouldn't have remembered anything about him except maybe his height. Except now, she'd always remember he'd been willing to save her life. What kind of man, even drunk, marries a stranger?

She decided to pick one thing, one feature that she liked about this man. Then, no matter how hard the coming months were, she'd remember that one thing she liked. If he turned out to be mean, her world might go from bad to worse. If he were kind, the months would pass in peace, but either way, they'd pass and she'd be alone with her land before fall.

He had honest eyes. She liked that about him. He looked at her directly, which was more than most men did. They always acted like they could *catch* crazy from her.

"What do you do now?" Lindsey asked as she took Quentin's offered arm.

"We could go over to the hotel for breakfast," she said, thinking of delaying going back to the ranch for a while. Mamie, the old housekeeper, always came to Callie's cottage after breakfast. By now she was probably rushing to the main house to tell everyone that Crazy Callie was missing.

Lindsey shook her head. "I'd best get over to the school. No time for breakfast. I've lessons to get ready."

"I'll drive you," Quentin volunteered, already helping her into the wagon. He looked back at Callie Anne. "I'll leave the buckboard in front of the hotel after I've circled Lindsey over to the school."

Callie nodded. "We'll walk from here. It'll give us time to get acquainted over breakfast."

He didn't say a word as they walked, and she figured getting acquainted might not be as easy as she thought it might be. The town was waking with a few people already hurrying about. No one seemed to notice the odd couple walking.

Her husband covered her hand as it rested on his arm. "Nice morning," he said as if it wasn't near freezing.

"Yes," she answered.

At the hotel door, he hesitated and Callie remembered that Edna had said he'd drunk until his money was gone. She reached into the pocket of her jacket and pulled out the money she'd been saving in case she had to run. "I'd consider it a favor if you'd handle this for me, Mr. Morgan. We're going to be needing a few things before we head back to the ranch, so after we eat I thought we might stop at the mercantile. You might want to buy a few things."

He slowly took the money. "I'll pay you back from the cattle sale for anything I buy."

"Fair enough."

They reached the hotel café just as the doors opened for breakfast. He held her chair and waited until she was seated. In a low voice, he asked her what she liked here, then ordered for her when the waitress came.

Callie thought of telling him that she could speak for herself, but realized he thought he was doing her a kindness and kindness was something she'd had too little of in her life.

They ate in silence. When the waitress pulled the plates away, he ordered more coffee and asked if she'd like tea or coffee.

She smiled. "Tea," she said, remembering her mother used to have a cup of tea now and then. It seemed a very "married lady" kind of thing to do.

When the waitress left, he said, "You're very beautiful, Mrs. Morgan. Your hair catches the morning sun."

She didn't know how to take the compliment, so she answered, "Thank you, Mr. Morgan."

"Call me by my first name, Callie. We're married now. Call me Luke."

She liked his name. "Well, Luke Morgan, I didn't tell you when we met that it'll take two months of hard work to round up half my herd once the snow clears. Most of them are out on winter grass and some will need branding, which might be a problem if the ranch hands quit after my stepfather leaves."

He waited like a man sitting halfway up a mountain waiting for an avalanche to fall.

She kept to the facts. "When my father died, my mother put the ranch in my name. Since she died before I turned eighteen, the court appointed my stepfather as guardian. He threatened to have me committed to an asylum if I tried to take control of the ranch. I was happy to let him run the place as long as he left me alone at a little cottage on the far corner of my property, but his soon-to-be next wife wants me gone."

"So you found me. I'm now your next of kin."

"Right. Now he has to leave. But—I'd want it to look like we're married. I mean really married," she finished, hoping he wouldn't ask for details. "If my stepfather thought it was a trick, I'm not sure what he'd do."

She tried not to think about what would happen if she pushed Howard too far.

"I'll play my part," he said finally. "For this to work, we have to have a real marriage."

"When you leave, I'll just tell folks you left me. No one will be surprised." Even if he was a crook and took her for every dime she had before he left, she'd still thank him. She'd still have her land.

He reached across the table and covered her hand with his.

When she jerked, he held firm. "I'll keep my word, Callie, and when I leave, you paint me as bad as you need to for folks to put the blame on me. It won't matter to me, but it'll make life easier for you having to live in this town."

She nodded and stood, pulling away from his grip. "We'll need to buy you clothes for this part of the country."

"And you a dress," he said as they walked out. "A woman should have a new dress on her wedding day."

"I don't wear dresses," she said. "I spend most of my time working with animals, and dresses get in the way."

"Would you wear one for me?" he asked politely. "If only for today."

It was a foolish thing to ask, but she saw no harm. If they were going to have to act married until spring, she could give a little.

They shopped for an hour. She picked out his clothes, and he chose a dress for her. She giggled when he wasn't sure how to put on a Stetson, and laughed as she twirled in her new dress.

There was a kindness in his voice that tinkled like wind chimes when he spoke. She could see deep sadness in his gaze when he looked away from her. It was as if he saw no joy in his past or future.

The schoolteacher had been right; he'd had his reason to live knocked clean out of him by a heartless woman. Callie couldn't help but wonder if he'd cared about anything would he have married her.

"Thank you," she whispered as he held the door for her.

"You're welcome," he answered as if he knew she was thanking him for far more than opening the door.

When they walked back to the wagon, Howard Thornville and the sheriff were waiting for them. Luke might not know who the men were, but his arm slid around her waist, pulling her closer to him. The knowledge that someone wanted to protect her warmed her.

"Arrest this man," Thornville shouted, waving his finger at Morgan.

The stranger she'd married removed his new hat and shifted slightly to face the man before them wearing both a gun and a star.

Luke faced the sheriff without giving her stepfather a glance. "What crime do I need to be arrested for?"

Callie saw another man within the Luke Morgan she'd married. A stronger man.

"Mr. Thornville says you kidnapped his crazy daughter." Sheriff Adams looked bored. "He says you've probably already taken advantage of her."

"I married Callie Anne this morning." Luke's words shifted slowly to steel. "And I assure you she's not crazy, and she hasn't been kidnapped or taken advantage of." He winked at her as he said the last words and she blushed, which was exactly what he probably wanted her to do.

When he turned back to the sheriff, his voice hardened. "She's my wife and I'll not have her disrespected or talked about as if she's a person who didn't hear every word you said, Sheriff."

Howard Thornville swore and moved toward Luke, but Adams stepped between the two men.

"Now calm down, Thornville. I'll check this out, but

if what he's saying is true about them being married, I'd say she's no longer your problem."

"But he married her without asking me?"

The sheriff shrugged. "She looks to be of age and everyone in the county knows you've been trying to marry her off for years. So I suggest we get the facts."

The sheriff tipped his hat to Callie, something he'd never done. "Is this man your husband by law and by choice?"

"He is," she whispered and felt Luke's hand close around hers. "I married him for love, Sheriff. Lindsey Baxter and Quentin McCaffree witnessed it."

"Then I wish you the best, Mrs. Morgan." He turned and pulled Thornville in his wake. "Sorry to have bothered you folks," he added over his shoulder.

Luke's intelligent gaze told her he saw the whole picture and didn't need to ask more. He took her hand. "We need to do a few things to protect your interests, Sunshine. I think you're right. Your stepfather does mean you harm. Right about now he's realizing he'd have to pass through me to get to you, but there are other ways he might try to hurt you."

She almost hugged Luke. He believed her. Then she giggled. No one had ever called her "Sunshine," and this man said it like he meant it as an endearment.

They walked across the street to the town's only bank. Luke showed the banker their marriage certificate then asked that all the ranch funds be transferred to her name.

"You mean both your names?" the banker asked. "We usually put the husband's name on top, then the wife can sign on the account if the husband says it's all right." The banker nodded at Luke. "Knowing women and their little sense for business, you can put a cap on how much she can withdraw."

"No," Luke said. "This account is hers. She can do whatever she likes with the money. In fact, from this minute forward, she'll be the only one making withdrawals. Do I make myself clear?"

The banker straightened and nodded. "Yes, sir, Mr. Morgan."

That was about the time Callie Anne decided Luke Morgan wasn't half bad-looking. His strong jaw was set. He'd laced her fingers in his big hand now resting in her lap. Anyone could see he was comforting her as he made all the arrangements. The land and accounts had been in her name since her mother died, with her stepfather as the only one able to sign. At first it had seemed right, since he was her guardian, and later, with her being crazy, no one questioned the fact she couldn't even draw money on her accounts.

Now, everything had changed.

Luke's arm brushed lightly around her shoulder when they left the bank. Several people watched them as though expecting her to bolt and run at any moment. They glared at him. He was a stranger and therefore not to be trusted. Even if the folks in town thought Callie Anne was crazy, she was still one of them.

As soon as they were away from the crowd, Callie whispered, "Folks are talking about us. They're probably wondering where I found you."

"Do us both a favor and don't tell them," he said.

"No one would believe me anyway."

He stopped and turned her to face him. "I don't care what people talk about. Nothing in my life was real or like I thought it was. From now on I'm making up who I am. If you want me for a husband then that is what I'll be and call myself lucky for the chance."

She smiled, deciding he might be the crazy one. "All

right. I'll play along. I'll be the woman who loves Luke Morgan."

He smiled. "Only me?"

"Only you." She saw the need in his eyes then. He was a plain man whose love had been tossed away. Even if they both knew this was far from a real marriage, he needed to feel as if someone, even a crazy woman, cared about him.

Without any thought of the people watching, she wrapped her arms around his neck and pulled his mouth down to hers. At first the kiss was hard against his lips and she feared he'd pull away, but after a moment, he softened and let her kiss him.

When she broke the kiss, she smiled up at this stranger she'd married. "The preacher left that part out this morning."

He looked a little embarrassed that they were kissing in the middle of town, but he didn't move away. "Thank you for that, Sunshine," he whispered against her hair.

Hand in hand they went to a lawyer and then to all the stores in town that gave the ranch credit. At each stop he insisted on her picking out something she liked, saying that a bride should have wedding presents even if no one came to the wedding.

By noon the ranch was truly hers, and the buckboard was stuffed with things she'd always wanted to buy. Rocking chairs for the cottage porch. A new set of dishes that all matched. Quilts and sheets and towels that weren't hand-me-downs from the main house. A huge red clay pot for flowers in the spring and a long mirror framed in walnut daisies.

They spent the afternoon drinking coffee with Quentin in an empty bar until school let out. Then, all three walked over to the schoolhouse so Callie Anne and Luke could say thank you to Lindsey.

Shadows were long by the time he finally said it was time to head home. She'd been hesitating, fearing what she'd have to face at the ranch. Her stepfather knew the game was over; his chance of taking the ranch from her had disappeared.

"Thank you," she said as Luke helped her up.

"For what?" he asked.

"For the day. I think it's the best I've ever had."

"Me, too," he agreed, sliding in beside her on the bench until his leg brushed against hers.

The sheriff caught up with them when Luke collected his trunk from the train station. "You folks be careful," he said as he walked near. "When I last saw your stepfather he was fighting mad and heading back to the ranch. I told him he'd best be packing, but if I were you two I'd give him a day or two."

Callie closed her eyes, dreading having to face him. "We'll do that, but he'll know we're going back to the cottage."

Luke's fingers brushed her cheek. "Don't worry. He knows you're no longer alone."

"How about I ride out to the ranch headquarters and meet you two in the morning?" Adams looked like he could smell trouble. "Just in case."

Before Luke could say no, she said, "Thanks, Sheriff, we'll see you there for breakfast."

The sheriff nodded.

Luke touched his hat in salute to the sheriff and clicked the team into action.

"Tomorrow," the sheriff said as he turned away.

For a while, they just rode, watching the shadows grow longer as the road seemed to stretch all the way to the horizon.

"Tell me what you like," Callie said, more to pass the

time. She had no idea what he ate, or how he liked his eggs, or what time he turned in. Did he read by the fire or take baths in the stream? Did he go to church or smoke or write poetry?

Finally, he answered her question with one choice as if the others didn't matter. "I liked the way you kissed me."

"Oh." That wasn't what she'd meant, and she had no idea how to answer him.

Chapter 5

A S he turned in to the ranch, Luke was surprised at
the size of the place. From the look of her clothes
when they'd married, he expected a dirt-poor spread of
worthless ground and thin cattle, not rolling hills of grass
with enough buildings nestled in a valley to look like a
small town.

Callie leaned closer. "That's the headquarters with the
main house and a bunkhouse beyond. My grandfather
started it and my father added on. As folks who worked
for us retired, we added the small places along the creek
that runs past the main place. We also have three barns.
One for only horses and another for the milk cows. My
father thought he'd live long enough to have sons who'd
run the place, not an only daughter with no interest in
ranching."

Before they could draw any nearer, she directed him
off to a small trail a few hundred feet from the entrance.
"The cottage where I live is over there in the trees. It was

my grandparents' first place and where my parents lived the first few years they were married."

"Why'd you move out here?"

"I ran here when my mother died. I felt closer to her in the cottage. My stepfather just left me alone. The cottage was far enough away from him that he could forget about me. He'd send our old housekeeper out to check on me every morning, but Mamie doesn't help; she just comes to visit and report in to him that I'm still there."

"You didn't mind being all alone?"

"I'm not alone." Callie laughed. "I have my animals—they've always kept me company. My father had been a farrier before he married my mom. He not only shoed horses, he doctored them as well. He'd studied to be a veterinarian in England and when a school opened up in Iowa, I thought I'd study to be one, too. I was almost finished when my stepfather told me he would pay no more money to educate a woman too dumb to marry."

"I've read about veterinarians. You must be valued out here."

She shook her head. "No one will bring their animals to me. Thornville told them all that I torture anything wounded. The one time someone from town did stop by I'd just finished pulling a colt from a dying mare. The man saw me covered in blood and believed all he'd heard."

"But you have patients?" he asked.

"Ones I find, mostly. Now and then one of the cowhands on the ranch will bring me an animal they've found who's hurting. I don't think they believe the lies my stepfather tells. I've even healed a few of their horses when my stepfather would have put them down."

Luke followed the directions she gave without saying a word. He wanted to believe her, but the wounds left by the last woman he'd trusted were still too raw.

He didn't miss the effort she seemed to be making to act as if nothing were wrong, but since they'd passed the main gate, she'd been watching for movement or strange noises. She expected her stepfather to be waiting for her.

"Did he ever beat you?" Luke asked.

"Who?"

"Thornville."

She shook her head. "When he first married my mother, he didn't even notice I was around most of the time. We didn't have enough in common to bother speaking to each other. After she died, I made sure I was invisible. Now, I go up to the main house with Mamie once a week to clean. My momma would have liked her house kept in order. She and my grandmother both loved the main house. If I didn't help the old housekeeper, I think Howard would fire Mamie and get another. We have an unspoken agreement. When I'm there he stays away. If I need to say something to him, I have to go over to the bunkhouse or the barn to talk to him."

She stared at the cottage ahead of them. "He used to make fun of me in front of the hands. When I was younger, he'd laugh at how awkward or stupid I was. When I got older, he kidded me about being crazy. Even introduced me to new hired hands as 'my wife's crazy daughter.' I think he just wanted me gone, and the more I avoided him, the easier I was to forget."

A movement in the sundown light between them and the outline of the cottage porch drew Luke's attention, and every muscle tightened.

Callie patted his leg. "It's only Domino. I call him Dom for short. He thinks he's the castle guard even if he does have only one leg." She raised her hand and a prairie hawk landed awkwardly on her arm. "Domino, meet my new husband."

The hawk didn't look the least interested and flew away.

"He likes you," she said, but Luke seriously doubted it.

As he climbed down, Callie walked across the porch and opened the door to her cottage. A fox darted out, brushing her skirts as he passed. "That's Checkers; he roams the night."

Luke carried in two of the boxes they'd bought. "Are we living with many more board games?"

She didn't have to answer. He could hear the birds as he stepped over the threshold. A lazy old cat, with a multi-colored coat, rose from the rug by the cold fireplace and looked at him as if she were angry that someone hadn't lit the fire.

"Don't mind Marble." Callie laughed. "She thinks she lives here all alone. She was here before the crowd came."

As his new wife lit the lamps, Luke realized this cottage wasn't like anywhere he'd ever seen. Colorful quilts covered the walls, and beautiful, hand-carved furniture circled the main room. A huge loom framed one wall with lines of earth-tone thread stretched tight. A mammoth fireplace stood along the opposite wall made of smooth stones with holes and shelves built in all the way to the twenty-foot ceiling. The windows were built high and placed so that light would crisscross the room in morning and evening.

"This is beautiful," he whispered, almost feeling like he was in a church.

"My grandfather built it to catch the whole day's light. In winter I like to quilt and weave." She smiled at him, obviously proud that he approved of her home. "I'm never alone here. The memory of my family surrounds me and my friends."

A skunk waddled out from under one of the tables and walked out the front door as if he hadn't noticed them.

"He's fixed," Callie whispered, "but don't tell him. He still thinks he can make a stink."

"Don't talk to the skunk. I'll make a note of that." Luke fought down a laugh.

He almost told her of how dark and colorless his world had been for so long, but he didn't want to see her smile disappear. "I'll bring everything in from the wagon, while you put it up."

She nodded, suddenly looking nervous. "The bedroom is through that door. You can put your trunk in there."

She began unloading all they'd bought. Between trips he watched her unpacking the new sheets and pillows as if they were a gift and not something she'd bought.

When he brought in his trunk, she said, "Set your trunk over here, Luke." She pulled a rocker to the side of a window. "This is your room. I've already cleaned out the top drawer."

"Our room," he corrected loud enough for her to hear.

"Our room now, I guess," she repeated as he walked to the bedroom door. "I put the furniture back like it was when my parents were alive. My father always said he liked to wake up with the sun shining in his face."

"Then, we'll sleep in there," Luke said, taking a step to continue unloading.

She froze. "But I always sleep on the cot by the fire in the main room."

"You're my wife. You'll sleep with me now. I'll keep you warm."

She didn't look too happy about the suggestion so he tried to be kind. "Take your time getting ready for bed, but we sleep together. I'll wash up in the kitchen. In a house this size it shouldn't be too much trouble finding my way back."

He watched her carefully, fearing that she'd run or scream or finally turn into that crazy person everyone thought she was. But, to his surprise, she picked up her things and walked into the kitchen. "No. I'll change in the kitchen. I have to cover the birdcages and check on the animals in the barn."

Walking around in the little bedroom, Luke slowly placed his new clothes in the drawers, leaving his trunk packed. There wasn't much he'd brought that would be useful in this new life he'd awakened to, but all he owned in the world was in that one trunk.

He'd gone to sleep in that alley wishing he were dead, and by sunup, he was married to a woman he still wasn't sure saw the real world. He knew he was pushing her again, but he hadn't started this marriage. She'd asked him. They were married and married people slept together. It was as simple as that.

Stripping down to his long johns, Luke lit a fire in the corner fireplace and waited. The house creaked and shifted in the wind. This country was colder than he'd thought it would be, but then, he'd never really thought about the weather. All he'd wanted when he boarded the train was to get to Shallow Creek and find Dorothy. He had money for the trip back and a small, two-room apartment promised him in Richmond. The job at an old law firm downtown wasn't much, but it would pay enough to get by and be far better than working in a mine. All he needed was her. His Dorothy. The only woman he'd ever dreamed about. She'd looked so adorable in her bonnet at church that first time. She'd smiled at him and invited him to sit with her at the social, and he'd fallen hard.

Only, when she'd opened the door to him four days ago, she hadn't looked the same. The young, carefree girl he'd met had aged far more than three years, it seemed. Her warm brown hair had dulled and the blush on her cheeks was gone. She looked shorter and far heavier than he remembered. It took him a few seconds to realize that she was pregnant, and, by then, she was yelling at him with a voice that would have shamed a crow.

He hadn't told her he was coming and somehow that one wrong outweighed all that she'd done—in her view, anyway. Luke closed his eyes, remembering how he'd stood like a fool listening to her yell at him, wondering what had happened to the shy girl he'd met three years before and sworn to love forever.

She'd tossed his letters at him and called him a paper lover. A daydream, she'd said, nothing real.

Luke barely remembered picking up the letters and walking away. If he'd come and found her dead and buried, he would have mourned and gone on with his life, but she was alive and the only thing to mourn was the life he'd planned.

She'd ripped it away, leaving nothing. The job, the apartment waiting for him, all looked so dark and lonely without her. He knew he couldn't go back to Richmond, but he had nowhere to go forward.

When he'd wandered into the saloon, he'd thought only to wait for the train, but he was so drunk the first night he missed the midnight train heading east. The next night he'd been sick from no food and far too much whiskey. The third night, he no longer cared; he just drank until his money was gone.

He'd been a fighter all his life with one dream and now he felt hollow inside. If Callie hadn't found him, he wasn't sure he wouldn't have just forgotten to breathe once in that alley and died. Only she had found him and, crazy or not, she'd given him a reason to keep breathing.

Looking toward the door, he saw her standing there, her hair wild around her shoulders, her white nightgown draped all the way to her bare toes.

"Come on, Mrs. Morgan, it's time to go to bed." He lifted the covers on the side of the bed nearest to the fire and waited.

She didn't meet his eyes as she walked toward him and climbed in.

He tucked her in and circled the bed. Turning off the one lantern, he crawled in with only firelight brightening the room.

"Lift your gown," he said after he'd settled a few inches away from her. "You said you wanted a real marriage and that's what we'll have."

His wife didn't move.

Luke had no idea what to do or say next. He figured he wanted to mate with her only slightly more than she wanted to mate with him, but it was what married people did and he was willing to do his part.

Chapter 6

❧

CALLIE waited in the darkness knowing she should have talked about the sleeping arrangements before now. She should have set down some rules for the short time they were living in the same house, like no sleeping together, but she'd been the one who'd insisted they have a real marriage.

"What is it?" she asked when he didn't move.

"Callie," he said, "am I real to you? Real flesh and blood, I mean?"

"You are, Luke." She thought of saying thank you for all he'd done, but he would have just said he was earning his half of the herd.

"Good," he finally said. "That's a start."

"I'm not lifting my gown," she added.

"All right, but you should know that's what people who are married do. They mate."

She was glad it was so dark. She never could have faced him and talked about this. "I know. I just don't think

I'm attracted to you in that way." She'd liked the kiss, but she wasn't ready for more.

"I understand. You're pretty, Callie, real pretty, but you're not the kind of woman I'm attracted to, either."

A few minutes before, she'd thought she was exhausted, but now, after what he'd just said, she knew she couldn't sleep. Relieved but a little insulted, she asked, "What kind of woman are you attracted to?"

Again he took his time answering. "Short ones, with brown hair and eyes, I guess."

"Like Dorothy Trimble? So that means you like women who are well-rounded." Callie frowned. Dorothy was so well-rounded she was surprised the woman didn't fall forward when she walked.

He was so close she could hear him take a deep breath before he said, "I don't want to talk about Dorothy."

"Do you still love her?"

"No." He touched her hand that rested between them. "She never loved me, either."

"Good." Callie squeezed his hand. "Because I'm the one who loves Luke Morgan."

He laughed. "You don't have to say that when we're alone."

"I don't mind. I kind of like the idea of saying I love someone. Maybe I'll just decide to keep saying it. Seems to me if love was a decision and not a feeling, there would be far less problems in this world."

"I'd like that." He didn't turn loose of her hand. "You can say you love me whenever you feel like it." He took a long breath as if somehow they'd settled something between them. "Good night, Callie."

"And you can ask me to lift my gown, but I'm never promising such a thing."

"Fair enough." He sounded half-asleep.

"Good night, Luke." She rolled to her side so that his arm touched her breasts just to let him know that she might not be well-rounded, but she still had curves.

In the darkness they could be together, two people no one loved.

He'd saved her today, but the nightmare of what it would have been like to be locked away in an asylum haunted her dreams.

When her mother first married Thornville, Callie ran away, not wanting to face the thought of some other man trying to take her father's place. It had taken him all day, but he'd caught up to her and brought her back. He'd locked her in an old abandoned root cellar for two days before he told her mother that he'd found her. She'd thought she would go mad in the darkness, and his telling her he'd done it to teach her a lesson hadn't helped matters.

Thornville had told everyone he'd found her living like a wild animal down by the river, and she'd been too frightened and hungry to correct him. That day, he'd been the hero and she'd been marked as crazy.

They'd never talked of why he'd locked her away but she knew if she ran away again and he caught her, he'd let her die in that cellar. Even six years later the nightmare of being hungry and cold still haunted her.

As she dreamed of being surrounded by the smell of rotting food and the sounds of tiny animals moving around her, she cried out for help and felt Luke's arm circle her shoulder.

"It's all right, Callie. It's only a dream." He sounded more asleep than awake.

"I know," she answered, fearing that he might think she didn't know the difference. "But will you hold me until I fall back asleep?"

"Of course," he said against her ear. "I find I like touching you. I have all day, you know." His hand moved down her back in a comforting caress. "Since I've been grown, I've never had a woman to touch. It feels nice having you next to me."

"I know what you mean," she answered as she slipped into dreams. "I haven't minded at all. I like knowing you're near in the dark."

"Me, too. Maybe we can protect each other from the nightmares."

"I'd like that." She hesitantly placed her hand over his heart and drifted back to sleep without dreams haunting her.

When she awoke at dawn, he was gone and she wondered if she'd dreamed the way he'd held her.

Mamie stood at the foot of her bed watching her. "You have the dreams again, child?"

"Not so bad last night," Callie answered as she stood and began to dress. "I'll fix your coffee."

Mamie nodded. "There was a man in the kitchen when I got here. One of the hands said he's the new boss. That true?"

"That's true," Callie answered. "I married him yesterday."

Mamie took everything in stride. She and her husband had worked for Callie's grandfather when he first settled here and as long as Cramers had this place, they'd have a home. Mamie might show up for work every morning, but she wasn't able to do much more than dust and clean the birdcages. The bunkhouse cook made sure the old couple had breakfast and dinner. Callie always sent a lunch home with the old woman before she got too tired.

After she'd had her morning coffee, Callie walked out on the porch and found her new husband leaning back in one of the new rockers with his feet propped on the porch railing.

He held up a paper. "I've made a list of the things that need repair. When we go over to the main house to make sure Thornville is gone, I'll pick up supplies and start to work."

She hesitated. "You're not going to want to move to the big house?"

"I like it here." He grinned and winked. "And, since you made our new bed here, I'm guessing you do, too. So, unless you'd rather move, I'm happy right here. Any more than two rooms to a house would make me nervous."

He stood slowly in front of her and brushed a tear off her cheek.

"I thought you might want to move. I love it here."

"Then we stay," he whispered, brushing her damp cheek with a kiss. "You, me, and all your critters."

She looked up, deciding she'd been wrong. This husband she'd found in the alley was handsome.

Chapter 7

~~~~~

LUKE wasn't surprised to see the sheriff step from the bunkhouse as they pulled up to the main house.

As Sheriff Adams started walking toward them he yelled, "Thought you should know. The foreman said Thornville was here yesterday probably right after he saw you and Callie Anne in town. He stayed long enough to load a wagon."

Luke jumped to the ground and reached for Callie. She let him help her down from the wagon then ran into the house.

He followed her and the sheriff inside. The place looked like it had been raided. Chairs were overturned, bookshelves wiped clean of books, drawers left open. Even with the mess, Luke could tell the place had been a comfortable home. A far cry from his two rooms back in Virginia. He'd had a bed, a desk, and one chair. It had been the cheapest place he could find and he hadn't minded because he was saving every dime he could.

Now, he watched his new wife walk through the rooms crying silently as she righted a chair or smoothed a cloth back across a table as she moved. In one corner, what had once been a glassed-in display cabinet was now rubble on the floor. Tiny figurines lay among the glass, shattered.

Luke knelt and carefully moved a stick through the broken glass, hoping to find one of the little statues still in one piece, but they'd all been too fragile to survive the tumble.

"Can you tell what's missing?" the sheriff asked.

Callie sounded more dazed than angry. "My mother's pictures. Her jewelry. All the guns including my grandfather's old Colt Walkers. The money for the household expenses and all the money in the safe."

Adams looked angry. "Add the wagon and four horses he took from the barn along with a new saddle and I'd say we got enough to arrest the man for theft."

Callie shook her head. "He's gone. That's all I wanted."

The sheriff turned to Luke. "That all right with you, Morgan?"

Luke nodded. "It wouldn't be worth the bother."

"All right. If that's the way you want it, but if I know Thornville, he'll have what he took gambled away in a month and be back for more."

Luke picked up a stack of books and set them on the shelf. A tiny figurine of a little milkmaid rolled from behind the books.

He picked it up and handed it to Callie.

She smiled. "This one," she whispered, "was always my favorite."

Somehow the one treasure he'd found stopped her crying and made her smile.

Luke saw his chance. "How about we deal with this mess later, Sunshine? Right now I'd like a cup of coffee

while I meet the men working here. You want to intro-
duce me?"

She shook her head. "I never talked to them much. My
mother said a bunkhouse is no place for a girl."

"She was right, but as my wife and the owner of this
place, I think it's about time you met every man who works
for you."

The sheriff agreed.

Luke felt her hesitation as he took her hand and walked
with her across the yard to the bunkhouse. He introduced
himself to the foreman, then, as he learned each man's
name, Luke introduced them to Callie. Not one laughed
at her or made a single rude comment, but he kept one
hand at her waist and the other balled in a fist at his side.

The cook offered them breakfast, even though the men
were finished. Luke talked to the men, giving the cook time
to set a small table by the window. By the time the cowhands left, the bunkhouse was quiet as they ate and planned.

Luke thanked the sheriff when they walked back outside. The wind was kicking up from the north, reminding
them all that winter was still in full force. The lawman
offered advice, but everyone knew there was little he
could do to help. His job was in town and ranch folks
were expected to handle any problems on their own.

As they walked back to the main house alone, Luke
took Callie's hand.

"It's going to be a long day," he said in the stillness.
"Seems like a lifetime's passed since I looked up in the
alley and saw you looking down at me. We made it
through yesterday and we'll make it through today."

Then, without a word, they began cleaning up the
mess. Tossing out broken furniture and sweeping up glass.
By midafternoon, when he helped her into the wagon,
snow blew around in the air as thin as white dust.

"You folks aren't staying here?" the cook yelled from the bunkhouse door.

"No," Luke answered. "We're heading back home. If it snows, you may not see us for a few days."

The old cook smiled. "I kind of figured that." He lifted a big basket into the wagon. "I know the cottage is stocked, but I packed you a few more supplies. Kind of a honeymoon basket." He winked at Luke. "See you folks when it warms up and you make it back over."

Luke thanked him, but Callie seemed lost in her own thoughts. She stared at the main house as they drove away, holding the tiny little figurine in her hand.

When they got back, heavier snow had started falling. Luke took care of the horses and stocked up a few days' worth of firewood beside the stove. When he made his third trip out for logs for the fireplace, he saw Callie feeding her animals, who'd all moved inside for the duration of the storm. There were more than he'd thought and every corner was filled with a nest or bungalow.

She talked to them softly and he found himself wishing that she'd talk to him in that gentle way. All day she'd done little more than answer his questions in one-word sentences.

By dusk, the temperature had dropped to near freezing. She spread a quilt by the fireplace and they ate bread with the cheese and jellies the cook had sent. He asked her questions and she talked some, but he thought she looked tired.

When they finished eating, he took her hand and pulled her to her feet. "Where do we put your mother's little milkmaid so none of the animals around this place accidentally knock it over?"

Callie pointed to a high shelf. He held her waist as she stood on a chair and stretched to reach just the right spot.

Then, when she would have stepped down, he lifted her in his arms and carried her to the bedroom.

With only the light from the fireplace an open door away, they undressed on either side of the bed. He spread out under the covers first and watched her pull a ribbon from her hair and comb it out slowly. The light in the room seemed to dance in the curls.

When she finally slid beneath the covers, he felt almost drunk on her beauty. Without a word, he lifted his arm and she curled next to him.

He finally broke the silence. "Say the words."

She nodded, knowing what he wanted. "I'm the woman who loves Luke Morgan," she whispered.

"Will you lift your gown tonight?"

"No," she answered. "But I'd like to kiss you good night if you don't mind."

"I wouldn't mind at all."

The kiss was sweet, light, but they both knew it was the beginning of more.

Chapter 8

A T dawn the silence of the cottage was broken by an
animal's wild scream.

Luke jumped out of bed and ran toward the door. Deep
in the night he'd dreamed Callie was crying for him as
blood ran over the collar of her white gown. With first
light he thought his nightmare might be coming true.

His thundering stomps frightened two squirrels sleeping in the rafters. They darted like lightning bolts above
his head. Without meaning to, he stumbled over the shy
skunk curled by the rocker and woke the piglets Callie
had decided were too young to sleep out the storm in the
barn. Their screams woke several other furry animals he
hadn't known lurked in the dark, and they decided to
attack him, by flying, bumping, or clawing their way
into him.

He was halfway across the main room of their cottage
when Callie's laughter stopped him cold. For a moment
he didn't see her, then he saw movement in the corner of

the kitchen area by the cook stove. There his wife knelt in her nightgown in front of the big cat.

"Kittens." She laughed. "Two already. One black and one gray. Oh, Luke, they're so beautiful."

"Really," he managed to say as he tried to slow his heartbeat and pull the zoo off him. Without bothering to move in for a closer look, he walked back to the bedroom and pulled on his trousers, heaviest sweater, and wool socks. At least now if one of them bit him, they'd have to bite harder to draw blood.

When he returned to the kitchen stove, all the not-so-friendly forest friends had disappeared back into their hiding places. He sat on the floor beside Callie and pulled her bare feet out from under her gown. Shoving her icy toes into another pair of his socks, he said, "First I keep you from freezing to death, then I count the kittens."

She was too busy to notice what he was doing. "Want to watch the next one being born? The mother eats away the birthing sac."

"They're born in bags? That's interesting." In all his life he'd never seen anything born.

He pulled her into his lap and circled her with his arms. "I don't know if I want to watch, but I'm here to boil water or whatever is needed." He pushed his face into the wild curls of Callie's hair and breathed deep, thinking that if he could have taken just this one smell with him into the mines he wouldn't have minded living in the darkness forever.

For the next hour, they watched first the births, then the mother cat take care of each kitten, washing her newborn and pushing it into the warm fur of her belly.

Callie giggled and encouraged the cat as if Mother Marble could understand every word she said.

Luke rested his chin on her shoulder and enjoyed watching Callie far more than he did the cat. Finally, he said, "I had no idea how much work giving birth is. I never knew the mothers had to do so much. Somebody should have told Dorothy about this cleaning up and licking away the blood before she got pregnant."

He felt Callie's chuckle against his chest. "Oh, Luke, aren't they cute?"

He thought they looked far more like blind, wet rats, but he didn't want to hurt Marble's feelings just in case she understood human talk. "Yeah, real cute. You think we could leave them long enough to make coffee?"

She stretched in his arms. "I don't know, I'm happy right here."

He thought the same thing, for their bodies touched in several spots and he wondered if she paid any attention to how often he stroked her. Slowly, he was learning the curves of her body, the soft feel of her skin, the way she felt against him day and night.

With regret, he pushed her up. "Coffee," he said, directing her toward the pot a few feet away. "I'll build up the fire while you try to think up names for the new arrivals."

An hour later they had breakfast by the windows, watching it snow and laughingly arguing over names. Big, huge flakes turned everything to a wonderland and closed them away from the world.

The cottage was silent now with the birdcages still covered and the fox curled in a basket by the door. The three little piglets that she'd brought in from the barn were making grunt-snuffle sounds. They were sleeping on straw in the hip tub near the back door.

This was a peaceful place, he thought. A kind of heaven that he'd never known. The main ranch house was

big and cold and could have belonged to anyone, but this
cottage was warm and colorful and all Callie. Part
shadow, part light, but all bathed in warm harmony.

As the day passed, he read to her while she sewed,
then they played poker with the beans they planned to
cook for supper. When he lay down for a nap, she joined
him, and they drifted into sleep smiling.

In the afternoon a bit of sun came out and Luke dug a
path to the barn so they could check on the horses and
let the little pigs go back to their mother. He felt young
for the first time in three years, playing in the snow, then
running back into the house, deciding it was far too cold
to be outside.

They hung their wet clothes on a rod across the kitchen
space and ate supper again on the quilt by the fireplace.
As the evening aged, he read from *The Adventures of
Tom Sawyer* while she rested her head on his leg.

Finally, cuddled by the fire, they began to talk. Both
had grown up as only children. Callie, here on the ranch
with her parents and grandparents. Him, with only his dad.
Most of his memories in a mining town were of always
waiting for his father to make it home from the mine where
he worked six days a week. Then, on Sunday, they went to
church.

She talked of cookouts in the summer with barbecue
and fresh corn and beans. He remembered thinking himself lucky when he had an apple in his pail that usually
held only a hard biscuit. She told of riding and camping
out with her parents in the summer. Luke remembered
the seasons mostly by the number of layers he had to
wear. Her world had held such color and his seemed all
browns and grays.

When Luke was fifteen, he heard the mine bell sounding as he left school. There had been a cave-in. His father never come home.

A week later he'd been offered his father's job and Luke's dreams of going to school were forgotten. No one took him in or helped him. He hadn't asked. It was time for him to become a man.

"If I hadn't met Dorothy one Sunday at church three years later, I'm not sure I would have started studying. Until then I was just drifting through weeks that turned into years. The only thing I loved was reading. I'd buy a book or two on payday and read it so many times it fell apart. After I started writing Dorothy, I decided I had to change something in my life and studying at night seemed the only road out. A priest I'd met offered to lend me law books so I started there. By working nights I could sit through a trial now and then."

"So we should stop by and thank Dorothy? Let her know that you're still alive?" Callie pushed her toes beneath his thigh for warmth.

He shook his head. "I know I was never really real to her, just someone to write to and dream about, but maybe she wasn't real to me, either. I just needed to believe she was waiting for me to make something of myself." He grinned, quoting something he'd read a long time back. "She was the star I charted by, but not my destination."

"You're real to me, Luke. I'm glad you studied and saved. I'm glad you came here, even if it wasn't for me."

He leaned forward and kissed her nose. "Time for bed, Sunshine. Thanks for the best day of my life."

She rose beside him. "Me, too."

As they walked toward the bedroom, his hand resting lightly on the small of her back, she said, "Luke, could it always be like this between us? Easy and nice for as long as we're together?"

"I don't know. I think I'd like it if it were."

"Me, too." She stepped into the bedroom as he turned back, remembering to add one more log to the fire.

For a long moment he stared out into the night where all the world looked peaceful. Something strange was happening inside him. He could feel himself changing all the way to his core. He was coming alive.

When he finally crawled into bed, Callie was warm and nearly asleep. He pulled her close, loving the way she let him touch her.

"I love you, Luke Morgan," she whispered.

He kissed her forehead. "I know. Will you lift your gown?"

"No," she started to say as his mouth covered hers.

He kissed her deeper tonight, wanting more of her. Wanting all she'd allow.

He'd expected her to turn away, but she let him kiss her fully and he felt her waking. As she began to kiss him back, he leaned over her, pressing his body against hers.

When he finally broke the kiss, he could feel her rapid breathing against his chest. He stared down at her, giving her time to slow her breathing, loving the feel of her beneath him, loving the wetness on her lips and the way her eyes half closed in pleasure.

"I'll have another, if you've no objection," he whispered as he fisted his hand into her hair and lowered over her once more.

She opened her mouth in invitation and he kissed her again.

When he pulled an inch away, she gulped for air and smiled, her eyes closed, her chest rising and falling.

"Say the words again while you're awake and not half-asleep." He almost didn't recognize his own voice, rough and low with need.

"I'm the woman who loves Luke Morgan," she whispered.

He cuddled her close, making sure quilts covered her completely. "Go to sleep now, Callie."

Chapter 9

~~~~

THE next few weeks after the storm were busy, but Luke stood by her side. Fences were down, corrals needed rebuilding, and the stock had to be looked after. Every man on the ranch was needed. To Callie's surprise, Luke fit in at the ranch better than she thought he would. He had a great deal to learn, but his easy manner welcomed instruction and help. He worked as hard as any hand during the day and stayed up late most nights straightening out her books and teaching her how to keep everything in order.

She learned to trust his skills and admire his logic. He'd stepped into a way of life he knew nothing about, but he tried his best and that was more than she'd expected.

Some nights he was so tired and sore he didn't even ask her to lift her gown, but she never forgot to tell him she loved him. When he did kiss her, the passion surprised her, but he never demanded more than a kiss. He was like a man learning to breathe and each day he drew in deeper.

It was the end of February before they had time to go the few miles into town. After spending over a month outdoors, he'd changed. His face was tanned and he wore his western clothes like a true cowboy. The too-short hair now brushed over his collar in midnight curls and his strong jawline was framed with a short beard. She often teased him, saying he looked like a Roman gladiator. Even the Stetson he hadn't known how to put on the day of their wedding was now worn and fit like it had been made just for him.

Something else she noticed was the twinkle in his deep blue eyes. Luke was happy. All day he might be one of the men warrioring through weather and the work, but when he came home, he always smiled at her when he saw her waiting for him on the porch. They'd have supper, then he'd ask about her animals or read to her while she sewed.

She loved the way he read as if crawling into the stories and running through danger with the characters. And today she loved the easy way his hand rested on her leg as he drove into town. To all they must seem like an old married couple now. Folks waved their greetings and Luke always waved back. But to her, every day, every night with him was something new.

He pulled up to the line of shops on the one main street of Shallow Creek. "I'll check in at the bank and then go over to the sheriff's office. How much time do you need to shop, Sunshine?"

"Two hours," she answered. "I should have time to put a dent in the bank account by then. Mamie and the cook both sent lists and I need to order wool for the loom."

"Buy another dress," he said as he helped her down. "Though I'm fond of this one, it wouldn't hurt to own two."

As he swung her onto the boardwalk, he bent and

kissed her on the cheek. A tender kiss like she'd grown
used to every time they parted.

"Be careful," she whispered. They'd heard rumors that
her stepfather had been drinking in town after the widow
wouldn't take him in. He'd told everyone that his stepdaughter had ruined his life. He said he'd slaved over the
land and been left with nothing.

"Don't worry," Luke said. "I think I'll stop in at that
little law office I visited next to the bank and pick up the
facts on Texas law. How about I pick you up at the schoolhouse later? Maybe we could talk Quentin and Lindsey
into having dinner with us at the hotel."

"They wouldn't," she said, knowing her shy friends
well. "Folks would think they were stepping out with each
other. It's not that way between them."

"I'll ask Quentin anyway. We could laugh about the
wedding I barely remember." He raised an eyebrow.
"You're wrong about the way it is between them."

He was gone before she could ask any questions. He
was wrong, of course. She'd known Quentin and Lindsey
all her life. She would have noticed if there was something going on between them.

Callie stood watching him leave and thinking how
much her life had changed over the weeks. When she
turned to start her shopping, she saw Dorothy standing
in the doorway of a dress shop. She held a newborn in
her arms. Luke's old love looked puffy and tired and
unhappy.

"Well, if it isn't Crazy Callie." Her greeting wasn't
friendly.

"Hello, Dorothy." Callie straightened, not feeling the
slap of her nickname as much as usual. For over a month
no one had even hinted that she was crazy. There was
only one person now that counted and Luke didn't think

she was crazy. "That's a beautiful baby you got there. Has your hair."

Dorothy ignored the child in her arms as she nodded toward Luke. "I threw him away, you know." Her gaze followed the wagon moving away as she talked to Callie. "Didn't even let him step foot in my house."

"I know," Callie said slowly, not wanting to cause a scene. "I guess I got the hand-me-down husband you didn't want."

"What kind of man comes halfway across the country to be with a girl he sat in church with a few times?" Dorothy seemed to be talking more to herself than Callie. "I figured he was desperate, and apparently he was. He married you, didn't he? Probably no girl in Virginia wanted him if he had to come all the way out here."

Callie couldn't argue. Luke had surely been about as low as a man could get to agree to marry her. She'd always known that. But he had married her. He'd saved her and he'd been kind. She owed him.

"I love Luke Morgan, Dorothy. I have since the morning I first saw him." The words came out so honest and strong she knew they were true. She was no longer saying them just because he'd asked her to.

Dorothy, who'd always known just the right cutting thing to say since she could talk, was speechless. Finally, she managed, "Well, if that's all you want, Crazy Callie, I wish you well. You're welcome to him."

Callie smiled. "He's all I want." She walked around Dorothy and smiled, realizing that for the first time in her life she felt sorry for Dorothy Trimble. She'd always been the prettiest, most popular girl in school. In fact, Lindsey and Callie first became friends because they were so often the brunt of her jokes on the playground. Only today, she was just a woman, not a friend or an enemy. For once she'd tossed away something worth keeping and she had no one to blame but herself.

Callie spent the afternoon shopping, piling up bags and boxes to be picked up on their way home. She even bought another dress and decided to wear it to dinner that night, if Luke managed to get both Quentin and Lindsey to go out with them.

She told herself one dress was the same as another, but she picked one belted with a blue ribbon because Luke often played with the ribbon she wore in her hair.

When Luke finally showed up at the schoolhouse, he'd already picked up her bags and had Quentin in tow. The lanky bartender didn't look comfortable, but he nodded a greeting to both Lindsey and her.

"Luke says he's buying steaks, so I thought I'd come along," Quentin said without taking his gaze off Lindsey.

"Well, if it's steaks he's buying, I might go along with you." The proper schoolteacher didn't smile. "You offering apple pie for dessert, too?"

Luke brushed his hand along the ribbon at Callie's waist. "I guess I am. Since my wife is dressed up tonight, we might as well go all out. This'll be our way of thanking you two for getting us together."

At the hotel restaurant, the party mood continued. Luke even ordered wine with the meal, though Lindsey would not touch liquor in a public place. The school board would fire her for sure.

They laughed about the wedding and all took their turn complaining about the music Mrs. Winters had played.

Over dessert Quentin talked about the threats he'd heard Thornville make, but Callie knew her stepfather was more talk than action.

Luke told of his trip to the law office and how the

town's only lawyer offered him a job as soon as he passed the Texas bar. "I enjoy the fresh air and the ranch, but the smell of a book-lined office draws me."

"You going to go for it?" Quentin asked.

"I might. Practicing law has always been my dream."

Before Callie could ask any questions, the conversation turned to oil leases. Big companies were coming into this part of Texas and the Indian Territory looking to drill.

This year most of the open land was free to range, but wire was being strung and soon the big herds wouldn't have enough grass or a trail to drive their herds to market. Cattle would all be shipped and the cowboys would become cowpokes when they had to ride along on the train and poke the cattle to make sure they remained standing.

Oil was a gamble, but living in this part of the country had always been a gamble. Callie found herself wanting to talk to Luke about what to do next, where to turn, but now, in front of their friends, wasn't the time.

On the ride home, he talked about the law, and she realized he didn't need half her herd to make a new start. He was no longer that broken man he'd been weeks earlier. She'd found him when he'd stumbled, not when he'd been down for the count.

When he finally paused long enough for her to say something, she told him about running into Dorothy.

"I told her I loved you." Callie couldn't bring herself to add more.

"What did she say?"

Callie knew Dorothy was nothing like what Luke thought she was. If he'd known her at all he wouldn't have come so far to see her again, but she didn't want to spoil his image of her more than it already was. "She said she wished us well."

"Good." His words came slow and guarded in the shadows. "I wish her well, too." He was silent for a few minutes, then added, "I want you to understand something. If you kicked me out tomorrow, I wouldn't even go speak to Dorothy. If I ever see her again, it'll be by accident and not my plan."

"I understand." She linked her arm around his. He hadn't needed to tell her how he felt, but she was glad he had. Voicing the answer to a question she hadn't asked ended all doubt about how he felt about Dorothy.

Callie helped unload the wagon and then dressed for bed while Luke took care of the horses. She could hear him whistling when he returned, moving about the cottage doing all those things he did before turning in. One lately included threatening any of the animals hiding to stay where they were. He always made sure each was nestled in for the night.

He turned out the last lamp and she heard him pulling his clothes off in the dark. With the warmer weather he'd stopped wearing his undershirt and only wore the pants part of his underwear.

The first time she'd rolled over and felt his hairy chest, she'd squealed with delight. She was sleeping with her very own bear.

After that he'd growl when she moved her hand over his chest.

As he slipped into bed, she touched him just over his heart. "I'm the woman who loves Luke Morgan," she whispered.

"Lift your gown," he whispered back, sounding tired.

"No," she answered.

"Then I'll say good night with a full and proper kiss."

He rolled toward her and she moved back. "No," she said, pushing at his chest with both her hands. "First, I have to tell you something."

"You've already told me you love me, Callie. Thanks for that each night, but it's late and I'm about all talked out for the day."

She wished she could see his face. "I can't lift my gown, Luke, because I'm not wearing one."

He was silent for so long, she feared he'd fallen asleep. He didn't move. He didn't even seem to breathe.

She'd expected him to come to her, but he moved out of bed. When he returned, he rolled to his side but didn't touch her.

Waiting, Callie wondered if he had any more idea what would happen next than she did. She wanted him to kiss her. Maybe she should have let him do that and just find out she wasn't wearing a gown. Tears bubbled to her eyes and she wished she could start her telling all over again.

Finally, his hand moved into her hair, tenderly brushing the curls away from her face. He rolled closer, so near she could feel the warmth of his body. His fingers moved lightly along her cheek as if he cherished what he felt.

Slowly, like a man who'd touched his lover a hundred times, he moved his hand along her bare shoulder and down her body all the way to her knee. Then he lifted her leg until it rested at his hip and closed the distance between them.

"Now," he whispered against her ear, "we begin."

She wasn't sure what she expected, an attack, an awkward mating of two people who didn't know how to make love, giggles and bumps until they figured it out. But it was none of that. They kissed for a long while, letting a fire grow slowly inside them, and as they kissed, their bodies moved over each other like matching parts fitting together seamlessly.

She felt his warmth moving over her and enjoyed the gentle way he explored her. When they finally mated, her body was ready, but she didn't feel a fire, a need inside her. He was finished in a few moments and all she felt was happy that she'd pleased him.

Without saying a word, they slept, wrapped in each other.

Late into the night he moved over her once more, waking her to passion, real hunger guiding his movements for the first time.

"I can do this better," he whispered. "Mind if I try again?"

"No," she answered, "I don't mind."

The heat between them became a blaze and this time, when they mated, her mind exploded along with her body. He held her tight against him as they tumbled into a passion neither of them knew could exist.

Her body was his, just as his was now hers, and she cried for pure joy.

When he finally pulled an inch away, allowing her to take a deep breath, he kissed her tears. No words formed in her brain as she lay in his arms letting him touch her as if he cherished her and kiss her tenderly, telling her how he felt without saying anything.

She drifted to sleep knowing she didn't need to dream of heaven, she'd already been there in his arms.

When she awoke long after dawn, she cried again, now missing him beside her and knowing that if he left her, she'd never stop longing for him. They hadn't talked of forever. Not once since the day they'd married.

In the midnight hours they hadn't talked at all, but they'd bonded. For as long as she lived she'd think of him as her man.

She dressed and found the wagon hitched and waiting for her. As was becoming his habit, he'd ridden over before dawn to meet with the hands, leaving her to sleep another hour. The kindness he'd shown her meant more than words.

Every morning, lately, Callie fed her animals and drank coffee with Mamie before heading over to the main house. She went about all her chores, but her mind was in the tender shadows of night, remembering what they'd done and how wonderful he'd made her feel. Without saying a word, he'd convinced her that she was wanted and loved. Even when he slept, his hands still brushed over her, covering her, cherishing her.

As she worked in the big house, moving books to his study so he'd have a wall to pick from to read at night, her mind might try to concentrate, but her body remembered the way he held her and molded her against him.

She closed her eyes, wishing that she'd lifted the hem of her gown weeks before. Then, she'd have a store of memories and she'd be a woman well and completely loved.

When one of the ranch hands came in to tell her the boss said he was held up and would meet her at the cottage, Callie almost cried. The news meant it would be after dark before she saw Luke.

She drove home alone, took care of the animals, and then made a soup for supper.

It was full dark when she heard him step onto the porch.

When she opened the door, he bent and kissed her cheek, then tossed his hat and gloves down and went straight to the sink. She watched as he stripped to the waist and washed. Nothing to say came to mind. What had happened between them the night before made small talk seem out of place.

When he didn't face her, Callie began putting the food on the table. It was long past suppertime and the soup seemed thicker than it needed to be. The corn bread was burned on the bottom from warming on the stove.

As she tried to straighten the table, he moved up behind her and wrapped his arms about her. "There's something I want more than food." He pushed her hair back and kissed her neck and his arm tightened just below her breasts. "You," he whispered, "only you."

She turned in his arms and smiled, dropping the silverware on the table.

He lifted her up and carried her to the bedroom. When he set her down by the bed, he kissed her lightly. "Be undressed by the time I lock the front door."

Callie tried, but he came back too quickly. He didn't seem to mind helping her.

When they were under the covers, he pulled her to him and kissed her with such passion she thought she might faint. As before, their bodies moved together. Tonight he took his pleasure first, then took his time pleasing her. It was almost midnight before they settled exhausted in each other's arms.

Luke pulled the covers up and noticed several tiny sets of eyes watching from the foot of the bed.

"Friends?" He lowered the covers so Callie could see.

She nodded.

He leaned up. "No audience. Scram."

All vanished except a lazy raccoon who waited until Luke growled before disappearing.

"Stay out of this bed, all of you," he warned. "I'm the only one who gets to sleep with her." He leaned back laughing.

As she played with the hair on his chest, he asked, "Any chance the squirrels haven't eaten our supper?"

"No," she answered, "but I could probably find something to eat. I'm starving." She moved away, but he pulled her back against him for one more touch.

"I was starving for you tonight. I hope you don't mind.

Being away from you wasn't easy. I thought the day would never end."

"I know. I felt the same." She thought about all the hours she'd spent that day trying not to think about him.

"You didn't mind us making love first?"

She shook her head. "I didn't mind at all. I belong to you, Luke, just as you now belong to me. That's what married people do, remember."

"I've always known, but I'm glad you finally figured it out. Bedtime just might turn into my favorite time."

They tugged on enough clothes to be almost presentable and dodged critters as they made their way to the kitchen looking for food. On the quilt by the fireplace, they ate cheese and bread and talked. Then they went back to bed and made love slow and easy as if it might take them all night long.

. . . And it did.

Chapter 10

LUKE had just managed to burn three eggs when Callie finally came out of their little bedroom. She looked adorable in the nightgown she hadn't bothered to wear to bed and one of his socks in her hand. Her hair was the wild sunshine he'd grown to love.

She studied him with tired eyes. "Is it always going to be like that?" she asked.

He smiled, knowing she'd been a full participant in what had happened and not a spectator. "You complaining?"

"Yes. At this rate I'll be dead from lack of sleep before summer."

He laughed and poured two cups of coffee. "I don't know how it's supposed to be." He sat down at the table. "I just know I've been up an hour and I'm already fighting the need to take you back to bed. I need to check something. There may have been one spot on that body of yours I forgot to kiss last night. I got distracted a few times so it might be wise for me just to start over. I'm not a man who neglects his duty."

"No." She waved the one sock as if it were a weapon. "I'm keeping my gown on until I get sleep and food and sleep and . . ."

He held his hands up. "I'll not touch you," he promised. "Come here and I'll even share my breakfast."

When she passed, he tugged her onto his knee and fed her a bite of eggs.

"Those are terrible," she mumbled as she stole a slice of bread.

"I know, but I couldn't wake my wife to help, and I've never been able to scramble eggs. So, looks like there is a good chance you'll die from lack of sleep and I'll starve to death. This marriage obviously wasn't meant to last more than a few days."

"How'd you eat eggs when you lived alone?" she asked, forcing down another bite and showing no concern for his problem.

"Boiled, always boiled." He took a bite of the eggs. "I hate boiled eggs so bad these even taste good."

By the time they'd finished off his breakfast, they were both laughing, when the raccoon wandered by and refused to eat a bite of the eggs that had landed on the floor.

Luke tugged her out on the porch so he could kiss her one last time before he left. "Sleep today. I promise I'll be home by dark and you'll probably need the rest because I don't plan on ever sleeping again." He settled his Stetson on his head. "Say the words before I go."

She smiled up at him. "I love you, Luke Morgan."

"I know and you do it so well."

There was so much more he had to say to her, but now wasn't the time. He needed to be at the main house. Yesterday he and his men had found fences down in several places and more than one man said the herd looked light. Someone was rustling their cattle. With the roundup still a month away, half the herd could be gone by then if he didn't do something.

When he got to headquarters, more bad news waited for him. During the night more cattle had been driven through another downed fence. The men were looking to him for answers, and Luke didn't know enough about the business to tell them what to do. Whoever was doing this knew the ranch; they had to know every path to be moving so quickly. Thornville had fired several men the previous year. A few might be getting their revenge.

It crossed Luke's mind that Callie's stepfather might be behind the robberies, but, from reports, it appeared Thornville was still hanging around in town as if waiting for her to beg him to come back and run the ranch. He'd told everyone who would listen that he was the reason the ranch had grown and prospered. If he hadn't married Callie's mother, the widow and her crazy daughter would have lost the place within a year.

Luke didn't miss the fact that no man on the ranch seemed to argue with Thornville's claim.

Quentin said Callie's stepfather stayed drunk most of the time and was sleeping with one of the doves a few doors down from the Watering Hole. Word was, he'd spent most of the money he'd gotten from selling off all he'd taken from Callie's place. But, if Callie was right and there had been half a year's savings in the office safe, he still had money to burn.

At about midafternoon, Luke decided to ride into town and talk to the sheriff. He also needed to hire more men to ride the fence line, but he had no idea who to trust.

Adams wasn't much help. Thanks to the drilling, men

looking for work were few. The sheriff even suggested that Luke think of raising wages on his place or he might lose those he had.

Luke rode back home and headed straight for the bunk-house. A drizzle earlier that had been bothersome had turned into a full storm. The men would be back at the headquarters soon working in the barns, so Luke stopped by the big room at the side of the main house that Callie called his office.

He didn't like the room, even though she'd added a wall of books and taken away most of the deer and bear heads. The place reminded him of the boss's office back at the mine. Built to impress, but hollow. Any man called in for a talk was probably in trouble. Maybe that was why Luke always went to the bunkhouse to talk to the men. He didn't know enough to be an equal to most of them, much less the boss.

As he tossed his soaked Stetson at the hook on the door, he swore. If Thornville was right and Callie and her mother would have lost the ranch, what chance did Luke have of saving it? Callie's mother had probably done the only thing she could think of to save the ranch: She'd married a cattleman. Her daughter hadn't been so lucky. Luke liked the outdoors and the hard work didn't bother him, but he wasn't sure he'd live long enough to learn all he needed to know to survive in cattle country.

At the rate they were losing the herd, they'd be lucky to have enough left to pay the bills through next winter. He'd checked in with the lawyer about getting an oil company to come out and test on the land, but that could take a year, maybe more. By then, the Cramer ranch might be owned by someone else.

Luke stared at the books. Thornville had made money, but he'd also spent it. The bank accounts would carry the ranch for maybe six months, into fall, but not through the winter. If he let half the men go and cut back, maybe another two months, but then there would be no money to start over next spring.

The worry over Callie and her ranch chilled him. If he could make sure she was safe. That she'd hold the ranch. That she'd be able to live. That she could make it.

Then, he told himself, he could leave in peace, but he already knew it was too late for him. No matter how he left, he'd be leaving his heart behind. No matter what happened between them, he had to fight now, for her sake.

If he sold off most of the herd, he'd need men to keep what was left alive and healthy. If he sold them now, while they were still winter thin, he'd take a loss.

Thunder rolled across the sky like a runaway stampede of thousands of head.

Figuring this out was harder than hammering through stone.

Luke stood and grabbed his hat. One thing he'd learned in the mines was that if he kept swinging, eventually the rock would crack. He'd worked with the ranch hands long enough to know they'd help and it was time he asked for just that.

The men were sitting down to supper when he walked in. Luke didn't waste time. He told them every detail while they ate, and by the time the cobbler was served, men were tossing around ideas hoping to lasso a solution. A few left the table saying they didn't have any idea what to do, but those who stayed gave it a try.

It was late when he left to ride home. Luke had a half dozen ideas worth considering. All were long shots, but that seemed all that remained.

For the first time since he'd left the cottage he let Callie completely fill his thoughts. Tonight he'd take the time to tell her how he'd been wrong about saying that she wasn't his type. She was all he would ever want in a woman. He loved everything about her. The way she laughed and how she talked to all the birds and animals. The way she made love and never hesitated to say the words he so needed to hear.

When he turned into the trees near the cottage, he was surprised the lantern was not burning on the porch. In fact, all the lights were out.

Maybe she'd gone to bed without him.

His heart stopped. Maybe she'd left . . . stepping out of his life as quickly as she'd stepped into it.

Chapter 11

CALLIE waited, wrapped in a quilt on the front porch as she watched the sunset blinking among the trees as if playing peekaboo.

Luke had said he'd be in by dark, so she wanted to see him as he rode up. How could a man come to mean so much to her in just weeks?

She'd liked him from the first. She admired that he was polite and never judgmental. He was kind and listened to her. They'd become friends and she'd learned to trust him and enjoy his company, but now it was far more. Love didn't seem a big enough word to tell him how she felt. She wanted to beg him to stay. She wanted to truly be his wife and deep down she knew he wanted the same thing. He wanted her.

Only, she feared if she let out all her feelings for him, she would finally convince him that she was as crazy as everyone said she was. When she'd said she wanted a real marriage, she was thinking about how it had to look to others. She never dreamed that a real marriage was exactly what he'd give her.

If she didn't show him how much he meant to her, he'd be gone and she might never have the chance.

The back door creaked behind her and Callie smiled. He was coming in through the back to surprise her. He'd probably walk up behind her and swing her into his arms.

Excitement wouldn't let her be still, but she cuddled beneath the blanket waiting for his first touch.

Seconds ticked by. Then her animals began to scurry and she smiled, remembering how he'd startled them the morning the kittens were born and they'd attacked him.

Don't slow him down now, she almost shouted, knowing that all he'd have to do was grumble at them and they'd call off the alarm. Even in the darkness, they'd know his voice.

The prairie hawk let out a shrill cry and flew from the low branch beside the cottage straight into the open doorway.

Callie stood, alarm climbing up her spine. The animals thought something was wrong. They were circling and growling like a mother protecting her nest.

Then, from the blackness of the main room, she heard a hiss, a cry, a yell of pain.

Her animals were attacking Luke. She dropped the quilt and ran into the darkness, wishing she'd thought to light a lamp inside. She hadn't even lit the fire, thinking they'd do that after they'd said a not-so-proper hello.

Another low animal growl, then a thump as if something had been kicked against a wall. The high, frightened screams of the birds filled the room as wings batted against cages they fought to escape.

Callie fumbled with the matches, knowing she had to get light to the room fast before one of the animals hurt Luke, or worse, he fought back and killed one of them.

On the third strike, the match flamed and a moment later light filled the room.

Callie's eyes focused on the bundle of fur in the corner. Checkers, her fox, was lying on his side as if he were a broken toy and not a living thing.

She made it two steps toward him when a hand grabbed her arm and whirled her around.

"It's about time we had a talk," a hard, familiar voice shouted. "Forget about your pet. We've got things to settle."

She shook violently, then tried to pull away, but her stepfather's grip was iron. Like an animal, she wanted to kick and bite and fight, but he'd always been strong and the little reason left in her brain told her if she fought, she couldn't win.

He shook her hard, making her teeth rattle as he bruised his handprint into her arm.

"Now don't go all crazy on me, girl. I'm not here to hurt you. I just figured we need to talk. All you got to do is see the facts of what's right and I'll be on my way."

A ball of fur flew from the rafters straight into his neck.

Thornville yelled, knocking the squirrel away but not before he'd ripped away an inch of flesh.

"Damn," Thornville yelled. "I'll kill every one of your wild pets, Callie. Never thought your mother should have let you have them anyway. She always did spoil you. Never made you do one thing you didn't want to do. Even if I'd had the time to teach you, she wouldn't have let you learn the ranch."

Callie tried again to break the lock he had on her arm, but it seemed hopeless. If she pulled any harder, her bone might snap.

He held his throat with one hand while he shook her again. "I'm going to shake some sense into you, girl, whether you like it or not. You can't just go ruining a man's life and think you can get away with it. And now you'll drive this ranch into the ground, making all my work worthless as well."

She had no idea where to start with him. Screaming that she'd hated him from the day he married her mother seemed a little too far back, so she picked his last crime. "You threatened to have me committed." The words came out higher than she'd intended, making her sound mad even to herself.

He tugged hard and sat her down in one of the chairs at the dinner table. "I was just doing my duty as your father. You're crazy as they come, girl, you always have been."

Callie closed her eyes. It was no wonder she talked to animals and danced with birds. He'd been telling her she was crazy for so many years she almost believed it.

"I needed to get on with my life and it wasn't like I was planning to take you out behind the barn and shoot you like you was a rabid dog. I checked into it. That asylum in Austin is the finest in the country. You'd like it there. They even said you could take a cat if you wanted to."

"You just wanted me gone off my own land."

"I worked it for years. I figure it's more mine than yours, girl."

Callie knew if she could stay calm, she might be able to talk to him long enough for Luke to make it home. Thornville might be strong, but he would be no match for Luke in a fight.

"I can smell that you've been drinking. Why don't you come back when you're sober and we can talk?"

"I haven't been sober since you ran me off my land. The sheriff, who's been my friend for years, threatened to shoot me if I wasn't gone within a day." Thornville let go of her arm and dug his fingers into her shoulder. "He don't know how crazy you are, or how determined I am. I'm not a bad man. I never hurt you, not once, but a person can only be pushed so far."

"You locked me up." He seemed to have forgotten that.

"It was for your own good. I couldn't be chasing after you every time I turned around. I had a ranch to run." He swore. "I still do. If I don't take over here, that husband you found is going to run the place into the ground before he has time to get you pregnant. The few hands loyal to me tell me that he's doing more wrong every day than right."

He leaned down behind her chair and looped one of her wrists with a leather strap. Before she could fight he'd caught the other wrist and pulled it into the tight knot of thin leather cutting into her flesh. "Now you just sit still, girl. This will all be over in a while."

When she inhaled to scream, he closed his bloody hand around her throat. Lack of air made her still and she thought he might kill her right then, but when he felt her go limp, he released her throat.

"I ain't going to hurt you. I promised your mother I'd never lay a hand on you and I'm a man of my word." He wiped the blood from his hand over the collar of her white gown. "What's going to happen here tonight will remove all doubt about whether or not you need to go to that asylum."

Callie would have sworn that her panic could climb no higher, but it did. "What are you planning?"

He scrubbed his face as if trying to sober up. "I ain't got it all worked out, girl, but I'm thinking on it. The way I see it, I got two major problems. One, you, but you've been a thorn in my side so long I'm about used to you. And, two, that husband of yours. Nobody knows him, so

I figure if he dies or disappears nobody's going to spend much time worrying about where he's gone."

"You're not going to kill him." She closed her eyes, realizing something worse than death might happen.

Thornville laughed. "Hell no, girl. I ain't going to kill him, but if I can just have a few minutes to think about it, I can figure out how you're going to kill him. It makes sense, you know. Folks won't even be surprised. Crazy Callie kills the only man in the state willing to marry her."

When she tried to scream, she only got out a squeal before he clamped his hand over her mouth. "Now stop that. You may not have to kill him, we'll just tell folks you did. I've got money. I'm thinking if we offered him some, he'd take it and disappear. He don't belong here. It's not his home."

"He won't leave," she mumbled beneath the hand covering her mouth.

"Then you'll have to convince him. Tell him you've changed your mind. You don't want to be married. Then you can tell folks he just left."

"And you'll tell them I killed him." Callie could see the future. She'd played this game with Thornville before. No matter what really happened, he'd spin his web of lies just enough to make folks wonder.

"You'll like Austin." Thornville seemed to be trying to calm her. "I hear tell they have music in the asylum and you can learn to paint. It's not like being locked in the root cellar. You'll be happy there."

He looked tortured. "It's my only option. I thought I could just let you live here at the cottage, but no woman is going to marry me with my ex-wife's crazy daughter still on the property."

Callie might have felt sorry for him if she hadn't hated him so much. All he'd ever thought about was himself.

Chapter 12

LUKE hid his disappointment when Callie wasn't waiting for him on the porch, telling himself that maybe the rain had driven her inside. He could also hear the birds in the cages along the front window and wondered why she hadn't covered them for the night.

The worries of the ranch weighed heavy on his mind but all he wanted to do right now was curl up in bed with Callie. They'd talk the future out while he touched her. If he had to sell the ranch, they'd keep the acres around the cottage. He could work as a lawyer and they'd have a good life.

Only she'd married him so she could stay on her land. Would she still stay with him if that were gone?

He put his horse up for the night and walked toward the house thinking about loving his wife.

When he walked in, he saw her sitting by the little table in her white gown and a quilt wrapped around her shoulders.

"Evening." He grinned, noticing her bare feet. "You already ready for bed?"

She looked up at him with huge, frightened eyes. With a slight shift, the quilt slipped from around her throat and he saw blood.

"What?" He made it one step before the barrel of a gun jabbed into his back.

"Easy now," a rough voice said from behind him. "She's all right. That ain't her blood you see. It's mine. One of these damned animals took a bite out of me."

Luke turned slowly until he saw Thornville's face. "What are you doing here?"

The gun didn't leave his back. "Why don't you just have a seat across from your wife? She got something to say to you and she wanted me here to make sure you heard every word."

Luke knew the man was lying, but he didn't want to do anything foolish. If Thornville fired, the bullet could go anywhere and might hit Callie.

He studied her closely, far more worried about her than himself. She looked frightened, but she didn't look as if she'd been hurt. "What is it?" he asked as he faced her with only the table between them.

"I want you to leave. The marriage is over. My stepfather has convinced me that this is the best for all. You leave tonight."

Luke couldn't seem to form words. He felt his insides caving in around his heart.

Thornville moved behind her, still pointing the gun at Luke. "We've talked about it and, if you leave now, I've got a thousand dollars to pay you for your time. I'll even take you east to the next train station. You can be on your way back to wherever you came from a few months ago and you'll never hear from us again."

Luke didn't look at Thornville. "Callie, is this what you want?"

"Yes. You knew from the beginning. A thousand is only half of what you'd have gotten for the cattle, but then you only stayed half the time."

She was talking to him, but her eyes stared at the center of the table. It crossed his mind that she must know that the ranch was in trouble. Maybe she'd gone after her stepfather and made a deal with him. If the ranch was the all-important thing, maybe she saw this as the only way. After all, she'd married a drunken stranger to stay; maybe she'd made a pact with the devil this time to keep the land.

Every part of him told him she was lying now. She still loved him. Only—he'd been fooled before by a woman and maybe he was simply too dumb to learn.

He stood slowly. "I'll go," he said. "If you'll say the words."

She didn't move. The room was silent. Thornville might have coached her, but he obviously had no idea what Luke was talking about.

"Say the words."

Finally she raised her gaze. "I'm the woman who loves Luke Morgan."

He saw it all in her eyes. The truth of what she said. The knowledge that she'd die if she lost him, just as he'd be dead without her.

Slowly, he turned to Thornville. "I'm not leaving, but I'll take your thousand dollars in payment for every cow on this ranch."

"What?" Thornville lowered his gun. "You must be as crazy as the girl. The cattle on this place are worth three or four times that."

"You built the herd. You take them. I'm sure the widow

will take you back. You can graze them on her land and open range until they're fat. The ranch belongs to Callie, but you're right, Thornville. The success of this place goes to you. Take the cattle. Leave her land and we'll forget you were ever here."

He moved closer to Callie and noticed her hands behind the chair. He didn't need to see the binding. "Cut her free."

Thornville bent and slashed the leather. A moment later she was up and in Luke's arms.

"It's all right, Sunshine. It's all over. Howard Thornville will never speak to you again." Luke met the man's stare. "If he ever does, I swear I'll kill him."

Thornville looked angry and lost, but even drunk, he wasn't a fool. "Why are you doing this? The cattle are the wealth of this place. Without them this ranch isn't worth much."

"I want the hatred between you and my wife to end here and now. When or if you ever mention her again, you'll call her Mrs. Morgan and there will be no talk of her being crazy. If it wasn't for her kindness and love, I'd have killed you tonight, but I don't want another bad memory haunting her. Do you agree the bargain we set is fair? Take the cattle. We'll survive and you'll have your start."

Thornville nodded.

"Then leave the money on the table and go. You've been paid in cattle for your years of work. Callie is no longer connected to you in any way. She's my wife."

Thornville hesitated as if trying to find the hole in the bargain. "All the cattle?"

"Every cow on the ranch and every one you come up with that has wandered off in the past few days."

"I'll need the men to round them up."

"Hire the ones who want to work for you. I'll not need them."

Thornville left mumbling something that sounded like he always knew crazy was catching.

Luke stood on the porch, his arm tight around Callie as they listened to him ride away. All the fright and panic bottled up inside her bubbled over into tears and he never once told her to hush. He let her cry.

When finally she gulped down one last sob, she whispered, "How'd you know I was lying?"

"Because you couldn't say the words unless you meant them. I could see it in your eyes. If you'd said them as you told me to leave, your heart would break."

He kissed her then and carried her inside. While he built a fire, she doctored her fox, wrapping his rib cage and laughing when he licked her hand.

Without talking they ate a small meat pie Mamie had brought that morning from the cook. They shared a glass of milk and the last of a loaf of bread, then he carried her to bed.

Finally, when the house was quiet and the door locked, they talked.

He told her about how they could live on the thousand dollars and the little money saved while he began his law practice. "I'm not a rancher, Callie, no matter how hard I try, but that doesn't mean I can't be a good husband. We'll keep the land. Who knows, one of our children might inherit the skills."

"We'll live here?" she asked.

"Until we run out of room, then we'll decide between town and the main house here."

"So, you're staying?" She pushed away from him and sat up, her gown open almost to her waist.

"Say the words, Sunshine," he said calmly.

She smiled. "I'm the woman who loves Luke Morgan."

"Then that settles it. I'm staying, 'cause I'm the man who is crazy about Callie Anne Morgan."

Epilogue

❧

FOUR years passed before Luke and Callie Anne moved to the big house, remodeling it to fit their ever-growing family.

They were married nine years when Luke Morgan became a judge in Hemphill County, and three years later they moved to Austin, where he served as a state senator. Callie spent her time there doing work at the state asylum, helping patients work with animals.

Twenty-five years, to the day, after they married, with the last of their children in college, they moved back to the cottage and their two oldest sons began ranching the land that had been in the family for almost a hundred years.

Some in town said that the love they had for each other spread out over everyone they met. A crazy kind of love that takes hold and never lets go. Even Quentin and Lindsey caught it. The bartender and the little teacher married a year after Luke and Callie had, to the very same terrible piano music and the same old preacher. Their oldest daughter married the oldest Morgan son, joining the two families in love and friendship . . . and, of course, shared grandchildren.

All who knew Callie Anne and Luke swore he repeated "Say the words" every day of their fifty years together.

Jodi Thomas is a certified marriage and family counselor, a fifth-generation Texan, a Texas Tech graduate, and a writer-in-residence at West Texas A&M University. She lives in Amarillo, Texas. Visit her online at jodithomas.com, facebook.com/JodiThomasAuthor, and twitter.com/JodiThomas.

Don't miss her next Harmony novel, *Betting the Rainbow*, coming April 2014 from Berkley. Turn to the back of this book for a sneak preview.

NAT CHURCH AND
THE RUNAWAY BRIDE

Jo Goodman

*For Susan Fry and Raymona Preston because they
are so tickled when they see their names in print
and it's not because they're in trouble.*

Note to Readers: Some of you will recognize Nat Church as the fictional adventurer of the dime novels mentioned in *The Last Renegade*. His exploits are also referenced in *True to the Law* and in the upcoming *In Want of a Wife*. When the opportunity was presented to me to contribute a short story for this anthology, I didn't hesitate. This dime novel had to be about Nat Church because he did not exist outside my head until I committed him to bytes.

Falls Hollow, Colorado

THE first thing Nat Church heard when he walked into the Falls Hollow Sheriff's Office was a harmony of voices, some sweet, some strident, all of them pitched in the alto and soprano range. The women—for surely this choir was composed exclusively of the female sex—were not crowded around Sheriff Joe Pepper's desk. Joe sat hunched in his chair, his head tucked between his shoulders, his eyes squeezed shut, and he was alone in the front office. It was the cells in the back room that were occupied.

Nat didn't call attention to himself. Joe hadn't heard him come in. It was hardly surprising, given the volume of the vocals. Nat recognized the tune as "Mary Had a Little Lamb," but the words were unfamiliar to him. He stopped just inside the door to listen.

Harry had a little dram,
   A little dram,
   A little dram,
Harry had a little dram,
   from a bottle marked eighty proof.
And everywhere that Harry went,
   Harry went,
   Harry went,
And everywhere that Harry went,
   drink made his belly pouf.

Pouf? Nat stopped listening. One of his black eyebrows was already lifted in a perfect arch. He wondered
how many words they'd found to rhyme with "proof," or
how many verses the Temperance women had composed
while waiting for husbands, brothers, fathers, or sons to
bail them out. Judging by the suffering, discomposed
expression on Joe Pepper's face, it was likely this choir
of angels had been unnaturally creative.

Nat shut the door hard enough to raise Joe's head above
his shoulders and open his eyes. Nat thought the sheriff
looked relieved to see him.

"Nat Church," Joe said, shoving away from his desk
and rising to his feet. "About goddamn time. Tell me
you're here for *her*. I've had a parade of good citizens
come through here this morning. Paid the fines for their
womenfolk. The hell of it is, the women won't leave until
her fine is paid, and no one's been willing to do that. Not
when it's clear as gin that she comes from money. I'm
thinking she could have paid everyone's fine right off, but
she never made the offer. Standing on principle is what I
heard her say." Here, Joe Pepper rolled his eyes. "What
principle? That's what I'd like to know. A man's got a

right to have a drink now and again. It's women like her that drive us to it."

Nat didn't agree or disagree. His dark eyes moved past Joe's left shoulder to the door behind him. The voices, the melody, the words slipped under the door.

Harry drank most every day,
    Most every day,
    Most every day,
Harry drank most every day,
    and beat his wife quite senseless.
There came a day when Harry hit,
    Harry hit,
    Harry hit,
There came a day when Harry hit
    but his wife was not defenseless.

Nat's gaze shifted to Joe. "Do they know any other tunes?"

Joe shook his head. "Just the one. I'll hear it in my sleep tonight."

"How many women are there back there?"

"Seventeen women. One she-devil."

On brief acquaintance, Nat Church was said to have eyes so dark they were impenetrable. Those few people who knew him better could sometimes see past the black and catch a glimpse of curiosity, interest, or, on rarer occasions, amusement. Nat was amused now. The right corner of his mouth kicked up a fraction and something glinted in his eye. It might have been a twinkle, although no one had ever suggested that.

"Sure," Joe Pepper said, raking his thinning hair with one hand. "Easy to laugh where you're standing. Me? I've been listening to 'Mary Had a Little Lamb' since six o'clock this morning."

"That's when you arrested them?"

"That's when they woke up. I arrested them at a rally in front of Sweeny's Saloon around ten last night. I didn't want to arrest them, mind you. Mike Sweeny didn't ask me to do it, but they wouldn't be moved, and *she* commenced to marching back and forth across his doors. Next thing I know, the marching stops, the ladies are holding hands, blocking the entrance, and no one's getting in or out. Now, Sweeny don't care if customers can't get out, but he cares a great deal when they can't get in. I had no choice. *She* dared me to put her in chains. Mostly I was interested in gagging her, but a tablecloth isn't large enough to stopper that Grand Canyon of a mouth."

Nat cocked his head to one side to better hear the individual voices. Which one was *hers*? Strident? Smooth? Sweet? Was she the slightly husky contralto or the clear-toned mezzo-soprano?

"So?" asked Joe Pepper. "Who are you here for?"

Nat unbuttoned his beaten, buttery-soft brown leather duster to reach inside his vest pocket and retrieve a photograph on heavy card stock. He stepped up to Joe's desk. If his tarnished spurs jangled as he approached, he couldn't hear them. He admitted to himself that he preferred their sound to the choir. The women seemed to be indefatigable. He could appreciate Joe Pepper's pain.

Nat turned the photograph around for Joe to study. "You know I could be here about any one of the bounties tacked to your wall, Joe. As luck would have it—and I'm thinking it's your good fortune, not mine—I'm here for one Felicity Ravenwood. Is that your she-devil?"

A broad smile split Joe's face as he looked down at the photograph.

Watching Joe, Nat sighed. "I figure that grin means she is."

"Photograph hardly does her justice, though," said Joe.

"Because that ridiculous hat hides her horns?"

Joe chuckled as he slid the photograph toward Nat. "Well, there's that. Maybe it's just knowing that you're taking her off my hands that has me thinking she's prettier than what you got there."

Nat did not glance at the photograph as he returned it to his vest. "How much is her fine?"

"Fifty dollars."

Nat whistled softly.

Joe shrugged. "Food and bedding accounts for five dollars. Thirty is for public disturbance. Sheer aggravation is the rest of it."

"Can't fault you for that, Joe."

"Didn't think you would."

Nat counted out the money and laid it on the desk. He asked Joe for a receipt.

Joe returned to his seat to write out a slip. "This isn't going to do you much good if you can't keep her."

"Just being thorough."

"Who is looking for her, Nat?"

"Not for me to say."

"But you'd tell me if she's a felon, wouldn't you?"

"It's a little late to be asking that question, don't you think? I just paid her fine." He took the receipt from under Joe's fingertips and pocketed it. "I just paid for her." In spite of Joe's relief to be rid of his she-devil, Nat could see that the sheriff was wondering if he'd missed an opportunity. Nat took pity on him. After all, the man had been listening to a Temperance-inspired nursery rhyme for the better part of the morning and hadn't shot anyone. He deserved some peace.

"She's not wanted, Joe. Not by the law. I'm doing some-one a favor."

"Careful you don't get your spurs caught crossways, Nat. Mark my words. She is going to make you wish you'd asked for money. A lot of money."

"You're probably right, but it's done. You want to spring her?"

"My pleasure." Joe got up and took the ring of keys hang-ing from a hook by the entrance to the cells. As soon as he opened the door, the singing stopped. "All right, ladies," he called, shaking the keys. "Fines are paid in full. Yours, too, Miss Ravenwood. Everyone can go home. In your case, Miss Ravenwood, you can go back to where you came from."

Nat Church hitched a hip on the edge of the sheriff's desk and stretched out one leg for balance. He sighed, folding his arms across his chest. If Joe's intention was to rile Miss Ravenwood, he had chosen the right words. He could practically hear the woman's feathers ruffling.

"I imagine you meant to be insulting, Sheriff. It hardly becomes a man of your stature. It belittles your office and your oath. You took an oath, didn't you?"

To his credit, Joe did not respond, although Nat sus-pected the man's ears were turning crimson. He heard the keys jingling and imagined Joe giving them a good shake to remind the women that he had power if not stature.

"I want my day in court. We all do. Isn't that right, ladies?"

Nat heard murmurs of agreement. As an endorsement, it was a mild one. He suspected Miss Ravenwood's Tem-perance followers were growing weary. When Miss Rav-enwood spoke again, Nat finally identified her voice as the husky contralto. He thought it had a fine timbre. A man would be grateful to hear her whisper in his ear. At least this man would.

Joe said, "You've had your day. Actually, your morning.

Judge Wilcox passed sentence when he came in to get Mrs. Wilcox. Found you all guilty, set the fine, and left here fit to be tied when Mrs. Wilcox would not be budged."

Nat heard a new voice and felt confident he recognized Mrs. Wilcox as the speaker. "But did he go home, Joe? Or did he go to Sweeny's?"

Joe's silence was telling.

"I thought so," Mrs. Wilcox said. "Let me out, Joe Pepper. The judge will need some help finding his way home, and he has a trial in Blackwater tomorrow."

"Right you are."

Nat heard the keys jangle again. The noise stopped the moment Felicity Ravenwood spoke up. "I'd like to know who paid my fine."

"Well, as to that," said Joe, "I can tell you I was sorely tempted, but fifty dollars is dear to a lawman."

"Fifty dollars!"

Nat could hear the women stirring. Fabric rustled as they rubbed shoulders and skirts in the small cells. Their voices were hushed. The whispers were unintelligible as a whole, but there was a snippet here and there that let him know that no one else was levied with such a steep fine. Apparently Judge Wilcox had gotten a little of his own back, and Nat recalled that Joe Pepper had added a tax for the grief she'd given him. Who could blame them?

"That is outrageous," Miss Ravenwood said.

No one disagreed with her.

"We were exercising our right to assemble and speak out against the demon rum."

"Yes, ma'am," Joe said politely. "I'm thinking you have better than a nodding acquaintance with demons."

Several women spoke up then. Nat heard the judge's wife among them. "Shame on you, Joe Pepper. You want us to start singing again?"

Nat had listened to enough. He pushed off the desk and crossed the office to the open doorway. He set his right shoulder against the jamb and casually looked over the eighteen women crowded into two cells. There was a third cell, but it was empty. Nat supposed that was purposeful. Joe didn't want his prisoners to be too comfortable. What he'd done was just make them mad.

Wet hens. That was the first thought that came to Nat's mind. It was hard to look any woman in the eye when their hats demanded his attention. Straw hats. Felt hats. Velvet and satin hats. Broad- and narrow-brimmed hats. No two were alike. The adornments distinguished them. He saw a garland of bloodred roses, a trelliswork of pearls, velvet ribbons, gold braid, beaded lace, and everywhere his eyes settled, there were feathers.

Pheasant. Ostrich. Peacock. Baby birds nested among feathers and fir cones. The colors were outside what he knew to exist in nature. At least, Nat did not think there was an ostrich alive that sported olive-colored plumage or had its fine feather tips dipped in gold or black or silver. These feathers bobbed and weaved and floated as the women turned their heads in unison to stare in his direction.

"Ladies," he said. His eyes settled on Felicity Ravenwood, or rather Felicity Ravenwood's extraordinary hat. The color was the first thing that set it apart. No one else was wearing anything in that same deep shade of claret. The high, stiff crown and wide, sloping brim were trimmed with claret velvet ribbon. An abundance of white ostrich feathers sprouted from the right side like sea foam, dipping and rising in waves as Felicity tilted her head. Nat could not decide if the hat was a work of superior millinery or a construction fashioned from the leavings on the milliner's workroom floor. Separate from its owner, he was certain it would look ridiculous. He was disconcerted when the word "fetching" flitted through his mind.

Nat removed his well-worn, pearl gray Stetson, nodded politely in way of a greeting, and ran his fingers through his unruly black thatch of hair just once. He doubted it did much to improve first impressions, yet it seemed as if he should try to ease this gallery's mind. Generally it was not something that concerned him, but he had a ways to go with Miss Felicity Ravenwood, and looking disreputable would not inspire confidence in him. Now that he could see past the flock of hats, Nat recognized some of the faces in the room. These women would speak well of him, or at least they could assure Miss Ravenwood that he wasn't a criminal. It was unfortunate that they could not say that he wasn't a killer.

Nat made eye contact with the women he knew and addressed them in turn, reserving his seldom-seen smile for the judge's wife.

Mrs. Wilcox stepped closer to the bars. "Why, Nat Church. You might just be the last person I was expecting to see this morning."

"And here I was thinking the same thing about you. Joe treating you right?"

"About as well as I deserve, I expect." She had an accusing glance for the sheriff before she turned back to Nat. "There *is* an empty cell we could have used."

Nat nodded. "Yes, ma'am. I see that. Your hats look a bit crowded. Joe, how about letting the ladies out now?"

"Seems like I was about to do that once already," Joe grumbled. He started to insert the large skeleton key into the lock of Mrs. Wilcox's cell. "Stand back, ladies. There's no need to stampede."

"Wait!" Mrs. Wilcox thrust her hand through the bars and curled her fingers around Joe's wrist. "What about Miss Ravenwood? You haven't told her who paid her fine. Was it one of our menfolk? Surely I want to know that."

Nat thought his presence answered that question, but apparently Mrs. Wilcox had not made the connection. "I paid the fine. I am going to accompany Miss Ravenwood back to her private coach, where we will wait for the next train. There will be no more protesting in front of Sweeny's Saloon, or rather no protesting that includes Miss Ravenwood."

As Nat expected, no one except Miss Ravenwood voiced an objection. Feathers parted to allow her to move to the front of the cell, and she did so with great dignity: chin up, shoulders back, and green eyes that never wavered from his.

"Mr. Church, is it?" she asked, tilting her head ever so slightly.

Nat nodded, fascinated that her hat remained in place. He wondered that the weight of it did not pull her off balance. The fountain of ostrich feathers was looking more like Old Faithful. He returned his hat to his head and, out of habit, carefully ran his hand along the brim to make sure it was set just so.

"Well, Mr. Church," Felicity Ravenwood said. "I don't know you. I thank you for your kindness in stepping forward to pay my fine, but it was unnecessary. I could have paid it myself, but there was a principle to honor. Since there is going to be no public trial, I am quite happy to reimburse you." She raised one hand to show the beaded reticule dangling from her wrist. "In fact, it has always been my intention to pay the fines for all of my sisters here."

Joe Pepper looked pained. "I told you, we're all square with that. Besides, if you want to pay people back, it's the menfolk you owe."

"Yes, I know, but I want to give it to the ladies. Now, what was the individual fine?"

Joe's attention was suddenly all for the toes of his boots. He muttered, "Five dollars."

"I see. I must have sorely aggravated you and the judge. Good. It was all of a purpose, and, more often than not, success comes at a cost." She opened the reticule and extracted a bundle of bills. She handed it to Mrs. Wilcox. "I would be pleased if you'd peel away five and then pass it along."

Nat thought the judge's wife had a smile on the sly, secretive side. He figured Miss Ravenwood's largesse came as no surprise. It was clever, really. Husbands, brothers, fathers, and sons paid the fines. That was five fewer dollars they had to spend at Sweeny's if they strayed in that direction, and five dollars for the women, who were hard-pressed to come by money outside of what their men gave them. There was a certain justice in their scheming that Nat could appreciate. He waited until the bills had circulated between the two cells and the remainder was returned to Miss Ravenwood before he spoke up.

"The door, Joe. The money's been settled."

The sheriff managed to turn the key this time. His attempt to open the door was thwarted when Felicity Ravenwood grabbed the bars in her slender, kid-gloved hands and held the door in place.

Watching from his vantage point in the doorway, Nat merely shook his head. Delicate hands aside, she was strong. He decided that desperation more than principles contributed to her strength. She did not want to leave the cell.

"Joe," said Nat, "open the other door."

"Good idea." The sheriff went to the second cell, inserted the key, and twisted.

As Nat had anticipated, once Joe was otherwise occupied, Felicity Ravenwood eased open the door to her cell and gestured to her companions to leave quickly. There was a brief hesitation before they complied. It was clear they did not want to abandon her. Felicity squeezed their hands as they filed out.

Nat moved out of the doorway to let the women pass into the front office. Felicity managed to close her cell door before the second group of women marched by. In a show of solidarity, they brushed her curled fingertips as they passed. When Joe saw that Miss Ravenwood was still in her self-imposed prison, he started for the door.

Nat put out a hand, suggesting that he stop. "Make your peace with the ladies in your office, Joe. You still have to live in this town."

"Don't I know it." He jerked his head in Felicity Ravenwood's direction. "You'll take care of her?"

"I will." Nat regarded Miss Ravenwood. Her green eyes had narrowed, and her wide mouth was set with a certain menace. Clearly, she did not embrace the notion of being taken care of. "How about some coffee, Joe? Tea might suit better. Isn't that right, Miss Ravenwood? Do you prefer tea? I find that tea introduces a level of civility that might otherwise be absent in conversation."

Felicity Ravenwood stared at him. "Who *are* you?"

"You know that, ma'am. Nat Church. Joe Pepper here will vouch for me. So will half a dozen of your newly formed sisterhood, not the least of whom is Mary Wilcox."

Sheriff Joe Pepper slipped behind Nat on his way out. "You brought this on yourself, Church," he whispered.

"God help you." He shut the door behind him and Nat heard him greet the ladies still milling about his office. "Can I impose on one of you to make a pot of tea?"

FELICITY Ravenwood kept her hands curled around the iron bars. When Nat Church stepped closer to the door, she felt the urge to back away. She fought it and held her ground. In a show of force, this man could easily wrest the door away from her, drag her out by her hair if he had a mind to, and frog-march her back to where her private railcar was waiting on a side track at the station. Relief warred with suspicion when he stopped within half an arm's-length distance and remained there, his hands resting relaxed and open at his sides.

He stood with his feet set slightly apart. His scarred leather duster hung loosely from his shoulders, but she had glimpsed his gun belt when he moved out of the doorway. She wondered about the gun holstered at his side. A Colt? A Remington? She did not know guns. Weapons were her father's particular interest, not hers. Neither was she interested in a man who wore a gun as comfortably as he did his Boss of the Plains Stetson. She imagined he no longer felt the weight of it against his leg. Its absence would be more bothersome, like the tingling of a phantom limb. That troubled her. In her experience, a man was only easy with a gun if he knew how to use it with an economy of motion and a true aim.

She glanced down at his scuffed brown boots. A fine layer of dust covered them. She raised her eyes slowly and saw the same thin film of dust on his long coat and pearl gray hat. Was he weary? If he was, nothing of it showed on his face. Except for a narrow smile, his features were without expression. He had dark, hooded eyes, a Roman nose, and a squared-off jaw. A shadow suggested there might be a cleft in his chin, but she could not be certain. The coarse stubble along his jaw hid the evidence from her. His rough beard seemed to be the consequence of not taking time to shave, but what accounted for his haste?

Dread knotted her stomach. An uncomfortable pressure settled against her chest.

Felicity took a deep breath and exhaled slowly. "I hope you can appreciate that your name does not of its own accord inspire confidence. As for the sheriff or my sister companions endorsing you, it is not all that helpful. Truth be told, Mr. Church, I know them little better than I know you. I only arrived in Falls Hollow three days ago."

"Imagine what you might have accomplished in four."

Felicity's full lips thinned slightly. "Do I amuse you?"

"After a fashion, yes."

"How do you mean?"

Nat shrugged lightly. "Have you ever seen the way a cat plays with a mouse before he pounces?"

"Yes. It's unpleasant."

"I suppose that depends on your perspective. You amuse me like that."

Felicity's cheeks flushed pink.

Nat turned his head toward the door and called out, "How's that tea coming, Joe?" When the sheriff called back that it was almost ready, Nat gave Felicity his full attention. "To my way of thinking, it can't come too soon."

"I'm not hopeful we can achieve civility," said Felicity. "Not if you won't answer my questions."

"I thought I just did. You didn't like my answer."

This time the breath that Felicity drew was much

shorter. She exhaled huffily. "Why are you here, Mr. Church?"

"Now, ma'am, that's a different question. I'm here to spring you."

"Spring me?"

"Pay your fine and get you out. I've accomplished exactly half of that. I suppose you have your reasons for wanting to stay where you are."

"I do. One of them being I don't go off with strangers."

"You feel safer here?"

"Yes."

"All right," he said. "I'm going to see about that tea."

Felicity watched him disappear into the sheriff's office. There was nothing for her to do but wait. For obvious reasons, the jail did not have a rear door. She didn't think fleeing was a solution to her problems anyway. Where would she go? Her Pullman car was hardly a sanctuary, not when that was where he wanted to take her. She would not be merely falling in with him. She would be leading the way. It would take very little effort to find her if she returned to the hotel where she'd stayed before her night in jail. He might have even gone there first.

Felicity was musing over how Nat Church had found her when he came through the door carrying two tin cups. He passed one through the bars. She hesitated, expecting a trick. He held the cup steady and waited her out. At last she took it.

"I took the liberty of adding sugar," he said. "I hope that's to your liking."

"It is," she said. There was another hesitation, then, "Thank you."

"You're welcome." He raised his cup, toasting her. "To civility, Miss Ravenwood. Drink up. I promise you, I won't remain a stranger much longer."

Felicity felt oddly calmed by that. It was the last thing she clearly remembered.

N AT Church looked up from cleaning his gun when he heard Felicity stirring. She was not awake yet, but he thought it would not be much longer. She had changed positions twice in the last ten minutes and was now lying curled on her side facing him. The bed at the rear of her private Pullman coach was not ten feet from where he was sitting. He had folded back the privacy screen so he could keep an eye on her. He wondered what she would consider the most egregious violation: That he had watched her sleep? Or that he had removed her hat?

He idly rubbed the ivory handle of his Colt Peacemaker while he watched for some faint movement beneath her eyelids. Not for the first time, it occurred to Nat that Sheriff Pepper had a gift for understating a truth. The card-stock image of Felicity Ravenwood that Nat still carried in his vest pocket did little justice to the woman he'd met in the Falls Hollow jail. Even sleeping, her features had more to recommend them than the sepia-toned photograph could suggest. Awake, she was vibrant. Sleeping, she merely glowed.

Nat's lip curled slightly, mockingly. Had he ever thought a woman glowed? He wondered if he was waxing poetic. Waxing pathetic was more accurate, he decided. He set his Colt down on the table beside his gun belt. He drew the leather holster closer and began to oil it. The trouble was, keeping his hands busy didn't necessarily occupy his mind, and his eyes followed the gist of his thoughts, straying at regular intervals in Felicity Ravenwood's direction.

In sleep, there were none of the hard edges the camera

had captured. Here her features were softly composed.
Nat imagined she had not been an easy subject to photograph. He did not think that sitting still came naturally.
Waiting while the photographer fiddled with lighting and
lenses had probably been painful for her, and the camera
caught her impatience. The effect was to make her look
stern, almost harsh, but to Nat's eye, even that could not
mask her deep unhappiness. The lush, full line of her
mouth was lost. Her chin jutted forward with no hint of
the tilt that made her seem equal parts coquette and mil-
itant.

The hat she wore for her studio sitting was equal to the
extraordinary creation he had removed from her head. He
wondered if wearing it was a battle won or lost with the
photographer. The feathers had created a slight shadow
across the upper portion of her face that made her eyes
appear deeply set and penetrating but without much suggestion of a sentient being behind them. In contrast to the
extravagance of the hat, the face that stared out from
beneath it seemed more plain than pretty, more dull than
distinctive.

The photograph could not indicate that her dark eyes
were a shade of green closer to emerald than jade, and
the camera had failed to find their brilliance, but these
oversights were failures of the invention and its mechan-
ics, and Nat had been prepared to meet a woman who
was something more than she appeared.

Her hair, though, was a revelation.

Until he removed the hat from her head, he could not
have claimed with any certainty to know the color, length,
or texture of her hair. Upon seeing it, he decided the hat
was guilty of a criminal offense. Nat supposed that if he
had been pressed, he would have said she was a brunette.
It was true but hardly accurate.

Sunlight flickered through the windows as the Pullman coach rattled rhythmically along the tracks. At regular intervals a sunbeam would glance off her hair and lift a wash of deep red to the surface. Auburn, he thought it was called. If he'd been asked, he would have named it autumn. It had that kind of warmth and glow . . . and he was waxing poorly again.

Shaking his head, Nat finished oiling the holster. He stood, strapped on the gun belt, and replaced the Colt. He put the oil and cloths back in his saddlebag before he sat again. There was a fashion periodical lying on the table that he had been deliberately avoiding, but now, given the fact that she was still sleeping, he picked it up and riffled through the pages. Clearly he had found the source of inspiration for her hats. He looked up from the magazine to stare at the stove. It was tempting to toss it in. It would have provided a brief, yet satisfying burst of flame. He resisted. Felicity Ravenwood was going to be furious. It was probably better if he didn't add fuel to that fire.

Nat stretched his long legs as he leaned back. He found an article that discussed what fashionable women would be wearing this winter when they went ice skating in Central Park. He had never been ice skating. He wondered if Felicity had. She would be better than merely competent, he thought, which was the best he could hope that he might achieve. It was easy to imagine that she would be graceful. Her long legs would lend her an elegant line, and she would glide effortlessly across the frozen pond. He had a picture of her in his mind wearing an ermine-trimmed skating costume that showed off slender ankles. Even better, she was hatless. Except for two silver combs to keep her hair from falling forward, it was unbound. It moved as she did, the cascade of long, unruly curls swinging slightly from side to side. She was enchanting, and Nat Church was mesmerized.

That was how it came to pass that the hero at Harrisonville and Broken Bow, the solver of the mystery of the Chinese Box, the winner of the Shooting Contest, and the man who put the Best Gang behind bars, to name only a few of his accomplishments, was completely blindsided by the shoe flung at his head.

The pump heel smacked him squarely on the forehead. The kid leather shoe, dyed claret to match Felicity's gown, bounced off his head and fell on the table, its landing softened by the open pages of the fashion periodical.

"That's some aim you have," Nat said. There was no rancor in his voice. He lifted his arm slowly and rubbed his forehead with the heel of his hand. "I suppose you think you have your reasons."

Felicity threw back the covers and pointed to her feet. "You suppose? You *suppose*?" Heat flushed her cheeks pink. "I have more reasons than Carter has Little Liver Pills. You put me in leg irons!"

Nat stopped rubbing his head and held up an index finger. "One leg iron. Singular. Would you like your shoe back?" Because she looked as if she were prepared to pitch the other shoe at him, he decided it was better to keep it. "The shackle is a precaution, nothing more." When she stared at him with the malevolence that only green eyes of her particular hue could muster, it seemed to him that further explanation was in order. "In the event you wanted to throw yourself from a moving train."

She continued to stare it him, although her expression held less malice than it had a moment earlier. Curiosity was nudging her toward calm. "You are not quite right, are you?" She touched the side of her head with her fingertips. "Here, I mean. I am wondering what else accounts for your extraordinary behavior." She raised her shoeless foot a few inches and frowned at the uncomfortable weight that made it an effort to do so. "Please remove this. I entertain no thoughts of killing myself. I am not leaving my coach while it's moving."

"All right," he said, rising. He took the key from the same vest pocket that held her photograph and moved to the bed. He stopped just short of turning the key to look at her. "There will be regular stops for water and coal. Already had one while you were sleeping. Don't test me." He didn't ask for her word. He didn't figure he could trust it. The better course was to watch her and see what happened. Nat opened the shackle. The chain remained wound and locked around the brass foot rail. He pushed the restraint out of the way and returned to his chair. He watched Felicity massage her ankle and rotate her foot. He didn't comment. He knew she wasn't injured, and he gave her a few moments to assess the same.

Felicity stopped rubbing, but she did not release her foot. "Should I be afraid of you?"

"No." He watched her contemplate that. "There wasn't any point in asking, if you aren't going to believe me."

She closed her eyes briefly as she pinched the bridge of her nose. "I am just realizing that. Whatever you slipped into my tea is still muddling my brain. That's how you managed this, isn't it? You put something in my tea."

"Yes. Chloral hydrate. Only a few drops. I apologize for that, but you were set on staying in jail."

"I was set on not going anywhere with you."

"I understand. Still, it couldn't be helped."

"I don't believe that. You could have explained yourself." She let go of her foot and swung her legs over the side of the bed. She didn't try to stand. "Why didn't you?"

"Because you wouldn't have liked it."

She sighed, resigned. "I don't think I'm going to like it now. You really do know the judge's wife, don't you?"

He nodded. "And the judge. And Joe Pepper. Several other ladies as well."

"And they'd vouch for you?"

"Yes, ma'am."

"Then you really don't mean me any harm."

"That's right."

"And you're not abducting me for ransom?"

"No, ma'am. Not for ransom. This is more in the way of a favor, although I do hope I can collect on the fifty dollars I advanced for the cause."

"I can pay you back the fifty dollars."

"I know, but to my way of thinking, it would be like taking a bribe. Besides, I peeked in your reticule. You don't have fifty dollars left."

She waved aside his objection. "I can write a draft."

"Maybe you can, but maybe it won't be any good."

Felicity frowned. "Why in the world would you say—" She stopped suddenly. "My father's done something, hasn't he? Has he cut me off?"

There was no putting sugar on this. "Yes, ma'am. I believe he used those exact words."

"You're working for him?"

"Not working. Like I said, this is more in the way of a favor."

"You abduct women as a *favor*?"

"Not as a rule. This is what you would call a special circumstance."

"Oh," she said. "A special circumstance. I would like to hear about that. I surely would."

Nat didn't flinch from the sharp edge of sarcasm in her tone. There didn't seem any point in shying away from something when it was so deserved. "As a favor to my employer I agreed to meet your father and hear him out. I believe they knew each other well once and cross paths now and again on matters of business and politics."

"My father *is* railroads so there is no question of crossing political paths now and again. It happens all the time. He usually curries the favor of politicians. It is hard to imagine he asked for one."

Nat shrugged. "I only know what I was told. If I thought I could help, then my employer said he would be pleased if I did so."

"Truly? There was not perhaps some pressure brought to bear? You do not impress as someone who could be intimidated by Edward Ravenwood, so I have to assume my father did not storm and rant and threaten you into helping him. Why are you doing it?"

Nat considered showing her the photograph in his vest pocket. It was an inadequate explanation at best. How could he tell her that he was moved by it when he hardly understood that reaction himself? What he offered instead was: "The promise of a favor from Edward Ravenwood is worth something. Your father owes me, not my employer."

Felicity's eyes dropped away. She stared at her hands while she smoothed the fabric of her gown over her knees. She did not look at her abductor when she said, "Then he is even craftier than I thought."

"Or perhaps more desperate. I witnessed his anxiety."

"You mistook embarrassment for anxiety," she said, stealing a glance at Nat.

"I don't think so."

"I did embarrass him, you know. The wedding guests were seated, all of them turned in my direction. My fiancé was waiting for me. I was on my father's arm." This time she shrugged. "And I bolted. Just like that. I remember thinking in the moment before I ran that my feet would not carry me a single step, then I understood it was because I was trying to will them to go in the wrong direction. I had no trouble once I made the decision to retreat. I ran to the waiting carriage, ordered the driver to go to the train station, and grabbed the whip from his hand when he didn't respond quickly enough. My father shouted for me. I remember that. I didn't dare turn back. What if something I saw in his face convinced me to return?"

"This coach was specifically built for your wedding trip, your father said."

Felicity touched her cheeks with her fingertips. In contrast to the iciness of her hands, her cheeks were hot. "Yes, that's so. A gift. Jonathan and I were going to tour the West. I've been to Europe, you see, several times, and . . ." Her voice trailed off. "I don't suppose that's important."

"It might be," said Nat. The mild prompt was enough for her to go on and confirm his suspicions.

"It's just that Jonathan thought Europe was a more appropriate destination. More refined. Cultured. Did you meet him?"

"Jonathan Harding?" Nat shook his head. "No."

"Social conventions are important to him. He is very, um, correct."

"Stiff."

"I prefer 'correct.'"

"All right. Still, he agreed to the western tour."

"Jon has always been tolerant of my opinions, but it was my father's gift, not my arguments, that won him over."

Nat had had plenty of opportunity to investigate the sumptuously appointed coach. Everywhere he looked, he could see the evidence of attention to detail. It was there in the carefully beveled walnut wainscoting, the polished brass knobs and rails, and the heavy velvet curtains framing each window. It was an extravagant gesture, but having been invited to the Ravenwood mansion directly across from the park, this railcar was obviously no grander a gift than Edward Ravenwood could afford. What Nat said was, "I see."

"Do you, Mr. Church? I don't love him."

"I didn't think you left him at the altar for any other reason."

"It seems as if I *should* be married," she said after a moment. "I'm twenty-six, you know." When he didn't respond, she added, "Of course you would know. Father regularly laments that fact. It stretches credulity that he wouldn't point it out. My mother was seventeen when she married my father, and her mother was seventeen when she married for the first time and twenty when she married for the second. I try to tell him we are living in different times, but the argument is not persuasive. There is hardly a woman in my set who is not married, widowed, or engaged. Certainly no one with as many prospects as I have had."

Felicity sighed. "I am depressing myself. I need a drink." She stood, tested her balance, and discovered she was steady on her feet. Except for a troubling lapse in her memory, she could identify no other lingering effects of the drug he had given her. "Would you like a whiskey?"

Nat blinked. This was unexpected. He had found the drinks cabinet but had assumed it was Jonathan Harding who had a taste for spirits. "You haven't forgotten you recently led a Temperance rally, have you?"

"Oh, that. Yes, well, that was the impulse of a moment. I heard the ladies chattering from my hotel window, and I was curious. I listened for a while and thought I should lend my expertise to their cause. They had no organization, and I am rather good at it. They had passion of purpose but no plan. It was remarkably easy to take them in hand, and I believe they were grateful."

Felicity opened the cabinet, removed a decanter of whiskey, and paused to look at Nat over her shoulder as her hand hovered over the cut-glass tumblers. When he nodded, she took out two and placed them side by side. She poured generously into each and carried them to the round table, where he was still comfortably stretched. She held them out and let him choose before she pulled out the other chair and sat.

"I have no particular objections to drinking, Mr. Church, but I particularly object to drunks."

It was a sentiment worth toasting. Nat Church raised his tumbler a fraction and waited to see if she would join him. She arched an eyebrow, but after a brief hesitation, she did the same. They took their first swallow together. The whiskey went down smoothly, and his mostly empty stomach accepted it without protest.

Felicity set her tumbler on the tabletop and turned it slowly. "What is the exact nature of the favor you are doing for my father? I am not going to marry Jonathan. I can't."

"Your father has made peace with that."

"Truly?"

"I believe so, yes."

A small crease appeared between her eyebrows. "Then what . . . ?"

"This was not your first engagement."

Her grip on the tumbler tightened. "I wondered if he shared that. I hope he explained that I ended the two previous engagements before the invitation list was sent. I should seem very cruel otherwise."

"He made certain I understood. It seemed important to him that I know you are not heartless by nature. He believes your mother would have taken you in hand."

Felicity's smile was rueful. "He invokes my mother when he is at a loss. She died when I was very young. I only have vague memories of her, and perhaps there is something to what he says if you believe my behavior requires a tempering influence, but I like to think she might have encouraged me to lead with my head and follow my heart." She sighed softly. "Father was so pleased when I agreed to marry Jon. Genuinely happy. I've often wondered if I agreed to the proposal because I knew how much joy it would bring to him. Regardless of my motives, knowing that I would hurt him made it all the more difficult to go back on my promise to Jon."

Nat watched as Felicity eased the pressure of her fingertips on the tumbler. She began to turn it again. "Do you remember what you wrote in your last correspondence to your father?"

His question made her breath catch. "He shared that letter with you? It was personal. It was the explanation I owed him. It was my farewell."

Nat glimpsed the sheen of tears in her eyes and sensed the depth of the betrayal she felt. "I'm sorry," he said, and meant it.

Felicity said nothing for a long time. She rolled the tumbler between her palms but never lifted it to her mouth. "I wrote that I would rather live by my wits and off the land than sacrifice my name to a man who cared for my money but nothing at all for me."

That was the precise phrase Edward Ravenwood had asked him to commit to memory. "Your father believes you meant it."

"I did," she said. "I do."

Nat nodded. "Then you understand why you've been cut off?"

Felicity raised her tumbler to her lips and drank deeply. She returned the glass to the table with only a splash of whiskey remaining. "I understand." Tilting her head to one side, she regarded Nat Church with candid, curious eyes. "Do you think I am spoiled, Mr. Church?"

Nat took in their plush surroundings before settling on Felicity again. "I think you are privileged, Miss Raven-wood. I can't say about the other."

"That's fair. You don't really know me, do you?"

"No."

She sighed softly. "Did you at least pay the hotel before you drugged and abducted me? I was there two nights."

"I left money with Joe Pepper to settle the bill."

"Good. I will add it to the debt I already owe you. Fifty for my release from jail and another . . . ?" She looked at him expectantly.

"Twelve."

"Very well. I owe you sixty-two dollars." Now it was Felicity whose eyes roamed the railcar. "Do you have any use for the painting above the bed? The frame is easily worth more than sixty-two dollars, and the painting is the work of Camille Pissarro. *The Outer Boulevards*. I purchased it in Paris. Jon said looking at it made him think there was something wrong with his eyes. The style is called impressionism. I quite like it."

Nat had studied the painting earlier. The application of oils to the canvas was done in a manner that disregarded clearly defined lines. The effect on close examination was a blur of color, but, regarding it from even a short distance, the brushstrokes took form and shape and left no doubt of the artist's view.

"I've seen something like it in the Metropolitan Museum of Art."

"Really?"

"Careful, Miss Ravenwood. The skepticism in your tone hints at snobbery." He saw she had the grace to blush, and he let her squirm for a moment. After all, compliments of the mirror above the washstand, Nat knew he was barely on the right side of disreputable. He had washed up while she slept and found a brush to pull through his hair, but his clothes and boots carried a fine layer of dust from days of hard riding to intercept the train. His long leather coat, hat, and saddlebag were still lying over the arm of an overstuffed chair. Caring for his gun had been more important. He was that kind of man. He thought she should probably know.

"It's all right," he said. "Your doubt is warranted. I was there to steal a painting, not to admire the gallery." Nat held her stare. He could see that she was trying to decide whether to believe him. The truth, and the frank manner in which he told it, left her more uncertain than she had been before. It was a reaction he was used to.

Felicity said, "Does my father know that?"

"I didn't tell him."

"I don't know if ignorance explains his trust in you."

Nat found he was moved to a smile by her wry tone. "It probably doesn't."

Felicity's eyes grazed his mouth. The amused slant of his lips did not change, and when she met his eyes, there was something more than darkness there. "What else do you do, Mr. Church, besides stealing paintings and abducting heiresses?"

"Former heiresses," he said.

"Yes. You are right to remind me."

Nat finished his drink and pushed his empty glass

toward hers. "What I do is not complicated, Miss Raven-wood. I lend a hand where I can. I help people."

"Is that how you justify abduction and thievery?"

"As a rule I don't justify myself. I see no reason to make an exception now."

"That is convenient."

He shrugged and watched her mouth flatten disapprovingly. She looked full of starch. Except for the shoe on the table and the other one on her foot, he might have smiled.

"What are your intentions, Mr. Church?"

Nat drew in a deep breath. His cheeks puffed slightly when he exhaled slowly. "Well, I saw your hip bath behind the screen over there. I thought I might use that to wash away the grit." He knuckled the stubble along his jaw. "I figure a shave wouldn't do me any harm, either. If I time it right, we'll be stopping for water near Sidney. There's an eatery at the depot. I'll order and we can dine here. You're hungry, aren't you? I am."

"What are your intentions *toward me*?"

"Now, see, that's a different question. I only have what's called an inkling about it now. I expect that after a bath, a shave, and a decent meal, it will be a fully formed notion."

"You're amusing yourself with me again, aren't you?"

"A little." Nat pushed himself upright, nudged the fashion periodical and shoe out of the way, and set his folded hands on the table. "You can still travel anywhere you like, Miss Ravenwood. Your father means for you to have use of this car providing you don't leave it. Set foot on a platform anywhere, at any time, and the conductor and porters have strict instructions not to let you board again. I gave them those instructions, but I had them in writing from your father. Any or all of them could lose their jobs if they act counter to his wishes."

"I think I preferred the Falls Hollow jail."

Nat made no comment about the accommodations. "Regardless of what he's done, your father is still concerned for your safety."

"And yet I am sharing my new cell with you."

"It is an imperfect world."

"Are you my keeper, Mr. Church?"

"That's a fair description."

"Have I grasped the situation correctly?" she asked. "I have no money and few resources while I am a passenger, yet if I leave the train to look for gainful employment, I will not be permitted to return, even if my search comes to nothing. All the while, you will be living in my empty pockets and, I imagine, making some sort of report to my father."

"In a nutshell."

"I see." Felicity stared at her hands. "I think he believes I'll return to New York without ever having stepped off this train. Perhaps he is not as resigned as you suppose to my elopement and he means to teach me a lesson."

"That's certainly possible." More than possible, Nat thought. It was likely. She knew it, too. He had already spied a glint in her eye, and it made him uncomfortable. What had Joe Pepper said? *You brought this on yourself, Church. God help you.*

Felicity rose from her chair and stood at the washstand so she could observe her reflection in the mirror. She fingered the gold locket at her neck while she turned her head this way and that. She pinched her cheeks and tidied her hair by twisting the long cascade of curls into one fist and securing it to her head with a pearl-studded ebony comb and pick. She smoothed the skirt of her gown and tugged on the sleeves before turning back to Nat and presenting herself for inspection.

"You mentioned an eating house at the Sidney stop. I think I could be a Harvey girl."

Nat groaned inwardly. Harvey girls were becoming as ubiquitous along southern train routes as water towers. They were employed exclusively in the eating houses and hotels owned by Fred Harvey, and he had exacting standards.

"I have read the ads," said Felicity before Nat spoke. "Mr. Harvey advertises in all the city newspapers." She quoted from memory. "'White young women, eighteen to thirty years of age, of good character, attractive and intelligent.' Is it too vain of me to suppose I meet all of his qualifications?"

Nat offered a grudging response, most of it under his breath. "You meet them."

"That's good, then, isn't it? And I could manage on what I'm paid." Her short laugh was a trifle self-conscious. "I admit the advertisements fascinated me. The promise of adventure and meeting new people all the time, I imagine. Room and board is provided, and the wage is seventeen dollars and fifty cents each month."

"Plus tips," said Nat, and then wondered why he'd mentioned it.

"Plus tips? I hadn't realized. That is splendid. I think I should do very well for myself." When he didn't say anything, Felicity flushed. She amended her boast. "Or at least well enough."

Nat decided to squash this notion before she was off the train with no chance of returning. He'd have no peace in his bath if he thought she was going to get off as soon as the train slowed, and he did not relish the idea of shackling her to the bed again.

"The eatery in Sidney is not a Harvey establishment." He saw Felicity's immediate disappointment was quickly replaced by suspiciousness. Before she asked, he said, "Yes, I've eaten there. There's no hotel. There's no reason to build one since Sidney is not a town where travelers are inclined to linger. The train will stop for twenty minutes, give or take, and the passengers will scramble to get a hot meal but accept a cold one if it's all that's available. I don't think I've ever seen anyone tip the biscuit shooters. There isn't time."

Felicity's chin came up. Even though she still wore only one shoe, there was a certain dignity in her step as she walked back to the table. "All right," she said. Picking up her shoe, she retreated to the bed and sat down to put it on. "There are other establishments along the route. If they aren't suitable, I know there are Harvey restaurants in Kansas, New Mexico, and Arizona. I can have this car uncoupled and added to a train taking the southwestern rails. That is not against the rules, is it?"

Nat gave her full marks for putting her wits to good use. "I should probably get clarification from your father."

"I know what that means, Mr. Church. My father did not anticipate that I might want to stay in my car but change trains. He made no provision for it; therefore, I believe I am playing well within the rules. You think so, too. I can tell."

Nat wondered what he had done to give himself away. He would think about that later, preferably while he was soaking in a hot bath. "All right. I won't ask him about it. There is no point in alarming him."

"Exactly." Felicity pointed to the hip bath. "The porters can fetch you hot water. You reach them by pulling on that cord by the forward door. I assume it's been properly connected. You will find soap, sponges, and towels in the washstand. The wardrobe to the right of the bed still has Jon's clothes in it. It is very small of me, but I was waiting to see if he would request them."

"It's only been three weeks," said Nat.

She nodded slowly. "It seems much longer. I'm not sure why."

"Perhaps it was the night in jail that changed your perspective."

Felicity chuckled. "Perhaps. Tell me, how did you get me from the jail to the depot? Surely you didn't carry me."

"I slung you over my shoulder long enough to get you to the back of a buckboard and drove it here. I had to leave my horse with Joe, but he'll get a good price for it and wire me the money."

She regarded him curiously. "I know it means something to you to have my father in your debt, but don't you think you should have asked for advance money as well?"

"I don't decide who I will and won't help by how much they can pay me. I have nothing against being paid, and getting paid a lot is better than a little, but it matters more if the assignment interests me."

"Stealing interests you?"

"Stealing from the Metropolitan interested me. It hadn't been done before."

"So it was a challenge?"

"Yes."

"Am I challenging you, Mr. Church?"

"I think you know you are." He pushed his chair back and stood. "I'm going to have that bath now."

FELICITY sat on the padded window bench alternately thumbing through *Peterson's Magazine* and looking out on the broad, flat plain of high grass and meandering

streams. She ignored—or tried to—the sounds of water
lapping against the sides of the tub. It meant Nat Church
was shifting, stretching, sluicing, and there would be
water sliding over his shoulders and chest in rivulets.
Soapy droplets would cling to his collarbones. Steam
would curl and spike the ends of his dark hair. Her first
impression was that it was overlong and badly in need of
cutting. When she saw him again, without his hat this
time, she amended her opinion. It suited him perfectly,
and she decided that the change in her thinking proved
she could be flexible. Jon had accused her of being intrac-
table, and while he framed it as a tease, she knew it was
not. She could even allow that there was some truth in it,
but she was also aware that intractability in a man was
considered principled, while a woman was thought to be
willful or stubborn.

Nat Church had said she was a challenge. He had not
said it with his usual directness, but she could infer it
from their exchange. More importantly, he did not seem
to mind. If she understood him correctly, it made her
interesting. He could mean that she was a curiosity, a
specimen to be poked and prodded and pinned to a board
for further study—she had not forgotten his cat-and-
mouse remark from earlier—but she did not think that
was so. He was intrigued.

Felicity wondered why.

DINNER was beef stew and biscuits. The stew was
rich with meat and potatoes but had few vegetables
and very little seasoning. The biscuits were hard. Felicity
and Nat softened them by dipping them in the stew and
washing them down with beer.

"You're very quiet," Nat said. He eyed her half-eaten

plate of stew and compared it to the one he had wiped clean. "And not very hungry."

She pushed her plate toward him. "Help yourself."

He did. "What's on your mind?"

"If you're certain you want to know, I'm wondering how I am going to repay you for dinner."

"Is that why you ate so little? Do you think I'm going to charge by the bite?"

"I don't know. We haven't discussed it."

"You offered me the Pissarro."

"You didn't say you would accept it."

"Didn't I? Well, I will. It will be a pleasure to look at now and again, and it will square your debt and pay for your meals for a very long time. Does that improve your appetite?"

Felicity stopped him from pushing the plate back to her. "It's all right. I'm still not hungry." She raised her beer and regarded Nat over the rim of the mug. "Where will you hang it? The painting. You said it would be a pleasure to look at. Where will you hang it?"

Nat's gaze narrowed on the painting as he studied it. "The Metropolitan Museum of Art."

"You mean you'll *visit* it?"

"Sure. So will lots of other people, I expect. I don't exactly have a place for it."

"Why is that? Where do you live?"

"Depends on what I'm doing. Hotels mostly. Boardinghouses occasionally. Outdoors when what I'm after is living there, too."

"Are you a bounty hunter?"

"Some folks might say so. I wouldn't."

"What would you say?"

"I don't mostly." He held up a hand, palm out. She pressed her lips together and gave him a chance to swallow *and* think. "Repossession," he said finally. "Repossession and recovery."

"That does sound better than theft, abduction, and bounty hunting." She sipped her beer. "Your employer makes unusual demands, Mr. Church."

"Nat," he said.

"Nat," she repeated. "Nathaniel?"

"Only if you're my mother. I'm Nat to everyone else."

"Nat, then. Since you will be sharing this car with me for the foreseeable future, you may call me Felicity."

He repeated her name and watched her eyes dart away. He even thought she might have blushed a little. He wondered about that. "Did your Jon Harding call you Felicity?"

"Of course." She knew she had answered quickly, too quickly, judging by the way Nat was watching her. Quietly, in the manner of a confession, she amended her answer. "Sometimes. Not often. Jon was fond of using endearments."

"Did you like that?"

The question startled her. Jon had never thought to ask her. She was not certain what she would have told him if he had, but she had the sense that nothing less than the truth would satisfy Nat Church. "It seemed careless," she said. "As if he couldn't be troubled to use four syllables when two would suffice. Darling. Dearest. Sometimes I wondered if he simply forgot my name. So, no, I didn't like it." Her smile was a trifle wistful. "Jon was frequently occupied with matters of business. It was important to him to continue to impress Edward Ravenwood."

"He works for your father?"

"He does. It was one of the reasons Father was so delighted by our engagement and hopeful about the marriage."

"So your father wanted a son. Anything else?"

Felicity sighed. "Grandchildren."

"And you, Felicity? What do you want?"

"Something different."

"You don't know?"

"I'll know it when I find it. And when I find it, I will seize it with both hands and not let go until the breath leaves my body."

Nat believed her. She made him believe her. He understood why the Falls Hollow Ladies Temperance League had followed her into jail. He even understood why they didn't leave her there when they had the chance. What he did not understand was why his arrangement was with her father and not Jonathan Harding.

Night fell like a velvet curtain over the countryside. When Felicity looked up from her knitting to mark the railcar's progress, she saw very little beyond her reflection in the window. Nat had lit every lamp, and the effect was to make their car visible to anyone standing along the route, but to make the route invisible to her. She had often done the same in the evening, and it had never bothered her. Now she wondered about the towns she could not see and what opportunities she might be missing.

Felicity's gaze moved slowly from the bank of windows to where Nat Church was sitting at the table playing solitaire. From where she was sitting in one corner of the small sofa, it was his profile that presented itself to her. She had looked over many times to study him and never surprised him studying her. It was difficult to know whether to be relieved or insulted and finally concluded she was a little of each.

At dinner he had worn a jacket he'd selected from Jon's wardrobe. Because it was a bit snug across the back and perhaps an inch too short in the sleeves, it was an adequate, not perfect, fit. Felicity thought he probably wore it as a concession to some sort of formality that he believed she required. He had removed it after the porter took away their dishes and the remnants of their meal, and now he played cards in one of Jon's crisp white shirts with the sleeves rolled up to three-quarter length and a dark satin vest embedded with flourishes in silver thread. The shirt and vest were a better fit than the jacket, and he looked as comfortable in them as he did in his own skin.

She watched him gather up the cards and begin to expertly shuffle them, his lean fingers deftly snapping the cards and squaring off the deck. She wondered if he played poker and supposed there was not a man alive who didn't.

"Are you married?" she asked. Felicity managed not to drop a stitch, but only just. She had not known she was going to ask the question until she heard it, and upon hearing it, marveled that her voice had pitched itself in a soprano's range. When he looked up from his cards and regarded her thoughtfully, Felicity made sure she returned that regard steadily while pretending that a tide of warm color was not washing over her face.

"I am not," said Nat.

"Oh." The *click-click* cadence of Felicity's needles did not falter, but she had no idea where she was in the row. She startled herself with another question, though it seemed to her that Nat Church expected it. "Have you ever been engaged?"

"No." He set the cards down and absently flicked the deck with his thumbnail. "There was a girl once, but nothing came of it."

"You didn't propose?"

"No. She saw it was coming and gently headed me off.

It wouldn't have worked. I know that now. There were too many years between us."

"She must have been very young."

Nat shook his head, his slim smile edged with amusement and regret. "The opposite. I was twelve. Miss Templeton was a little more than twice that."

"About my age, then," said Felicity. "I imagine she was flattered."

"I don't know about that. Embarrassed and uncomfortable probably better describes it."

"I would have been flattered, even charmed."

"In other circumstances perhaps she would have felt the same, but she was my younger sister's governess, and if either of my parents thought she had encouraged me, she would have been dismissed from her position."

"Of course. I didn't realize." Felicity's eyes darted toward the bed. She had straightened the linens and smoothed the blankets while Nat was gone to get their dinner. The rumpled bedclothes had called attention to themselves in a way that Felicity found disturbing. When she looked back at Nat, she saw his slim smile had deepened. There was nothing to do but say what was on her mind.

"Have you determined where you will be sleeping this evening?"

Nat's smile did not waver. He looked deliberately toward the bed and then back at Felicity. He thought she might have stopped breathing. "Are you really harboring some doubt about the answer to that?"

"I wish you weren't amused," she said after taking a careful breath. "Or rather, I wish I did not amuse you. I wouldn't have posed the question if I knew the answer."

The narrow lift of Nat's mouth that defined his smile vanished. "Of course. I intend to sleep here."

"In that chair?"

"In this car."

"Yes, but *where*?"

Nat raked his fingers through his hair. "Well, I figure I asked for that. I don't suppose I've given you much reason to think I can act the gentleman or even that I was raised to be one."

"You did drug me."

"Carried you off and shackled you, too."

"You did all of that." Felicity saw him nod, acknowledging the truth of it. What she did not see was regret. Without regret, there would be no apology. She did not wait for one and was not entirely sure one was warranted. "So?" she prompted.

"I plan to sleep on the floor," he said. "That's assuming you won't begrudge me a few blankets. If that's the case, I'll sleep in the bed and you can have the floor."

Now that her mind was eased, humor tugged at Felicity's lips. "You may have as many blankets as you like. A pillow also."

"Easily better accommodations than I had these past two nights."

It was not said accusingly, but Felicity knew she was responsible. "When did you realize I asked for this coach to be put on a spur in Falls Hollow?"

"When I received a wire from your father while I was en route from Denver to Cheyenne. I had to get off and take another train going south, and then when I couldn't get a connecting train to Falls Hollow, I had to ride for three days to intercept you before you left."

"So Father is following my progress."

"Every mile."

"Of course. When I was traveling in Europe with friends, he sent two men to watch over us. It would have been better if he had told me. I wouldn't have reported them to the gendarmes. There was a lot of fussing before we straightened it out." Felicity offered up a Gallic shrug and moved her knitting from her lap to the basket at her side. "He could have had this car returned to him at any time. There isn't an engineer on a rail line anywhere that would not have cooperated. Instead, he sent you because he has conceived this lesson for me, and it doesn't seem that he wants me back until I've learned it or surrendered. I do not believe he will waver. It is like him to see a thing through to the end."

That was Nat's impression also, but he refrained from commenting. He asked, "Are you tired? I can put the screen in place if you would like to ready for bed."

"Please." Felicity rose at the same time he did and went to help him. She liked that he accepted her assistance without comment even though he was quite capable of managing alone. She would rather be an ally than an albatross.

Nat returned to the table and took up the cards again. He made a point of keeping his eyes on his game. He could imagine what was going on behind the painted silk screen without looking at it. When Felicity emerged, she was wearing a white linen shift beneath a dressing gown of ruby silk. In contrast to the delicacy of her sleepwear, she favored heavy gray woolen socks to more fashionable slippers.

Felicity caught Nat staring at her feet as she approached the bed. She stopped, lifted the hem of her shift as she looked down, and wriggled her toes. "They get cold," she said.

He raised both hands in a gesture of innocence. "I didn't say anything."

Felicity made a small sound at the back of her throat

and dropped her hem. She opened the trunk and set some blankets on the floor beside the bed and then dropped a pillow on top of them. "You can have any part of the floor that you like," she said. "I'm not assuming you will want to sleep here."

"There is just fine."

She nudged the stack of blankets a bit farther to the left. "In the event I get up in the middle of the night," she said. "I don't want to step on you." Turning her back on him, Felicity swept the bedcovers aside and sat down on the edge of the mattress. When she extinguished the lamp secured to the wall at her bedside, she saw Nat get up to take care of the other lamps in the coach. He left one lamp flickering on the table so he could resume his game and prepare for bed when he was ready.

"Good night, Felicity," he said when she stopped turning under the covers and lay still. "Pleasant dreams." He chuckled when his words were immediately followed by a distinctive thud. Metal crashed against wood as Felicity kicked the leg iron out of her bed.

ONE day passed without incident. Then two. On day three Felicity paced the length of the railcar so often that Nat threatened to shackle her. She eyed his gun but never revealed if she was considering shooting him or herself. Nat would not have blamed her for attempting either, but only because the real target of her frustration was her absent father. Nat restrained the impulse to point it out and invited her to play cards instead. She won more games than she lost until he introduced liquor into their play. After that she won them all.

Nat woke with a sore head on day four. Felicity was relentlessly cheerful. As a strategy, Nat decided it was diabolical. And, as he had an appreciation for the diabolical, he liked her more for it.

A week in, Felicity presented Nat with her plan to find work in a dance hall. She was only marginally discouraged when he told her the steps she had mastered for the ballroom would not serve her on the stage. That night, behind the privacy screen, she practiced fan kicks. Nat watched the shadow play, the flutter of her petticoats, and imagined he could see up the length of her bare leg all the way to the Promised Land. He took out his gun and began cleaning it.

Day to day, Felicity wondered at the patience of her jailer. She had not tortured him with variations on "Mary Had a Little Lamb" as she had done to Joe Pepper, but she had rearranged every piece of unsecured furniture several times, cheated at cards on three successive evenings, and read aloud to him from at least one article in every ladies' periodical he procured for her. It was hard not to appreciate, even admire, the man's equanimity. Whether it was his intent or not, he helped her make peace with her situation, at least until night bore down on them.

She had never known loneliness in her bed until he was sleeping beside it. She often inched toward the edge and stayed there, alternately fearing and hoping he would understand it was an invitation. If he knew it, he never acted on it. There were times he only pretended to sleep, and she accepted it because saying she knew otherwise would compromise them both. He was something more than he would have her believe, and something less as well. For all that her father trusted him, Felicity was of the opinion that Nat Church stood dangerously close to the wrong side of gentleman. For her part, she was aware she was flirting with ruination. Her sleep was disturbed by dreams that made her regret waking.

In spite of that, she gave no conscious thought to testing him. If she had, she would have dismissed it as foolish. Instead she searched for common ground and found it was almost always underfoot. They both were seasoned travelers. She, because her education had been abroad; he, because experience had been his education. They often talked during dinner but fell silent when they shared a drink. Quiet suited them. They both read. She knitted. He played solitaire. She plotted her eventual escape. He plotted the route that made escape undesirable, even impossible.

They were twenty-three days living in each other's shadow before Felicity began to calculate the chances of surviving a jump from the train.

"I'm getting off at the next station," she told him. "This is not the western tour I had in mind. We are taking a circuitous route to nowhere. Do you think I don't know what you're doing?"

Nat was reclining on the short sofa with his calves dangling over one arm. He was wearing his pearl gray Stetson except that he had settled it over his face and not on his head. He poked the brim with the tip of his forefinger and lifted it just enough to uncover his mouth. "What do you think I am doing?"

"You're making sure I have no opportunity to find a suitable position. You have coupled and uncoupled this car at least six times that I know of. I would not put it past you to have had it done while I was sleeping. In a week it is possible to get from San Francisco to New York, and yet we have not been east of the Mississippi nor west of the Great Salt Lake. In ways I cannot begin to understand, you have been successful in bypassing all major cities between here and there and back again."

"But the countryside's been pleasant, don't you think?"

"I want off this train, Mr. Church."

"I understand."

"Do you? Because I have not seen the evidence for it. You would not goad me as often as you do if that were true." Felicity ceased pacing when she reached the back of the sofa. She leaned over with the intention of plucking the hat from his face and tossing it to the floor. She even entertained the idea of stomping on it. Nothing like that came to pass. Her wrist was seized in a grip every bit as secure as the leg iron had been. When she tried to pull away, she merely helped him sit up. The hat fell forward, but he caught the brim in his free hand and flicked his wrist. The Stetson sailed toward the table, landed, and slid just as far as the edge and no farther. The ease with which he accomplished it was the end of enough.

Felicity Ravenwood burst into tears.

Nat Church did not believe for a moment that he was hurting her, and that left him at a loss to explain her reaction. He didn't know many men comfortable with a woman's tears, and he didn't count himself as an exception. He loosened his grip but not so much that she could pull free. What he noticed was that she didn't try. It required little effort to guide her around the sofa. When she was standing in front of it, he tugged once. With no more urging than that, she sat beside him. He found a handkerchief in his pocket and gave it to her. She held it against each eye to stem the tears, but when they continued, he lent her his shoulder. She crumpled the handkerchief in her fist and leaned into him with the ease of someone who belonged there.

Felicity closed her eyes. A few more tears leaked from beneath spiky lashes. She forgot about the handkerchief and knuckled her eyes. A swallowed sob shuddered through her. She hiccupped once and then was quiet.

Nat released her wrist and slipped an arm around her shoulder. He let her rest. She was still and silent for so long that he thought she had fallen asleep, but then he heard her long, indrawn breath and knew she had not.

"I cannot stay inside another day," she said. "It's cruel. I need fresh air and sunshine and room to do more than stretch. I need a destination and a purpose."

"I know."

"You *don't* know. You get off at every stop. You can walk the length of the platform and the length of this train. You talk to passengers. I have conversations with you and the porters. No one else. I see people coming and going at every station, and I can't be one of them. I don't understand. Has something changed? Are you making these decisions on your own or acting on my father's instructions?"

Nat looked down on the auburn crown of Felicity's hair and thought that if he inclined his head a mere fraction he would know its softness under his cheek. He refrained. Instead, he breathed in the scent of it. She favored lavender in her bathwater. The light fragrance infused her hair and lay lightly against her skin. His nostrils flared. It was the least of his body's responses.

"When I went to get our dinner that first night, I sent a telegram to your father. I informed him I had found you, that you were safe, and that you were entertaining the idea of becoming one of Fred Harvey's girls." He felt Felicity's head move from side to side. He did not have to observe her face to grasp her disappointment. "I expected he would have objections; what I did not expect was that he would not accept the risk that you might succeed."

Her brief, husky chuckle held no amusement. "That is because you believed he was resigned to my single state. He's not."

"I am not always right," he said. "But I am not usually so wrong. I misjudged him. I regret that . . . for both of us."

Felicity believed him. "My father is persuasive because he sincerely believes in the rightness of his arguments. You are not the first person to misinterpret his real motives. He wants me back in New York, but he wants me to believe it is my idea. It is a successful strategy in matters of business. He has a tendency to forget I am not one of his employees."

Felicity drew her legs up and folded them sideways under her gown. It caused her to lean more heavily against Nat. He accommodated the shift without comment. His arm continued to support her. His hand lay lightly against her upper arm. His thumb brushed her shoulder.

"Why does my father really trust you?" she asked.

It seemed to Nat that Felicity had plucked the question from thin air, but on brief reflection, he realized that it was likely she had only been holding it back. He had demonstrated that first night that her father's trust had not been misplaced and, at more than a little discomfort to himself, he had been proving it every night since.

Nat knew only one way to answer her question. He said, "I gave him my word."

"It means so much, your word?"

"Evidently your father thought so."

Felicity shook her head. "I mean no insult, but I doubt that. There is more to you than your name, Nat Church, so I'll ask you again and trust you will provide a better answer. Who *are* you?"

After more than three weeks in her lavender-scented company, observing her grace in circumstances that tested her good nature and his moral compass, the surest way to make certain he continued to sleep beside her bed and not in it was to tell her.

So he did.

"My employer," he said. "Your father trusts me because I serve at the pleasure of the president." Felicity pulled away sharply to gape at him. He gently nudged her jaw closed and drew her back into the cradle of his shoulder. "Yes," he said. "*That* president. I served his predecessor as well."

"Those things you told me early on and the crumbs you dropped here and there, were they all true?"

"What things?"

Felicity did not doubt that he knew. There were no holes in his memory. He was being cautious, as she had come to learn was his nature. She reminded him so he would know *she* had not forgotten. "That painting, for instance, the one you said you stole from the Metropolitan."

"A Renaissance work of art presented to our president by the Italian ambassador. It was already on loan to the museum when the Italians learned their ambassador had exchanged the gift for a fake. They were embarrassed and apologetic and asked for the painting's return before it was discovered to be a forgery by the museum's curators. The president decided that in the interest of preserving relations, the best course would be to steal it. That's what I did."

Felicity tilted her head so she could look at him. Her eyes narrowed as she tried to gauge how truthful he was being. "I never heard about the theft. I would imagine something like that would cause a stir." She paused as her gaze slid lower and caught the faint change in the shape of his mouth. "Unless . . ."

"Yes?"

"Unless you replaced the forgery with the genuine painting." She saw his lips twitch. It was so brief that in other circumstances she might have thought she imagined it. "That's what you did. I know it."

"If you say so."

"I do." She settled comfortably into the crook of his shoulder once more. "What else?" she asked. "You said there were people who would call you a bounty hunter. What about that?"

Nat considered what he wanted to say carefully. "The president receives correspondence from citizens every day. Most are letters expressing a concern. There are invitations, requests, and many that thank him for something he's done. It might surprise you to know that people write deeply personal things." He drew in a breath and released it slowly. "Then there are the threats. Too often it's not possible to know the author of those, but when it is, it falls to me, or someone like me, to find that person and judge their sincerity. Sometimes men who pen those letters are already in prison or have their picture hanging on a wall in a sheriff's office somewhere. If lawmen get the impression I'm a bounty hunter, I don't correct them."

"I've read and traveled enough to know bounty hunters are not generally well respected. It doesn't trouble you to be painted with a black brush?"

"I know who I am. People who matter to me know it as well."

And now she knew, Felicity thought. Did that mean she mattered to him?

"Is there something else you want to know?" he asked.

The question hovered on her lips. Did she matter? She knew herself to be a coward for not giving voice to it. Her friends thought she was brave, even fearless, but she knew differently. When it came to matters of the heart, it was easier to run from the truth than confront it.

"Have you ever killed anyone?" She thought he might put her away from him or choose not to answer. He did neither of those things.

"Are you certain you want to know?"

Was she? "Yes."

"Then, yes." He waited for the question that would inevitably follow. When it didn't come, he closed the short distance that separated his cheek from the crown of Felicity's head. Her hair was as soft as he had always suspected. "That's all?"

"It's enough." She did not need to have the specifics explained to her. Whatever small doubts she harbored, they had vanished with this last confession. This was a good man who was holding her, a good man who had been her companion these last twenty-three days. She could admit, at least to herself, that with increasing frequency she had begun to wish he were not quite so good.

Felicity felt his cheek against her hair. His palm still rested against her upper arm. His thumb made an idle pass across her sleeve. She could feel the warmth of his hand through the fabric. She was not merely comfortable; she was comforted. The distinction, and it was an important one, was borne home to her in a way it had never been.

"Where is home when you are not sleeping away from it?"

A quiet chuckle resonated from the back of Nat's throat. "You're so sure there is such a place?"

"You have written two letters since you've been with me, and since I know you use the telegraph to communicate with my father, I feel safe in assuming you are corresponding with family. Your sister. Perhaps your mother. You've mentioned both. I think you are more settled than you wanted me to believe at the outset."

"Very well. Washington."

"A boardinghouse?"

"A home."

"So you have a place you could hang the Pissarro."

Nat glanced over at the painting. "The library."

Felicity arched an eyebrow. "You have a *library*?"

"A crate of books, an old desk, and a scarred leather chair that lists to one side. Library is overstating it."

"I don't believe you," she said. Felicity smiled to herself when she felt him offer a careless shrug. "Why don't you want the painting? You don't like it?"

"I like it fine."

"So . . . ?"

Nat sighed, not impatiently, but as one resigned to revealing certain truths. "There would always be regret."

"Regret?"

"That I was looking at the Pissarro and not at you."

His words washed over her like a warm and gentle spring shower. The sentiment was novel, refreshing. It touched her heart and nurtured her soul. It did not make her eloquent. What she said was: "Oh."

Nat gave her shoulder a light squeeze. "Indeed."

They fell into a companionable silence, neither of them inclined to move or reflect more deeply on the moments just passed. Felicity felt herself fall asleep and did not fight it. It seemed right and proper that she should have the comfort of Nat's chest against her cheek, his arm around her shoulder. For his part, Nat simply waited her out, and even then he waited long after she was breathing in the even cadence of sleep to ease away and give her sole possession of the sofa.

IT was late by the time they ate dinner. In contrast to the earlier conversation, the exchanges they had before and during the meal were careful to the point of being stilted. After the meal was over, and the porter had come and gone, they simply ceased to talk. This silence did not pass as pleasantly as the earlier one. Threads of tension drifted in the air like dust motes, tightening their throats, making breathing seem labored.

Felicity selected a pair of hatboxes from storage under her bed and placed them on the table. Nat looked up from where he was cleaning his gun on the window bench to observe her remove two extravagantly adorned hats and regard them critically. He watched, fascinated, as she proceeded to shift feathers, discard fur, rearrange ribbons and braid, exchange pearls for jet beads, and in the end produce two different hats that were still every bit as extraordinary as the ones she'd pulled out of the boxes. She continued to defy natural laws of physics as he understood them by returning the hats to their respective boxes and closing the lids.

Felicity stood, a hatbox string in each fist, and caught Nat staring. "What?" she asked.

"I did not think they could possibly fit," he said.

"Then it is very good you didn't make a wager."

His eyes lifted from the boxes to her. "Why did you do that?" he asked. "Alter the hats, I mean."

"For the same reason you clean your gun," she said, moving toward the bed. "It calms me."

"I see."

"No, I don't think you do." Felicity gave him her back as she began to unfold the screen for privacy while she changed. "I intend to seduce you."

Whatever conversation was to follow, Nat thought he should put his gun away. He returned it to the holster and set it at his side. "Look at me," he said as she continued to fiddle with the screen. When Felicity merely gave him over-the-shoulder attention, he motioned with his index finger for her to turn around. She huffed softly to make her objection known, but complied, her defiant stare at odds with the hot color in her cheeks. He supposed that meant he had heard her correctly.

"Am I allowed to have an opinion about it?"

"Yes, of course you can, but you should keep it to yourself. Especially if you are in favor of it." Her chin lifted a fraction. "I know next to nothing about seducing a man. I mention my lack of practical knowledge so you will have a better understanding of the state of my nerves. However, I am well-read and if I can rely on the authors of such informed articles as 'The Pleasure of His Company' and 'In Pursuit of Happiness,' it is universally accepted that the nature of seduction is one-sided at inception. I believe I have to earn your cooperation, so if you give it at the beginning, then where is the challenge? There should be an element of challenge, don't you think? You are not alone in finding challenge interesting."

She had rendered him speechless. Nat required a moment to gather his wits. "Am I allowed to have an opinion now? Or is your question rhetorical?" Nat interpreted her pursed-lip response to mean that the answers should be self-evident. He took a chance. "There is nothing wrong with a challenge, but a proper seduction does not have a winner and loser."

"I mentioned earning your cooperation, didn't I?"

"Yes."

"Well?"

"What if you succeed?" he asked. "What if my cooperation comes at the expense of my better judgment? What then?"

"Then there will be regrets. Yours, certainly. Mine, quite possibly. And we will live with them as people generally do, but it will be easier than living with the regret of what might have been. *That* would be inviting cancer to reside in my soul. I think it would be the same for you." With that, Felicity disappeared behind the privacy screen.

Nat's dark eyes remained fixed on the spot where Felicity had been standing. He knuckled his chin, first to close his jaw, second to assess the rough state of his stubble. Should he shave? Felicity had fair, delicate skin. He recalled how the weight of the iron shackle had chafed her ankle. He had never apologized for that. At the time, it had seemed more important to assert his authority and make her understand the limits of her freedom. Besides, she had thrown a shoe at his head.

The memory made him smile. He had liked her for that. In truth, he liked a great many things about her, but most particularly he liked that she was never boring. Aside from the females in his family, he had never lived with a woman. There had been pleasant evenings with many, nights of pleasure with some, and on a few occasions, it had pleased him to stay for breakfast. Nat Church had had the company of women, but he had never known a woman as a companion.

Felicity Ravenwood had changed that. She was his companion.

The fact that he thought of her as *his* did not register at first, and when it did, he only considered it long enough to realize he wasn't troubled by it. Perhaps he should have been troubled by *that*, but if Nat had learned anything in his line of work, it was that time spent worrying about what couldn't be helped was time he could have spent helping.

He stood, rubbed the back of his neck as he rolled his shoulders, and then walked to the washstand, where he began sharpening his razor.

Felicity stood on tiptoe to look over the top of the

screen when she heard Nat get up. She followed his progress, dropping back to her heels when she realized what he was about. Her fingers fiddled with the satin sash at her waist while her conscience pricked at her resolve. Closing her eyes, Felicity let her conscience have its say, and although it presented a reasoned argument, there was still air enough in her balloon to tug her out from behind the screen.

Nat paused, the straight razor poised just above his Adam's apple, when he saw her approaching. Her heavy auburn hair was loosely bound and lay over one shoulder. She wore a cotton shift and the red dressing gown. An angel in scarlet. The devil's handmaiden in white. She was neither one nor the other. Felicity Ravenwood was both.

Felicity halted when she stood just behind him and a little to one side. She regarded him in the mirror. "I can do that," she said. Without taking her eyes from his, she held up one hand, palm out.

A glimmer of a smile touched Nat's mouth. "All right." He placed the razor in her hand and sat down in the chair she pulled out for him.

"Lean back. I know you have more than a nodding acquaintance with that posture."

Again, Nat complied. He closed his eyes, offered up his neck to the straight razor, and although he was not wholly relaxed, he did not so much as twitch when she laid the blade against his throat. Her first stroke was deft, competent, and his fingers uncurled from where he was surreptitiously gripping the seat. Clearly, she had practical experience here, and as an overture to seduction it played very well.

Felicity cleaned the blade expertly between strokes. She applied herself to the task with more care than quickness, giving his well-defined jaw its due, and paying special attention to the faint cleft in his chin. When she had cleared it of lather, she kissed him there. It might have seemed as if she was acting on the impulse of the moment, but it was something she had been thinking about for days, and his lack of response emboldened her rather than having the opposite effect.

She laid her lips against other places she had cleared: the hollow below his ear, the underside of his jaw. She carefully considered his face before she applied the blade again and chose the space above his upper lip so that when she leaned down and touched him there, his mouth was under hers. She did not linger long, so whether he might have responded was unknown to her, but she did feel his breath hitch and knew a heady satisfaction in that.

"Don't move," Felicity said. He didn't, and she wondered how he came by his unnatural composure as she examined her work. She returned the razor to the washstand and picked up the damp towel he had used to soften his stubble. She wiped away bits of lather at his ear and chin. "I've done very well by you. Would you like to see?"

Nat opened his eyes and found himself looking directly into hers. He had no desire to exchange that view for his mirror image. Instead, he ran his hand over his face as he moved his jaw from side to side. "Smooth as a well-worn saddle."

"Smoother," she said, tossing the towel aside. Because she wasn't certain what to do with her empty hands, she took his. With very little effort she drew him to his feet. She could not recall that they had ever stood face-to-face in such close proximity. He was tall, but then so was she, and she had always judged they would be a good fit. It was gratifying to learn that she was right.

Felicity inched forward, closing the gap between them.

She set his hands at her waist and then raised hers to his shoulders. She lifted her face, held his darkening gaze, and because she knew no way to be other than direct, she leaned into him and kissed him full on the mouth.

Nat's lips parted under hers, but he left it to her to direct the kiss. Her lips were firm and warm and tasted faintly of mint. The first press of her mouth was chaste, virginal. After a moment, she nudged his lips, changed the slant of her mouth, and sucked gently. With as simple a gesture as that, she unwound a thread of pleasure that spiraled all the way to his toes.

Nat's fingers tightened at her waist. He jerked her closer. He felt her grasp his shoulders for purchase as he set her off balance. Tension pulled their bodies taut. Felicity's mouth left his just long enough to suck in a ragged breath, and when her lips returned to his it was with a renewed sense of purpose and a better understanding of what was possible.

It was Felicity who moved them in the direction of the bed, inching backward until she felt the mattress behind her knees. She held the line there, forestalling his advance by placing her hands flat against his chest and applying resistance. With very little effort he could have pushed her down. He didn't. Just on the point of deepening the kiss, he lifted his head and regarded her with a question in his eyes.

Felicity had a sense of such intense longing that it was all she could do not to force his mouth back to hers. She wet her lips and waited for the tightness in her throat to ease. "I want to undress you."

It was unexpected, and it was not framed as a request. He wondered if she had gotten the idea from one of her ladies' magazines or if she had conceived it on her own. While he was trying to decide if a response was in order or even required, she said, "I am a Progressive," and began to unbutton his vest.

Nat offered minimal assistance, shrugging out of the vest when she eased it over his shoulders. She tugged on the tails of his shirt next, pulling it out of his waistband. He looked down and saw her fingers hover at his belt buckle, but evidently she reconsidered it and began to unfasten his shirt instead. Recalling her words about a challenge, he gave her no help in getting him out of it. She laid it over the vest at the foot of the bed before she turned her attention to his union suit. She opened it from his throat to his navel but did not attempt to get him out of it. Instead, she slipped her hands under the material and laid her palms flat against him. Nat's heart slammed against his chest once and then became a steady thrum.

Felicity spread her fingers wide and passed her thumbs back and forth over his skin. He was warm, but she was warmer. Touching him did that to her, and she wondered at it, wondered that what she felt was satisfaction and not shame. Of their own accord, her fingers walked lightly down his chest until they came to rest at his belt. This time she drew the leather tip through the keeper, tugged once to release it from the tongue, and opened the buckle. She let it hang there while she fumbled with the steel button closure on his waistband.

Nat sucked in a breath as Felicity's knuckles brushed his abdomen. His skin retracted. Her fingers dipped. His erection swelled, pressed hard against his trousers. Arching an eyebrow, he lowered his head until his forehead touched hers. He whispered, "Are you pleased with yourself, Miss Ravenwood?"

Was she? "I am, yes."

As confessions went, it was a brazen one, and Nat liked

her the more for it. He toppled her backward onto the bed and followed her down. The landing was awkward, and he lay heavily on her so she could not take a proper breath. What air she had in her lungs burst from her as an abrupt shout of laughter. Nat rolled onto his side, relieving her of his weight but not freeing her completely. She managed a gulp of air before his mouth came down on hers.

He addressed the earlier promise of his kiss by beginning this one where he left off. This kiss was a thorough assault on her senses, deep and wet and lasting just this side of forever, and she answered in kind, compensating for her lack of experience with enthusiasm. They twisted and thrashed, seeking purchase with their hands and heels until they lay lengthwise on the bed. They paused, each taking stock, and without a word said between them, attended to what needed to be done. Nat sat up to remove his boots. He dropped them over the side. Felicity untied her belt and squirmed out of her satin robe. She pushed it out of the way and it slithered over the edge of the mattress and made a scarlet puddle beside Nat's boots. Nat whipped off his belt and followed with his socks and trousers. Felicity rearranged the covers so she was under them before she loosened the ribbon that kept her shift modestly gathered at the neck, but when Nat lifted the covers to crawl under still wearing his union suit, Felicity shook her head.

"If you don't mind," she said, "I'd like to look first."

"And if I do mind?"

She sighed. "Then I shall be disappointed."

"Are you certain?"

"That I'll be disappointed? Yes, quite certain."

He cocked an eyebrow at her, not believing for a moment that she had misunderstood.

The challenging lift of Felicity's chin was at odds with the becoming shade of rose coloring her face. "It might be my only opportunity," she said. "After tonight, I'll be a fallen woman."

Nat rolled his eyes. "Even if that were true, that state would present rather more opportunities than less."

In response, Felicity turned on her side, propped her head on one elbow, and waited him out. Anticipation stirred her blood and deepened her blush. She did not look anywhere but at him.

Nat shook his head, but it was disbelief, not denial, that moved him to it. He stepped to the side of the bed, stood so that he was facing her, and shucked his union suit. He watched her blink once, slowly, and then nod as though in confirmation of something she had suspected. He had no idea of the nature of her thoughts, and he did not ask.

She had primed the pump and brought this horse to water. He was definitely going to drink his fill.

Felicity edged further under the covers as he eyed her with the intent of a predator. She was not prepared when he lifted the blankets and yanked. Her nerveless fingers could not hold them. She reached for them, but his hands lightly knocked hers out of the way. He stretched out beside her. His fingers scrabbled in the hem of her shift, raising it first to the level of her knees, then to the top of her thighs. He let it rest there while he slipped his hand between her legs and fitted his palm to the inner curve of her thigh. His thumb made a single pass across her skin. Then it made another.

"Breathe," he whispered, watching her. He saw her eyes dart to the lanterns burning around the railcar. She had not thought about turning back their wicks. "Too late," he said, not at all sorry for the oversight. "We'll leave the dark for another time."

Felicity swallowed. She had not thought beyond this time. She said nothing.

Nat leaned over her, kissed her again. She warmed to the touch of his mouth immediately. Her lips parted; her tongue made a sweep across the ridge of his teeth. He met her foray with his tongue, licking, darting, sucking. She moved restlessly now. She stretched and arched and rolled her shoulders. She sacrificed her neck to his mouth. He sipped her skin, laved the hollow of her throat. Her pulse fluttered wildly in her neck.

Felicity pushed her fingers into his hair. She cupped his head and held him there. She wanted him to know the taste of her; she wanted him to have this memory.

Nat's lips followed the neckline of her shift. He tugged on the ribbon with his teeth. Her fingers relaxed against his scalp, allowing him to drag his mouth lower. Her shift parted, and then his lips were at the rising curve of her breast. He nudged aside the fabric and exposed the coral aureole before his mouth closed over the nipple. He flicked it with his tongue. That pass lifted a small moan from the back of her throat.

Felicity ran her palms along his bare shoulders and then moved them to his back. Corded muscle bunched under her fingertips. She traced the defining lines and pressed her thumb along the length of his spine. His hips jerked. His erection was hot and hard against her thigh. It seemed he shifted only a few degrees, but it was enough to put him between her thighs. Until that moment, she was unaware of opening her legs to make that possible. He rubbed against her, hesitated, and then shocked her by lifting his hips and resting his hand on her mons. He slid a finger between her lips, then another. He spread them. Embarrassed by this as by nothing else, Felicity squeezed her eyes shut.

"I don't want to hurt you," he said.

She felt his breath on her cheek, but she didn't dare look at him. "There's something wrong with me. I think I must have—"

"Shh. There is nothing wrong with you. I needed to be sure you were ready."

Felicity's cheeks puffed as she blew out a breath. Her eyelashes fluttered. She stared at him. His hand still rested intimately between her thighs. "I thought I was. Now I'm not certain."

"It's all right. You will be."

And she was. He stroked, caressed, and took her mouth again. He lifted her to the exact pitch that caused every one of her nerves to vibrate. With no urging, she raised her knees on either side of his hips and cradled him. He would have eased into her, but Felicity would have it her way, and impatience made her bold. She thrust upward and was done with it. Her final act of seduction was drawing him into her.

Settled inside her, Nat did not move. He pushed himself up and looked down at her. She was biting her lower lip. He screwed his mouth to one side and cocked an eyebrow at her.

Felicity had no difficulty interpreting the look. It was not romantic. She released her lip and sighed. "I know," she whispered. "I know. I should have waited, but I am no good at it, and in my defense, you made me want you."

As defenses went, hers was not entirely unacceptable. Nat bent his head and gently kissed her bruised mouth. Her lips parted, and when she sighed again, he drank it in.

A rolling wave of tension pulled her muscles taut. She cleaved to him. Her arms, thighs, and calves contracted, and the same tightening was repeated where he was joined to her. She felt deliciously full and vaguely powerful, and although it was not in her nature to follow anyone's lead, she did so now and was rewarded in a manner she had not been able to imagine.

He moved slowly, deliberately, testing the limits of her tolerance—and his. She stayed with him, striking the same rhythm, finding the steady beat that supported their dance. Her fingers curled into the sheet when the first notes of pleasure touched her. She had barely caught her breath, barely had time to register the urgency she felt, when the crescendo began to build. There was no part of her that did not respond to the steady rise of pleasure. It was not only her body that was lifted; it was also her soul.

Felicity wanted to know every part of this experience. She remained fiercely connected to each moment so she would have the memory of the whole of it. She never closed her eyes. He branded her with his mouth, with his hands, and she wished she might always have the marks as proof that she had not only been loved once, but that she had been loved by him. She listened to him, to herself, to the rumblings of the railcar as it sped along the track. She pushed her fingers through his hair and pressed her face into the curve of his neck. She breathed deeply of his scent. Every one of her senses was engaged in this act.

She had always imagined that she would feel vulnerable, and perhaps that would have been true had she been with any other man, but what this man did to her, what she allowed him to do, made her feel the opposite of that. And when she thought he had wrung the last scintilla of pleasure from every one of her nerve endings, he carefully showed how very wrong she was.

The journey was a succession of peaks, not a long single climb. The pauses, those short moments where her body hummed but did not shatter, allowed her to catch her breath. Anticipation filled her much in the same way he did. Her eyes never left his face, and, watching him, she came to learn that his denial was in service of her pleasure.

She was afraid to think why that should be important to him. It was better to simply feel, and in the end, feeling was not a conscious choice. It was a state of being.

Felicity heard her voice, knew that she had cried out, but what she said was unintelligible to her own ears. Her body trembled; she pressed the back of her head into the bedding, exposing her throat. Her pulse beat wildly. She spread her fingers, extended her arms. Threads of fire unraveled in her belly.

She shuddered hard and then she was still. The sparks of heat that had made her body dance were quiet, softer, and what remained was a delicious sort of warmth that discouraged all thought of moving.

It did not appear to be so different for Nat. Pleasure had struck him down as well. Her cry had barely subsided when she'd heard him shout. His body shuddered with more force than hers; his final thrust drove him deep inside her. She had clutched him, cradled him, and now he lay heavily on her while his heartbeat slowed and his breathing calmed.

Felicity raised one hand to the back of Nat's neck. She stroked the nape lightly and then idly twisted a lock of his dark hair around her fingertip. She withdrew her hand when he shivered.

It was a long moment after that before Nat determined that he could actually move. He lifted his head and regarded Felicity from slumberous eyes. She was infinitely more alert than he was, but then so was a slug. Satisfied with what he saw, Nat grunted softly, withdrew from her, and rolled onto his back. Although he closed his eyes immediately, he had the sense she had turned on her side and was watching him. She would want to talk, he thought. Women frequently did. He never understood it.

Felicity did not talk, though. She waited for him to fall asleep and then she left the bed. The water drawn for her bath earlier was cool now, but it felt good on her heated skin. She eased herself into the tub. For a long time she just sat. The washcloth remained bunched in her fists. She held it against her chest, loath to use it, loath to remove his scent from her skin. Sitting there, water lapping at her naked shoulders, unwelcome thoughts intruded. It was not possible to ignore them.

Felicity laid the damp washcloth across her eyes and quietly wept behind it.

N AT could not recall the last time he had slept so deeply. Darkness shrouded the landscape on the other side of the coach's windows. Inside, the lamps were either extinguished or had had their wicks turned back. He knew it was Felicity's handiwork. He had not stirred.

Nat turned his head and examined the space beside him. It was empty. He sat up and looked around, felt his heart seize until he spied her curled on the short sofa. She was wearing her shift and using her red satin robe as a blanket. Her hair was loosely braided and lay in the curve of her neck and shoulder. It was tied off with a ribbon.

She looked at peace, and perhaps she was now, but her sleeping arrangements and her pale complexion suggested a troubled, exhausted mind.

Nat threw back the covers and stood. He padded silently to the washstand, cleaned up, and then put on his shirt and trousers. He had no intention of adding his vest, but he noticed its absence as soon as he lifted the other clothing from the foot rail. He glanced at the floor, then at the backs of the chairs. He lifted a sheet to see if it had gotten caught in the tangle of blankets.

There were few options left, and Nat had done enough repossession and recovery to know that sometimes a thing could be found hiding in plain sight. He turned, faced the short sofa, and saw his vest was folded neatly under Felicity's head. She would have found the photograph of herself in it. It would be reckless to believe differently.

He looked back at the bed, at the iron shackle that was still attached to one leg of the bed. He wondered if she had thought about using it on him. There had certainly been opportunity. She could have left the train. There had been at least one stop while he slept the sleep of the drugged or the dead.

Nat removed Felicity's knitting basket from the cushion of the overstuffed chair and sat down. He reached over to the drinks cabinet, took out the whiskey, and poured himself a drink. After a moment's reflection, he poured one for Felicity as well.

When he leaned back, one drink in hand, the other beside him, he saw that she was awake, alert, and watching him. "Good morning," he said.

"Is it either?" she asked. "Good? Or morning?"

So it was to be like that, he thought. "I poured you a drink. Would you like it?"

"Yes." Somewhat stiffly, she added, "Thank you."

Nat brought it to her as she sat up. She took it in both hands but did not lift it to her lips. Nat's eyes darted to his vest. "That's not much of a pillow."

Felicity shrugged. "It served. You may have it if you like."

Nat bent, picked it up, and knew immediately the photograph was no longer in the inside pocket. "What have you done with it?"

She did not pretend to misunderstand. "I put it here." She reached under the cushion and removed the photograph. She handed it to him with the image side face-down. "I did not want to pose for that picture."

Nat had suspected as much. "Was it a wedding portrait?"

"No. For the announcement of my engagement."

That explained her flat expression captured in the photograph, the dull eyes that stared back at the camera. "It is an accurate likeness," he said, "but it is not like you. Except perhaps for the hat. What made you choose that particular one?"

Felicity looked down at the tumbler she was cradling. "Jon told me he liked it, that he liked it on me. He was lying, of course, and I knew he was lying. It was a ridiculous hat. I chose it so that when he looked at that photograph he would be reminded not to lie to me."

Nat decided he would do well to keep that in mind. He kept the photograph but tossed the vest to the foot of the bed. He did not like standing over her, although she did not appear to mind. He returned to his chair and sat down. Rather than waiting any longer for her to broach the subject that was on both their minds, Nat asked, "Is it your father's handwriting on the back of the photograph?"

"Yes."

"I worked off that assumption." Nat glanced at the message on the back of the photograph, but it was Felicity who spoke them.

"'Save her.'" Her brief smile was rueful. "My father does not flatter me, does he? I am not sure he is even aware of the insult. His very worst offenses are couched in the language of protection, and he has a rationale that is impenetrable. He always speaks of my best interests. I have never doubted that he means well or that he believes his arguments. I have been encouraged to be independent minded, but not, it seems, if I stray too far from *his* thinking. I have never been able to make him understand that his choices will not necessarily be mine. Last night, *you* were my choice."

"To spite him?"

"No." She held his eyes. "No," she said again. "I was selfish. I acted in *my* best interests."

"Regrets?"

She was silent a moment, then, "I wish I had not found the photograph." Felicity finished her drink. She held the tumbler in both hands again while she looked at him. "You?"

"I wish you were beside me when I woke."

"You fell asleep."

"I regret that, too."

A faint smile lifted the corners of her mouth, but it did not linger. "Repossession. Recovery. You can add rescue."

"Aside from the pleasant alliteration, why would I do that?"

"You wanted to save me, didn't you? That's the reason my father is in your debt."

"Save you? No. God, no. Not in the way I think you mean. I don't suppose it occurred to you that I wanted to save you *for* me?" He set his tumbler aside, leaned forward, and rested his forearms on his knees. "No, I can see not. Felicity, among all the women I have known, know now, or am likely to know, there is no one less likely to require rescuing than you. The situation that you cannot extricate yourself from doesn't immediately spring to mind. Have you ever found yourself in something like that?"

Hesitating, uncertain, Felicity released a breath slowly. After another moment's careful consideration, she said quietly, "Not until I met you."

Nat was able to keep himself in his chair, but only barely. He held her unguarded stare. "You mean that first morning, when I shackled you to the bed."

"No."

"Then you're referring to my manipulation of our route."

"Hardly."

Except to make a steeple of his fingers, Nat did not move. "Say it, then, and say it clearly, but say it because it's true and not because you think it's what I want to hear."

Felicity pushed aside the scarlet robe that lay across her lap and stood. The floor was icy beneath her bare feet, but she tolerated it because this was not a declaration one should make wearing heavy woolen socks. It flitted through her mind that she should be wearing a hat, and the absurdity of that thought provoked a narrow, self-mocking smile. It faded as she approached him. There was no lift in her chin, no defiance in her carriage. Earlier she had wept because she thought she had come to the truth too late and despaired of ever saying it aloud. Now she owned this moment.

She said, "I love you."

It was a naked, guileless confession, and the simplicity of it moved Nat to take Felicity's hands in his. She came willingly when he drew her closer and then down onto his lap. There was adjusting involved, some shifting of positions to make the fit work, but a compromise was reached. As a metaphor for what would be their life together, Nat thought it was appropriate.

"I have no interest in working in any of your father's enterprises," he said.

A husky laugh vibrated in Felicity's throat. "You ruined Edward Ravenwood's daughter. I don't think you'll be invited to sit at the table."

"You don't mind?"

"That I'm ruined or that you don't want to work for my father?"

Nat gave her an arch look. "The latter. I did *not* ruin you."

"I beg to differ." Smiling, Felicity bent her head and touched her lips to his. "No, of course I don't mind. Why raise the point at all?"

"Because I thought it might be expected. Isn't it customary for the son-in-law to be offered a position in the family business?"

"I suppose, but Jon was already in my father's employ when he proposed, and so was—" Felicity's musings came to an abrupt halt. Her jaw snapped shut with an audible click.

Amused, Nat tugged on the tail of her braid. "In consideration of your ruined state, for which I am not responsible and frankly don't believe, you should say yes."

"Yes," she whispered. "I say yes."

"Good." He used her rope of hair to tip her head toward him and kissed her, softly at first to seal her agreement, then more thoroughly to signal his intent. In time, he led her to the bed, where they tumbled with less awkwardness and more abandon and pleasured each other to an agreeable state of exhaustion.

Nat said, "I love you."

Felicity turned on her side and raised herself on one elbow. A bead of sweat trickled down her back. Strands of hair clung to her nape. Her skin glowed. She laid her hand above his heart and lightly tapped his chest with a fingertip. "I thought you were sleeping."

He heard no rebuke, only gentle teasing. He put his hand around hers, held it there. "I love you," he said again.

"I thought you might."

Nat smiled. He squeezed her hand. "What you might not know is that as much as I love you, I like you more. That came real easy. There was the photograph to start. I admired the confidence of a woman who could wear that hat, and now that I understand why you wore it, I like you better for knowing it was ridiculous."

"It lacked editing."

"It lacked a lighted match."

Felicity's mouth flattened. The disapproving line dissolved when a bubble of laughter parted her lips.

Nat went on. "Then I tracked you to Falls Hollow and learned you were a resident of Joe Pepper's jail. That was more in your favor than against it, mostly because I had it from Joe Pepper himself that you were a she-devil."

"A she-devil? What is that exactly?"

Nat shrugged. "I don't know. I liked the sound of it."

"You are a man of peculiar tastes, Nat Church."

"I had some misgivings when I understood it was a Temperance rally that put you behind bars, but you put those to rest when you knocked back that fine whiskey you keep."

Fascinated, Felicity edged closer.

"You barely blinked an eye when I told you the terms that your father set for your return. You conceived the idea of becoming a Harvey girl before we had dinner and, by my count, hatched a half dozen other schemes over the course of that first week. Reporter, dance hall girl, barkeep, librarian, piano player, and actress. No single setback discouraged you. You remained optimistic, mostly pleasant—irritatingly so, if you want the truth. And you made peace with my company. I never understood how you did that; I still don't."

"Perhaps I was falling in love with you. Perhaps, just perhaps, mind you, I did not want to strike out as much as I said I did. That would have been a hard thing to admit, even to myself. I'm not sure I like the sound of it now."

Nat chuckled under his breath. "I'm sure you don't." He shifted so that he could tuck her head against his shoulder. Her hair lay softly against his skin. "At the next town big enough to have at least one preacher, I'm going to invite him to marry us."

"Here? In this car?"

"Of course. If you get off, you won't be allowed back on. That hasn't changed."

"What about my father? He might have objections."

"Might? I think it's certain, which is why I'll be calling in that favor he owes me."

"The favor of my hand, is it? One could be forgiven for thinking you had it planned."

"One could," Nat said without giving himself away. "We can take this car all the way to Washington, and once you're settled there, you can lend your organizing talents to as many rallies as you like."

"Suffrage?"

"My employer won't like it, but he likes Temperance even less."

Felicity smiled. "So do I." She turned her head to regard his profile. "Have you considered that my father could have had just this end in mind when he sent you after me?"

"I don't know how that's possible."

"I don't know, either, but he did not build an empire by refusing to take risks. Calculation and craft. They figure into it. He might just think you are in my best interests, Nat Church."

"What do you think?"

"I know you are."

He settled a kiss on the crown of her head. "Good. I will dedicate my life to proving you right."

Felicity jabbed him lightly with her elbow. "Dedicate yourself to finding my hat with the ebony-tipped feathers. I want your opinion."

"Now?"

She nodded and moved out of his way, sitting up as he rolled to the edge of the bed. He extended an arm, leaning over the side as far as he could without falling out. One by one, he pulled out the hatboxes he could reach. While he searched, Felicity stripped out of her shift. She removed the ribbon that secured her plait and quickly unwound her hair, combing it with her fingers as she went. Waves of auburn hair cascaded over her shoulders as Nat lifted the desired hat for her approval.

"That's the one," she said. "Hand it here."

Nat had not yet raised his head over the side of the bed. He kept the hat in her view, but he did not hand it over. "Are you naked, Felicity?"

"I won't be if you give me my hat."

Much encouraged, Nat passed the hat behind his back but not before he plucked one of the ebony-tipped feathers from the velvet band. He sat up in time to see Felicity settle the extraordinary creation on her head. Her siren's smile faltered when he said nothing.

"Well?" she asked. "What do you think?"

"I think that you are wearing that hat in the only place it is decent to do so."

She lifted an eyebrow. "It requires that feather to restore balance. May I have it?"

Nat held her darkening eyes. "I don't think so." He slowly twisted the feather between his fingertips so that it pulled her attention. When he stopped, her eyes returned to his. Nat's smile was wicked, deliberately so, and unlike the one she had practiced on him, it did not falter in the face of her silence. He touched the feather's ebony tip to the hollow of her throat and let it hover there, full of promise. So there could be no mistaking his intention, he said, "I have a particular purpose in mind for this feather, Miss Ravenwood. There is more than one way to restore balance."

Felicity was pleased to learn that Nat Church knew all of them.

Jo Goodman is a licensed professional counselor working with children and families in West Virginia's northern panhandle. Always a fan of happily-ever-after, Jo turned to writing romances early in her career as a child-care worker when she realized the only life script she could control was the one she wrote herself. She is inspired by the resiliency and courage of the children she meets and feels privileged to be trusted with their stories, the ones that they alone have the right to tell.

Once upon a time, Jo believed she was going to be a marine biologist. She feels lucky that seasickness made her change course. She lives with her family in landlocked Colliers, West Virginia.

Don't miss her next historical romance, *In Want of a Wife*, coming May 2014 from Berkley Sensation. Turn to the back of this book for a sneak preview.

THE SCENT
OF ROSES

Kaki Warner

S HE stood out like a swan among sage hens. Tall and graceful. An impossibly long neck. Sleekly elegant from the plumed hat and pale scarf covering her hair and most of her face to the flowing cream-colored dress and matching cape. Guaranteed to capture the attention of every man on the railway platform.

Not a dowager, Richard Whitmeyer decided, watching her through the soot-smeared window and the first tiny snowflakes drifting down from the slate sky. A sporting woman, perhaps. Maybe a card dealer. Certainly not a schoolmarm. No proper woman would be traveling alone and dressed so conspicuously.

He scanned the other passengers in the boarding line, saw nothing to arouse his suspicions, and swung his gaze back to her. He admired her air of assurance, the proud set of her head, the hint of rounded curves beneath the cape. Her scarf blocked his view of her face, but he guessed she was a beauty.

Maybe she was a madam. Or a confidence schemer. Or even a bounty hunter after the bank robber who had caused such an uproar in town late yesterday.

Unlucky for him that he'd still been here in Omaha City when the news broke.

With a sigh, he pinched the bridge of his nose to slow the knot of tension tightening behind his eyes. Already the newspapers were full of it, although, judging by the confusing accounts given by the employees at the Cattleman's Bank and Trust, no one knew who to search for, or even in which direction to look.

"Rangy," "skinny," "fat," "tall," "average," "short," the witnesses had told the *Omaha Sentinel* reporter. Only a few descriptions were consistent. The thief had carried a dark leather case and had been dressed entirely in black— gloves, boots, trousers, hooded greatcoat. A thick scarf had covered the lower half of the face, and tinted spectacles concealed the eyes. And the culprit had been deaf and dumb.

"At least that's what the card said," the teller had told the reporter. "Then he—or she, hard to tell—passed a note through the bars, asking if we had safety-deposit boxes. I said we did, and then he asked if he could look them over before he left his parcel. I said, 'Sure,' and took him back to the vault."

According to various accounts, the person in black had exited the bank several minutes later, still carrying the case. The teller was found an hour later, locked in the vault, sleeping off the effects of chloroform. Only two boxes had been opened, and while the newspaper didn't list the contents, Richard knew exactly what was missing: from one box, two hundred bearer shares issued by the New York and Ohio Railroad, and from the other, a yet-to-be-tallied fortune in unset jewels.

"Kingston Allied Insurance of Baltimore," the *Omaha Sentinel* article had concluded, "is offering a substantial reward for the safe return of the jewels. The police expect to apprehend the thief soon."

Not much hope of that, since they didn't know the gender, eye color, hair color, or voice characteristics of the perpetrator. But it did ensure that every insurance investigator, lawman, private detective, and bounty hunter within five hundred miles would be joining the hunt.

He hated when they offered rewards.

Seeing the late boarders come through the door at the front of his car, Richard took the precaution of removing his hat and setting it on the seat beside him before turning again to the window. The narrow wooden benches were uncomfortable at best, but more so for a man of his height.

He would have preferred the plush comfort of a sleeper, but there were no Pullmans on this train, or even a dining or parlor car, which would have afforded him an opportunity to move around and study the other passengers without drawing notice. Luckily, there were only two other passenger cars on this run, and they were almost filled. After checking them thoroughly and seeing nothing of concern, he had returned to this car and settled into the window seat on the last row. This car, coupled directly behind the tender, would be the last to fill since it was the noisiest and grimiest due to the soot and smoke coming off the engine stack. But it also offered the best vantage point to study new arrivals.

Still facing the window, he listened to passengers milling about in the narrow aisle. A moment later, footsteps slowed beside his row. He heard a *thump* when something heavy—a valise?—dropped to the floorboards, then felt a shiver go through the bench as someone sat down.

Frowning, he turned to find the swan sitting beside

him. Interest sparked. He supposed if he had to have a seatmate, she would be better than the farm boy with the chicken he had seen standing in the boarding line.

Without a glance in his direction, she retrieved a small book from the valise at her feet, opened it, and began to read.

"You're sitting on my hat," he informed her, wondering how she could have missed it. With its wide brim, the Stetson covered half the bench seat.

Careful not to bend the bleached ostrich feather poking out of her bowler, she pulled off the scarf, then turned and regarded him without expression. She had black hair pinned in a bun at her nape and astonishing blue eyes framed by lashes so dark and lush against her cold-reddened cheeks they looked like two small, black feathers caught on a pink bedsheet.

Definitely a beauty.

The lashes swept up and down. A smile tugged at her lips. Full lips, also reddened by the cold, with a slight upturn at the corners. The top was plumper than the bottom, which made her mouth seem swollen. It drew his eyes, sparked imaginative musing about what might have caused it. A lover's good-bye kiss?

"Am I?"

He forced his mind back on track. "You are."

Reaching under her skirts, she groped around, finally pulled out his flattened hat. "What was it doing on the seat?"

Snatching the Stetson from her gloved hand, he punched out the crown, pinched the crease along the edge back into shape, then returned it to his head. "I put it there."

"Why?"

"To discourage unwanted company."

"Ah." Her smile spread, parting those alluring lips to

reveal very white, evenly spaced teeth with a slight over-bite. "So I was correct."

"About what?"

"My choice of seats. I had hoped by your dour expression that you wouldn't attempt to draw me into tedious discourse. I'm pleased to see I was right."

Dour? He wasn't dour. Preoccupied, perhaps. Dour was for old men, not thirty-five-year-olds scarcely into their prime. However, before he could explain the distinction, she returned to her book, signaling an end to the conversation.

Disgruntled, he faced the window again as the last snow-dusted stragglers hurried to board—an elderly couple, the man wearing a black armband, the woman in full mourning, including veiled hat; the lumbering farm lad with his chicken; and a man with a bushy brown mustache, carrying a small satchel with a shoulder strap and wearing a Colt .45 Peacemaker in a holster on his hip.

The one to watch.

The train jerked, sending the swan against his shoulder. He pretended not to notice, although the softness of her arm against his and the flowery scent she left behind were difficult to ignore.

Roses? Something subtle. Expensive. Not what one might expect from a sporting woman. But then, she was a contradiction on so many levels.

Several more jerks, and they were rolling slowly out of Omaha City, headed west toward Wyoming, through the Wasatch Range of Utah, then on to California.

But he would be disembarking in Salt Lake, assuming all went well. He needed a break. This was his third job in less than a month. Maybe he would take a month off, backtrack south into Texas and New Mexico, revisit the wide-open spaces of his youth. He could certainly afford it.

How could she call him dour? He was distracted, that was all. To prove how wrong she was, he turned to her with what he hoped was a friendly smile. "Are you traveling far?"

She looked up from her book. Her eyes were a sharp, bright blue, the same shade as the aqua waters along the tip of the Florida peninsula. They were far too intelligent for such a pretty face. "*Now* you wish to talk?"

"Not particularly."

"And yet you persist in doing it."

"Only to correct you. You said I was dour. You're wrong."

One dark brow rose. "Indeed?"

"I'm not old enough. To be dour, I would have to be at least fifty years of age, which I'm not."

Amusement warmed the cool blue gaze. "Morose, then?"

He shook his head.

"Melancholic? Suffering dyspepsia? An earache?"

"Tired." Although, at the moment, he felt quite invigorated. And amused. How long since he'd had a conversation about something other than his current mission? Or been teased by a pretty woman?

"There's a cure for that," she said, that tilt at the corners of her mouth rising into a smile. "Go to sleep."

And before he could think of a snappy retort, she began reading again.

He blinked, astonished by her audacity. And intrigued. Not your average female, his seatmate. Too bold to be a timorous spinster, and too outspoken to be a compliant wife. Obviously, a woman who lived life on her own terms.

A madam, then. Who else would be so brazen?

He smiled at the thought. With a madam—especially one as smart as this woman appeared to be—he could avoid all the wearisome constraints of polite society and simply be himself. Talk without guarding his words. Tease her back a little. And if things went really well . . .

Still smiling, he watched snowflakes race past the window. The prospect of the long run to Salt Lake didn't seem quite so dreary anymore.

RACHEL James kept her eyes fixed on the book she held, even though her mind was focused on the man beside her. Why was he smiling? Had he guessed her intent in choosing this seat?

Sprawled as he was, taking up most of the narrow bench, his dark scowl daring anyone to come near, he had made it quite clear he wanted no company. Which was precisely why she had chosen to sit beside him. A man who made such a point of protecting his solitude probably had something to hide.

And she so loved to ferret out secrets. She had a talent for it. But this man might be more of a challenge than she had anticipated.

She had expected a taciturn cowboy. He had the size for it. And the face, with that sun-browned skin and those squint lines around his dark brown eyes. But not the hands, she had realized when she'd watched him straighten his flattened hat. She had never met a cowboy who didn't show evidence of his profession in his hands—bent or missing fingers, scars, callused skin, broken nails. This man's hands were more refined—long fingered and clean, but unmarred by hard work. That faint stubble of beard and his overlong dark brown hair gave him a rough, careless appearance, but his eyes told a different story. Despite his attempt to appear aloof, that dark, watchful gaze showed keen interest in his surroundings. And surprising intellect.

If not a cowboy, then what? A lawman? A bank robber? A gambler with a few extra aces up his sleeve?

Rachael prided herself on her intuition. More often than not, after a glance or two, she could pinpoint a person's age within a few years, ascertain profession and station in life, and determine if there was menace or threat in his or her manner.

Instinct and observation. They had served her well.

But this man gave off such differing tells she was unable to draw any firm conclusions. Although it could use a brushing, his suit was of good quality and tailor-made to fit his large frame. His rumpled shirt showed no food stains and she caught no odor of tobacco or whiskey. He was clean enough to be a doctor or dentist, yet seemed too standoffish. For the same reason, he would be a poor preacher or salesman. But with that air of authority he might make a passable rancher or lawman.

Or an excellent thief.

Certainly, a challenge. And as her late husband had once accused . . . she loved a challenge more than she had ever loved him. Sweet, plodding Charlie.

She snuck a glance at the other passengers, although she could see little but the backs of their heads. Cowboys, farmers, drifters, men with wives and children, that sad elderly couple in mourning, the farm boy with the chicken. Nothing to arouse suspicion.

Other than the man sitting beside her.

Wouldn't that be a twist?

Biting back a smile, she flipped a page and continued to read—or pretend to. The constant rock and sway of the railcar made it impossible to focus without becoming queasy, and the clatter of the wheels over the joints in the tracks was too distracting.

Beyond the window, farmland gave way to broken

terrain, then rising hills. They stopped every twenty or thirty miles to fill the tender with water or take on coal, and many of the passengers took advantage of the short breaks to stretch their legs or make purchases from enterprising locals peddling dime-box meals along the siding. But Rachel's stomach was too unsettled for a full meal, so she contented herself with small bites of the apple and crackers she had brought with her.

Her seatmate suffered no such malady. He disembarked at each stop—first one off, last one on. Wondering what he was up to, she watched him pace beside the idling train, looking up into every window between bites of his latest box purchase. He tried to be subtle about it, but she wasn't fooled.

He was looking for someone. Hunting, to be more precise.

When they stopped in Columbus, Nebraska, she decided to move to the second car. She had learned all she could here—the man beside her had not risen to the bait of indifference she had cast out, which normally elicited more attention than she wanted—and she needed to assess the travelers in the other cars. If she found nothing untoward, she could always come back to this seat later.

Rising, she reached down for her valise.

"You're getting off at this stop?" her seatmate asked in surprise.

"I'm moving to another car."

"You are? Have I offended you?"

"Actually, you've bored me."

That look of shock again. It was almost comical. "But you said you wanted to avoid conversation."

"*Tedious* conversation. And that was hours ago."

"But now you're feeling more sociable?"

Rachel hesitated, wondering why he was suddenly so desirous that she stay. Had she misread his aloofness for shyness? The notion amused her. Shy? A man this well-favored? Hardly. Then why didn't he want her to leave?

"Do you play poker?" he asked when she didn't answer.

"I don't gamble."

"But do you play? For fun?"

"I have on occasion." *For information.*

"Excellent." A grin broke across his chiseled face, involving everything from his lively eyes to a mouthful of white teeth, and adding two deep dents in his whiskered cheeks. *Dimples?* Rachel was amazed. Who knew such a handsome man lurked beneath that shuttered expression?

"Please stay," he cajoled and patted the bench beside him. "I'll behave. I promise."

She almost wished he wouldn't. Shoving the valise back under her seat, she smiled and held out her hand as she sat again on the bench. "Rachel James."

"Richard Whitmeyer." He gave her fingers a quick squeeze then reached into his pocket. "And I just happen to have a deck of playing cards right here."

And a gun, Rachel noted when his jacket gaped open and she saw the shoulder holster under his arm. A professional gambler, then. That would be a real challenge . . . besting a cardsharp at his own game, using information as currency. And the first thing she wanted to know was why, after five hours of silence, he was suddenly so anxious for her company.

"You deal first," she said with her most winsome smile . . . which, around him, wasn't that difficult. "And refresh my memory about what beats what."

"YOU'RE not even trying," she accused a while later. Richard looked up from his cards to find her studying him with that teasing glint in her pretty eyes. "Yes, I am."

"Then you're either a poor player, or a hustler trying to lure me into complacency. At this rate, I'll soon be out of questions."

His earlier suspicion that she was either a madam or a card dealer or both had grown with every hand he'd purposely lost—a man could often learn more from the questions asked than the answers given. She was too skilled to be a casual player, and he knew most bordellos also offered gambling and it wasn't unusual for a madam to deal at her own gaming tables. When he'd suggested cards, it had simply been a ploy to keep her from leaving; despite his initial reservations, he'd found Rachel James to be a perfect seatmate—easy to look at, silent, and sweet smelling. But now it had become less a diversion and more of a challenge to figure out who she was and what she was really after. "Perhaps I'm having a run of bad cards."

"Perhaps." Her smile widened, which made him lose his train of thought.

The woman was no dunce. She knew how to work her charms. At first he'd found it amusing to have to answer questions when he lost: *Where are you from?* Texas. *Are you married?* No.

But he was beginning to wonder what other games she might be playing. Earlier, he had seen her studying the other passengers while pretending to read, and he knew she had watched him whenever he'd left the car. Why? Was she setting him up as a mark in a confidence scheme?

That would certainly be a switch—the hunter becoming the hunted.

"Your question?" he asked, shuffling the cards.

"What brought you to Omaha City?"

"I had . . . business connections there."

"What kind of business?"

He looked up, felt himself sinking into those blue eyes, and fumbled the cards. "Isn't the rule only one question per win?" he asked, gathering them up again.

"Of course. My mistake."

He dealt them each five cards facedown on the folded newspaper balanced across their knees. This time, he had two tens, a trey, and a pair of sixes. "Another card?" he asked her.

When she shook her head, he tossed the trey, drew a four, then called. His two pair beat her two pair. He had his question ready. "Are you in business?"

"I have . . . business connections," she mimicked with a teasing smile. "But I don't run my own business. Yet."

"And when you do start your own business," he pressed, "what will it be?"

"Sorry. That's two questions."

Richard masked his frustration behind a bland smile. All he'd learned in the two earlier hands he'd won was that she was a widow and she was traveling to San Francisco to visit her sister. But he wasn't sure he believed her in view of all the inconsistencies.

For instance, her choice of forfeits—information— seemed odd, especially after her initial disinterest. Then the way she dressed. Her clothing was too showy for long train travel. Had her late husband left her financially independent, or was she earning money in another way? Confidence woman, madam, gambler, or simply a wealthy eccentric?

He figured madam. But that could be wishful thinking.

He pushed the cards toward her. "You deal. And let's try blackjack. Maybe it will change my luck." He regretted they weren't playing strip poker. That would definitely improve his playing.

"There's no such thing as luck," she said, dealing with

practiced efficiency. "Only mathematical probabilities. We drive our own destiny by making good or bad decisions based on those probabilities. Luck has nothing to do with it."

A philosopher, too? He looked at his first card. Five of clubs. "And if I draw a poor hand?"

"You fold. That would be the wise decision."

"But less fun than a bluff."

"Fun? That's a different game altogether." She surprised him by laughing. A soft, breathy chuckle that was as arousing as a touch.

He drew in a deep breath to distract himself from the sound of it, and watched her slide over his next card. He liked watching her deal. She had discarded her gloves, and her fingers were long and tapered, moving over the cards in an almost sensual way. He wondered if they were as soft as they looked. How they would feel against his skin. What a night with her would cost him.

"Shall I hit you?"

Startled, he looked up. "What?"

"Do you want another card?"

He blinked, having forgotten to look at his second card. Seven. "Yes."

She flipped up a king.

Twenty-two. *Damn.* With a sigh, he turned his cards facedown and awaited her question.

"Are you a lawman?"

He reared back. "Why would you ask that?"

"Curiosity. It's a woman's prerogative, you know."

"I thought changing your mind was your prerogative."

"It was, until I changed my mind."

A laugh burst out of him before he could stop it. Wit to go with that sharp intellect. The woman was a constant surprise. "No, I'm not a lawman." Not precisely.

She stared at him, her gaze fixed on his mouth. He tried to guess what she was thinking, but then she cleared her throat and thrust the cards at him. "It's late. I'm too weary to concentrate."

Then how about you sit on my lap for a while? Of course, he didn't actually say that. Instead, he glanced at the other passengers and was surprised to see that most were asleep. The conductor had come through after the stop in Kearney, turning down oil lamps and stoking the coal stove at the front of the car. But, judging by the chill, the fire had burned low. It was unsettling that he had let so much time slip away unnoticed.

"I enjoyed our game," he said and meant it. Women rarely got the better of him, but this one certainly had. Seven hours in her company and he still knew almost nothing about her. Tomorrow—after he looked over the other passengers, especially the one with the mustache and gun—he would try to break through that cool reserve. They were still a long way from Salt Lake, and he needed a diversion. And what could be more diverting than a beautiful madam who liked to play games?

WHILE Mr. Whitmeyer turned down the oil lamp above their window, Rachel pulled the cape closer and, using her scarf as a pillow, sat back and closed her eyes.

It wouldn't do. With nothing to brace against, her head flopped side to side with every sway of the railcar. With a hiss of irritation, she shifted sideways toward the window so that her shoulder and head rested against the back of the seat. Better.

Her seatmate remained upright, staring into the blackness beyond the window, one long, blunt finger idly running back and forth across his bottom lip.

A nice lip, she thought drowsily. And a nice smile. With a mouthful of unstained teeth, marred only by a small chip in the second on the right.

How long since she'd noticed a man's mouth or been entranced by a smile? And Mr. Whitmeyer did have a lovely smile. That, and a way of looking at her that made her feel pretty and clever and desirable. Plus, he made her laugh. She hadn't felt so lighthearted in a long time.

Too bad she couldn't trust him. Trust was a liability in her profession since she rarely knew who was a threat and who was an ally. She couldn't afford to let down her guard for a moment or waste time playing card games with handsome strangers and trying to tease stern-faced men into smiling. There was too much at stake to lose her concentration now.

But one thing was certain, she thought, stifling a yawn. She wasn't having fun anymore. She needed a new purpose. One that didn't keep her on the move all the time. She was lonely enough as it was. Her strong reaction to Mr. Whitmeyer had proven that.

RICHARD awoke with a start. He looked around, wondering what had roused him, then realized it was the silence and absence of motion. The train had stopped.

He peered through the window at a night lightened by a swirl of white. They must have been stopped for a while: Snow was already forming crescents on the lower half of the windows. Where were they?

Not North Platte. He vaguely remembered the train stopping there to add a second locomotive for the long climb up Sherman Hill. Had they reached the pass? He started to pull his watch from his vest pocket then realized he couldn't move his arm. Looking down, he saw a tousled dark head on his elbow. He frowned, tried to focus his sluggish mind. Rachel James.

Tilting his head for a better look, he saw that her hat had slipped and was now trapped between his arm and her cheek.

Smashed flat. Like his. Served her right.

She had slumped down so far she was half reclining on the bench, using her folded hands on his bent arm as a pillow. Her face was practically in his lap. *If only.* The incongruity of it made him smile.

He gave her shoulder a gentle nudge. "Ma'am."

No response.

"Mrs. James." Nothing. Slipping his arm free so that her head rested against his side, he ran his hand down her back. Even through her cape, dress, and who knew what assortment of lingerie a madam or confidence woman might wear, he felt the warmth of her body. The scent of roses teased his senses. Emboldened, he drew his hand higher, the tips of his fingers brushing against the side of her breast.

That did the trick.

Lurching upright, she batted at the hat hanging in her face, finally yanking it free—along with most of the pins that had held it in her hair. "W-what's happening? Why have we stopped?"

"I have no idea."

She looked ridiculous, blinking at him like a doe caught in a sudden flash of light, her hair in disarray and one side of her face crisscrossed with marks left by the wrinkles in his coat sleeve.

Ridiculous, yet oddly appealing.

Other passengers awoke, muttering and peering out the frosted windows until the conductor came in, his hat and shoulders white with snow. "Everything's fine, folks," he called out. "We made the Sherman Hill summit, but we're stuck in a snowslide. Cheyenne is sending locomotives with a Bucker plow and crew to dig us out. Until then, since it's snowing hard, I suggest you stay on board. Unless," he added with a hopeful look, "any of you want to help shovel the tracks so we can pull back into the siding? It might get us out of here sooner."

Unwilling to spend the rest of the night waiting in the cold, Richard motioned for Mrs. James to turn her knees to the side so he could get past her.

"You're going out there?"

Stepping into the aisle, he reached above her to rummage through his saddlebags on the overhead luggage rack. "I'm tired of sitting." After retrieving a wrinkled duster, he pulled it on, buttoned it, then dug in the pockets for his gloves.

"Take this." She thrust her scarf into his hands.

He stared at it, nonplussed. The filmy bit of cloth had the weight and consistency of a woman's underthing. What was he supposed to do with it?

"I know it's not much, but it might keep the wind from blowing off your hat."

Ah. "Thanks." He tied it over his Stetson then headed for the door, wondering if any of the other men would notice he wore a silk scarf and smelled like roses.

RACHEL waited until the door closed behind Mr. Whitmeyer, then stepped into the aisle. Rising on tiptoe, she lifted the flap on his saddlebag and ran her hand inside. Clothing, a penknife, a box of bullets, and a book. She pulled it out. *The Deerslayer.* No inscription. In the other bag, she found more clothing, toiletries, a tin of tooth powder, matches, and a stub of candle. No letters, no photographs, no mementos of a personal nature.

Not an acquisitive fellow, Mr. Whitmeyer.

Returning to her seat, she quickly straightened her hair and repinned her hat—minus the broken ostrich feather— then rose and walked toward the open platform at the rear of the car. When she pushed open the door, a blast of icy air almost sucked the breath from her lungs.

"Watch your step. It's slick out here." A man with a satchel hanging from his shoulder stepped into the dim light cast by the lamp over the door. Muttonchops, a bushy mustache, eyes that took everything in but gave nothing back.

"Hello, Harvey."

"I've been waiting out here for an hour, Rachel."

"I fell asleep."

He muttered something then let out a deep breath that fogged the air between them. "So what have you found out?"

"His name is Richard Whitmeyer, he's from Texas, he's not a lawman, and he had business in Omaha City. I haven't learned yet what that business was."

"That's it?"

"He's definitely not a cardsharp, and I doubt he's a bounty hunter."

"You doubt?" More muttering.

She had never felt comfortable around Harvey King. He had his uses and knew his business, but he was also volatile, officious, and prone to cruelty. For that, and the way she often caught him looking at her, he made her uneasy. Another reason she would move on after she got her share of the money she and Harvey would earn at the completion of this mission.

"Anyone else I need to know about?" he asked.

She shrugged. "They all seem harmless. Just travelers. Anyone in your car you want me to look over?"

"I'll let you know. Meanwhile, stay close to Whitmeyer. There's something about him that feels off. We'll talk again in Laramie."

Without another word, he opened the gate, stepped onto the platform of the second car, and went inside.

Rachel stayed out a moment longer, enjoying the silence, the stillness, the gently drifting snow that hid the world's ugliness under a glistening mantle of white. When dawn warmed the low-slung clouds to a faint pinkish glow and she was shivering so hard her teeth chattered, she finally went back to her seat.

RICHARD'S hands felt like blocks of ice dragging at the ends of his aching arms. His toes throbbed, his eyes burned, and his nose had been numb for an hour. But at least they were making progress. The switch frog was finally uncovered. If they could clear enough track to back the train into the siding, then the bucker plow and locomotives could come through without having to slow down . . . assuming no trees or rocks had come down with the slide and were now laying across the tracks.

As he worked, he thought of Rachel James.

Was she really a widow? A madam? Most madams started out as whores. But he had doubts she was a woman of negotiable virtue. She seemed too confident . . . too composed . . . too proud to allow herself to be used that way. And with her looks she could easily find another husband to take care of her.

Unless she preferred to take care of herself.

Either way, she was a puzzle. He liked puzzles.

Dawn came and went, barely noticed through the over-cast. But by the time the sky brightened from dark gray to sooty white, they had cleared enough of the siding to back in the train. And in the nick of time—above the rhythmic exhalations of their idling locomotive they could hear Lucifer's own orchestra racing toward them in a deafening cacophony of screeches, whistles, clangs, and roaring engines.

"Take cover!" the conductor yelled, running behind their train.

Frozen in place, Richard gaped at the immense ice-crusted apparition hurtling out of the mist, spewing a cloud of fire and brimstone into the morning sky. Like great arched wings, walls of snow rose from either side of the giant plow, and vibrations from the churning engines rattled windows and shattered icicles hanging from the passenger cars beside him.

Clapping hands over his ears, he ducked under a wave of snow as the rescue train sped past, side rods clanking, whistles howling, the pounding heartbeats of six loco-motives at full throttle making the ground shudder beneath his feet. With a thunderous clatter, the plow slammed into the snow piled over the tracks. The strain-ing engines drove it as far as they could before losing momentum, then they stopped, pulled back, and ran at it again. Over and over they drove into the snow, carving a path through the drift by sheer force. When they finally broke through, the diggers waved their shovels and gave a great cheer, echoed by those watching from the railcars.

It was the most amazing thing Richard had ever seen.

The conductor waved them aboard. Stomping off snow, he and the other diggers turned in their shovels and climbed into the passenger cars, glad to be out of the cold.

"Did you see that?" Richard said a few minutes later

when he flopped into the aisle seat beside Rachel James. "Wasn't that astonishing? I could feel the heat of the engines on my face. It was unbelievable!"

"It was. Would you mind taking off your coat? You're dripping snow."

"What? Sure." Still talking, he pulled off his duster and gloves and put them, along with his damp hat, on the luggage rack overhead. "Can you imagine the power?" he went on, sitting down again. "Six locomotives at full speed. The ground shook when they went by. And the noise! My ears are still ringing." He laughed, excitement still coursing through him. He'd been enamored with trains ever since he'd seen his first one go by over a decade before. After all of his rail trips since, he would have thought he'd outgrown his fascination, but he hadn't. "I've never seen such a thing. Amazing." Realizing he still held her scarf, he handed it to her. "Sorry it's wet."

"Good heavens, your hands are like ice!"

He looked down at his reddened fingers, tried to flex them, but could only bend them halfway. He noticed then how cold they were . . . especially when she clasped them in her warmer ones.

"You should have come in earlier." She began to rub his right hand vigorously between her palms. "You could lose your fingers."

He probably would if she kept rubbing them that hard. Much as he enjoyed her attentions, he pulled his hand free before she peeled away skin. "They're fine."

"They would warm faster if you slipped them under your shirt."

"I'd rather slip them under yours." Had he said that out loud? Her expression said he had. *Damn.*

"I meant you should put them under your arms," she said stiffly.

"That's what I meant, too." He smiled innocently.

She picked up her valise. "Let me out, please."

"I'm sorry, Mrs. James. It just slipped out. Probably the cold."

"Must I crawl over you?"

Oh, please do. But instead of adding to his indiscretions, he rose and politely moved aside so she could sweep into the aisle. "Poker later?" he asked hopefully.

No response, other than the slamming of the door behind their bench as she exited the rear of the car.

His earlier euphoria fading, he slumped against the window. Who knew madams could be so sensitive? Unless she wasn't a madam. *Hell.*

A scream from the back platform brought him to his feet. Flinging open the rear door, he saw Rachel hanging by her gloved hands on the other side of the railing, her feet dangling in air. "What happened?" He stepped toward her, slipped on the icy deck, and careened into the railing beside her, narrowly avoiding flipping over the side as she apparently had. Righting himself, he braced his feet against the supports and peered down. "Are you all right, Mrs. James?"

"No, I'm not! Help me!"

"You want me to take hold of you?"

"Of course I do, you nitwit!"

"I wouldn't want to offend you again."

"Hurry! I'm slipping!"

"If you're sure . . ." Bending over the railing, he gripped her under her arms and hauled her up and over. As he set her on her feet, he gave a broad smile. "It seems you're going to warm my hands after all."

"Oh!" She tried to jerk away, started to slip, and grabbed his jacket.

"Be careful, Mrs. James. It's icy out here." He continued to hold her, his palms pressed against the sides of her breasts, which were warming his hands nicely. "Imagine how much more dangerous it might have been had the train been moving. Or if you had been more than a foot above the ground. A nasty fall."

"I despise you."

"No, you don't. Your heart wouldn't beat this hard if you did."

"My—?" She looked down, saw where his hands were, and gasped.

Which made him laugh. "Just a bit of fun, Mrs. James. No harm."

"Release me!"

"You'll fall." But he let her go, keeping his hands up and ready to grab her if she slipped. She didn't, and managed to keep her footing to the door. "Shall I get your valise?" he asked. "I believe it's just there, in the snow."

She looked up at him, blue fire in her eyes. "You're a hateful man."

"You're welcome. Meanwhile"—reaching into his jacket, he pulled out the deck of cards—"you'd best deal. My hands are still too cold."

"Go to the devil."

Richard retrieved her valise and returned it to their bench, where she sat, glaring out the window; then, to allow her time to get over her snit, and since the train hadn't started moving yet, he took a stroll through the other cars.

Many of his fellow shovelers were recognizable by their red noses and cheeks. Not so, the fellow with the sweeping mustache and sideburns sitting alone near the rear of the second car.

Richard sank down beside him, accidentally stepping on the satchel by his foot. "Sorry," he said, slipping his hand inside as he brushed it off. Only papers.

Muttonchops snatched it from his grip and stuffed it between his hip and the window. "That seat's taken."

"I won't be long. Just waiting for the lavatory."

"What lavatory?"

Richard bent over to straighten his trouser cuff, then twisted in the seat to look behind him. "I was told there was a lavatory at the back of this car."

"You were lied to."

"Hell." With a sigh, he sat back. The train jerked, then rolled slowly forward in the wake of the locomotives and bucker plow, which had gone ahead to clear the rest of the track between Sherman Hill and Laramie.

"Where you headed?" Richard asked after a while.

"West."

"San Francisco?"

A terse nod.

"What a coincidence." Shifting in the seat, Richard extended his right hand. "Richard Whitmeyer. Texas, mostly."

After a slight hesitation, Muttonchops took his hand, gave a single shake, then released it. "Harvey King. Omaha City."

"Hear about the bank that was robbed day before yesterday?"

Harvey shot him a glance. His eyes were as dark as an empty mine shaft, and about as welcoming. "What bank?"

"Only one in town. Cattleman's National, I read."

"Read where?"

"*Omaha Herald.* Surprised you didn't hear about it, you being from the town where it happened. But not everybody can read, I guess."

"I can read. Just don't have time for it."

"A businessman? What do you do?"

"This and that."

"I'm between jobs myself. Maybe I could look you up when we get to San Francisco, see if you're hiring. Have you any business cards?"

"No. And I'm not hiring."

"That's too bad." He sat a moment longer then pushed himself to his feet. "If there's no lavatory, guess I should go back to my seat. Perhaps we'll talk later."

No response.

That was odd, Richard mused, fighting to keep his balance as the train picked up speed. For a resident of Omaha City, Harvey King knew little about it—such as that there were several banks in town, none named Cattleman's National—and the town newspaper was called the *Omaha Sentinel,* not the *Omaha Herald.* Nor had he met a legitimate businessman with the hands of a bare-knuckle street fighter who carried no cards, but did carry two guns, one on his hip and one in an ankle holster. And what were those papers in the pouch he guarded so vigilantly? Wanted flyers? Stolen stock certificates?

He would have to keep an eye on Harvey King.

"You're still aboard?" Rachel asked when he slipped into the aisle seat beside her. Despite the sarcasm, her tone had softened. Probably too weary to sustain her resentment. It had been a long twenty-four hours for both of them.

"I was visiting." He eyed the cracker she held. "Is that all you have to eat?"

"It's the only thing I can tolerate while we're moving." She broke off the corner of the cracker and slipped it between her lips . . . lips that weren't as red as when she was cold, but still delightfully plump. He hoped to kiss her soon to find out if they were as soft as they looked.

"I'm glad you decided to sit with me again," he said.

"I had no choice. The other car was full."

Not strictly true, but he didn't argue. "I'll behave." Picking up the cards and newspaper she'd left on the seat, he began to shuffle. "Blackjack or draw?"

She chewed her morsel of cracker. "Visiting with whom?"

"Blackjack it is, then. A man in the second car. Harvey King. Odd fellow." He checked his cards. Two queens. Excellent. "Stand or hit?" When she didn't answer, he looked up to find her staring at him in the strangest way. "Stand or hit?" he asked again.

"Hit. Odd in what way?"

He flipped over a nine of spades. "He's a liar." While she studied her hand, he told her about the discrepancies. "If he's from Omaha City, he should know the name of the only newspaper and the name of the Cattleman's Bank and Trust. Another hit?" he asked, his question already forming in his head.

"I'm bust." She sat back. "Maybe he only recently moved there."

"I doubt it." He showed his winning hand. "So my question is . . . when do you want me to kiss you?"

"W-what?"

"And don't say never. Never is a long time, and we've only a limited time until I get off in Salt Lake City."

"You're outrageous."

"I'm interested. Surely you know when a man is interested in you. In your line of work it probably happens all the time."

Her beautiful mouth opened then closed then opened again. That blue fire came back into her eyes. "My line of work?" she asked, showing teeth, but not in a friendly way. "What is that supposed to mean?"

Hell. He'd erred again. "Perhaps I made assumptions I shouldn't have."

"About what?"

He smiled weakly. "How you earn your money."

She did that gasping thing again. "What? You think I'm a . . . a . . ."

"I realize now I was probably wrong," he cut in before she started shrieking.

"Probably? *Probably?*"

"Definitely. I was *definitely* wrong." He tried for a contrite look. "Clearly I'm the nitwit you think I am."

"Clearly!"

He gave her a moment to calm down, then said, "About that kiss . . ."

"I would rather suck venom from a leper's leg."

Richard shuddered at the image. Disgusting, but not an outright no. There was still hope.

RACHEL simmered in silence until the conductor came in two hours later to inform them they had a hotbox on the rear tender truck—whatever that meant—and would be delayed in Laramie until Cheyenne sent out a replacement axle. "Two days at most. Maybe five. I recommend the Grand Hotel. It's near the depot, the rooms are mostly clean, they have a decent dining room, and this time of year it's practically bug free. We should arrive within the hour."

Mr. Whitmeyer shifted on the seat. She could sense him studying her, but refused to give him her attention.

"It's because of your clothing," he finally said. "And your poise and beauty." When she didn't respond, he continued. "Not many women of means would be daring enough to travel alone, especially dressed the way you are."

"What's wrong with the way I dress?"

"Nothing. Not a thing. In fact, you look stunning. But the fineness of it does make you stand out among all these other drab travelers. For that reason, and because of your confidence and intelligence, not to mention your rare beauty—"

"You already did mention it."

"What?"

"My beauty. You listed it twice. But, pray, do continue."

"Yes, well." He cleared his throat. "For all those reasons, I assumed you were in business, the sort of business that would provide wealth and independence while allowing you full control. I could think of only one."

A pretty speech, even if only half of it were true. "You're wrong. There are many positions open to women."

"I know. I've made a grievous error and I'm deeply sorry. Perhaps you'll allow me to atone by taking you out for a real meal when we reach Laramie."

She studied him, trying to gauge his sincerity. He did seem remorseful, but she saw amusement behind the contrition, and that made it hard for her to keep a stern expression. The man could charm his way out of anything. "You think I'm beautiful?"

A smile tugged at the corner of his mouth. "Very."

"But immoral."

"'Immoral' is rather harsh. I prefer 'available.' It was—and still is—my ardent hope that you are. Available."

"Perhaps I am." She watched a spark flare in his dark eyes and happily quashed it. "For dinner. No more."

He grinned, not looking quashed in the least. She would probably need a hammer to do it properly.

"Excellent. Shall we meet in the Grand Hotel dining room at six o'clock?"

"Or thereabouts." First, she had to talk to Harvey King and find out what had gone on between him and Richard Whitmeyer.

THE Grand Hotel was like a hundred other western hotels that had sprung up alongside the tracks when the Union Pacific came through over a decade prior. New enough to still have the piney scent of freshly milled lumber, but old enough to show a bit of wear and tear. Rachel suspected that as towns grew and rail travel became more common, these wooden structures would give way to brick and stone hotels boasting grand lobbies decorated with chandeliers, velvet drapes, and thick carpets. It had already happened along the east coast, and refinements were quickly spreading across to the west.

Alas, they hadn't reached as far as Wyoming Territory. Even so, the Grand boasted a full washroom and hip bath on the ground floor, and a community convenience on the second level.

Knowing there would be a rush later, she went directly to the washroom. The old couple got there first, but she didn't have to wait long. After a quick wash and change of clothing—into something more sedate to assuage Mr. Whitmeyer's sensibilities, although why it mattered, she couldn't say—she went up to her room. She had just put away her things when she heard a knock on her door.

"I checked with Omaha City," Harvey said, stepping past her. "Nothing new. Still no description." Crossing to the window, he pushed aside the curtain and peered out. "They seemed to be concentrating east, rather than west. Takes some of the pressure off of us."

"Mr. Whitmeyer said he spoke to you earlier."

"Sat down beside me, chatty as a schoolgirl." Letting the curtain fall, he turned to face her. "I don't trust him."

"He doesn't trust you, either." She listed the inconsistencies Whitmeyer had mentioned. "You need to be more careful."

"You're lecturing *me*?"

"He's not stupid." Seeing that belligerent look come over Harvey's face, she softened her tone. "I'm having dinner with him tonight. Is there anything you want me to find out?"

He grinned nastily, showing a snaggle of broken teeth, a legacy of his fighting days. "Getting chummy, are you?"

"You told me to stay close to him."

The grin faded. He waved a knobby-knuckled hand in impatience. "Then do what I asked you to do and find out for sure if he's a bounty hunter, so I can get him out of our way if necessary. And I want to know what his business was in Omaha City, who he's working for, and why he's heading to San Francisco."

San Francisco? He had told her he was getting off in Salt Lake City.

Harvey crossed to the door. "I'm in room two ten down on the right. If you learn anything tonight, let me know or slip a note under the door." He reached for the knob, then hesitated. "You still carry that little Remington derringer?"

"Always."

"Good. If Whitmeyer gives you any trouble, don't be afraid to use it."

"I'm not afraid." Not of Richard Whitmeyer, anyway.

But Harvey King was another matter.

At five minutes before six, she left her room and walked downstairs. Judging by the crowd outside the dining room, they would have a busy night in the kitchen. She hoped Mr. Whitmeyer had made reservations.

Apparently he had and was already seated.

The server led her directly to a table between a big window and a crackling fire in a huge, rock fireplace. The tang of wood smoke mingled with the smell of roasting meat. Her empty stomach rumbled.

He stood when he saw her. "You look especially beautiful in that pretty dress," he said, helping her with her chair before returning to his own.

"And hopefully less whorish."

His expression changed into something quite fierce. "I would never apply that word to you, Rachel."

"Immoral, then."

He frowned, his lips pressed in a thin line. Then the anger faded from his dark brown eyes. "I suppose I deserve that."

"I suppose you do. But in view of your seemingly heartfelt apology—"

"It *was* heartfelt."

"—I won't mention it again."

"Thank you." He let out a deep breath and gave a crooked smile that melted away her lingering pique. The man did have a way about him.

She studied him, thinking he looked quite handsome himself. It was amazing what a shave, a trim, and a freshly ironed shirt could do for a man—although she missed that shadow of beard on his strong jaw—it went so well with his roguish smile. It pleased her that he had gone to such effort, even though it also made it slightly awkward. After all, it wasn't as if they were actually stepping out, or forming an attachment to each other. Not really.

But then again, he had called her Rachel.

"HOW are your accommodations?" Richard asked after their server had placed the evening offering—venison stew with all the trimmings—before them.

"Quite nice. They don't move, which I find particularly appealing. And now that the clouds have lifted, I have a lovely view of the river and the mountains across the valley."

"Our rooms must face the same direction. I'm in two eighteen."

"Two fourteen."

He frowned. "Are you sure? I thought I saw Muttonchops coming out of that room earlier."

"You must be mistaken."

But she didn't meet his eyes when she said it, nor did she ask who Muttonchops was. And suddenly all those doubts circled back through his mind. If not a madam, then was she running a scheme with Muttonchops? Endeavors like that could be lucrative, and required careful thought and deception. The widow James was both wealthy and highly intelligent. Had he been duped by her beauty and his own attraction to it? Had he become that careless?

They ate without speaking—Richard, mulling over all he knew about the elusive woman across from him; Rachel, taking tiny bites of her meal and refusing to look at him. An air of reserve rose between them and Richard found himself trying to think of something to say that might bring back her saucy smile.

"What will you be doing in San Francisco?" she asked, breaking the long silence. "Visiting family?"

"Salt Lake City. Looking for someone." Odd that she would mention San Francisco so soon after his talk with Muttonchops.

"An old acquaintance?"

"Someone I've never met."

"Sounds quite mysterious."

"It isn't. Just business." Instinct told him he was being gently interrogated. Not sure of the reason for it, he changed the subject. "Would you care for dessert?" he asked, seeing she had finished her meal.

"It depends on what they have."

At his signal, the server removed their plates then wheeled over the dessert cart. Richard selected a dish of berry cobbler. She chose bread pudding.

Around them, noise rose and fell as the dining room filled and emptied and filled again, but Richard was reluctant to speak. He wasn't sure he wanted answers to the questions bouncing around in his head. He admired this woman. He didn't want to learn she was an enemy.

Liar. He more than admired Rachel James. He was smitten. Being with her created within him an anxious, edgy feeling he hadn't experienced in . . . well, ever. He wasn't certain he liked it. But he couldn't seem to stay away.

He watched her take two bites of her dessert, dab a drop of creamy pudding from those lips he so admired, then sit back, her expression unreadable.

"You said earlier you weren't a lawman. Could you be a bounty hunter?" She smiled as she said it, but he sensed the answer was important to her.

Pushing away his empty plate, he took a sip of coffee, found it cold, and set the mug back down. "The notion of hunting down a human being for money is distasteful to me."

"But isn't that what lawmen do?"

"It's certainly a part of their job, but not the whole of it. And they receive no added recompense for the criminals they apprehend. In fact, I'd wager the yearly salary of a sheriff or federal marshal is a fraction of what a bounty hunter makes."

"If that's the case, why do they do it?"

He gave a wry smile. "Why, indeed?" Leaning forward, he braced his elbows on the table and studied her over his laced fingers. "Maybe you're the bounty hunter."

"Me?" She laughed. That husky, breathless sound that heightened his awareness of her all through his body.

"You're certainly clever enough," he went on. "And with your beauty you could easily lure a man into a trap."

"You make me sound rather devious, like a spider enticing unsuspecting prey into her web."

"It's not unheard-of for a woman to take on that role."

Her smile faded. "Perhaps. But I think I'd rather be the pursued than the pursuer. A fly has more freedom and can see the world from every angle, while the spider is confined to her dark, lonely corner. How dull would that be?"

"You crave excitement."

"If the alternative is boredom, then yes." Laying her folded napkin beside her unfinished pudding, she gave a weary smile. "But right now, what I crave is sleep."

Taking that as his cue, Richard rose and came around to assist her. As he pulled out her chair, the scent of roses drifted up to him. Potent. Heady. Reminding him how long he had been without a woman. Firelight shimmered in her black hair, reflecting back glints of red and gold, and he imagined the silky feel of those dark strands sliding through his hands.

One night. That was all he wanted.

A feeling of regret moved through him. Why couldn't she be a sporting woman? It would make everything so much simpler.

"It's been a lovely evening, Mr. Whitmeyer," she said, regaining his attention. "Thank you for the first true meal I've eaten since Omaha City."

"My pleasure, Mrs. James." He fell into step beside her as they crossed to the lobby. "Shall I walk you to your room?" he asked when they reached the stairs.

"That's not necessary. Perhaps I'll see you again before we resume our trip."

"Count on it." He watched her climb to the landing, his gaze drawn to the gentle sway of her hips, the proud line of her back. A remarkable woman, the widow James. If he wasn't careful, she could easily become his downfall.

Sighing, he turned and walked out of the hotel and onto the boardwalk.

RACHEL waited at the top of the stairs until she saw the lobby doors close behind Mr. Whitmeyer then hurried down the hall. Stopping outside the door marked 210, she knocked softly.

No response.

She continued on to her room, pondered what to do, and finally penned a note to Harvey: *Whitmeyer saw you come out of my room. Meet me at 9:00 A.M. at the depot. R.* Then she returned and slipped the note beneath his door.

As she walked back to her room, she heard footsteps behind her. Turning, she saw Richard Whitmeyer walking toward her.

"What are you doing still up?" he asked.

"I had to step out for a moment." She made a vague

gesture in the direction of the convenience, then realized it was at the other end of the hall.

He didn't seem to notice. "I'm glad I caught you." Stopping beside her, he smiled, showing those fine teeth and a faint shadow of new stubble on his chin. She had forgotten how big he was. He swallowed the light and blocked most of the hallway with his wide form, giving no chance of escape, should she want one.

Which she didn't.

"I saw the conductor," he said. "The axle is delayed. We won't be departing for several days. I thought perhaps we could meet for breakfast in the morning then take a stroll through town. There's not much to see, but you might enjoy the local shops. Say . . . nine o'clock?"

It was only because she needed more information—not because the idea of spending more time with Richard Whitmeyer added an odd jump in her heartbeat—that she nodded. "A walk sounds lovely. But nine thirty would be better."

"Nine thirty it is." His grin broadened, left deep creases down his cheeks where those dimples hid.

Having that smile and those deep-set brown eyes fixed on her with such intensity made Rachel feel a bit breathless. "I look forward to it." She turned toward the door.

A touch on her shoulder brought her around again. "About that kiss . . ."

She tried to speak, couldn't, and cleared her throat. "Mr. Whitmeyer—"

"Richard." He stepped closer.

She stepped back, her heels thumping against the floor molding.

Looming over her, he braced one hand on the wall above her head. "You did lose," he reminded her.

"Which allows you a question. No more."

"A question you never answered."

"Yes, well . . ." Her words trailed off when he lifted a hand to cup her cheek. His palm was cold against her heated skin, his fingers so long his thumb brushed her temple and his fingers reached around to the back of her neck.

"One kiss, Rachel." He bent lower, his breath fanning her eyelashes. "That's all."

"I . . . I . . ."

"Say yes."

She couldn't. But she did manage a breathless nod.

His lips brushed hers—softer than she expected—still cool from his walk. She tasted coffee, smelled wood smoke and damp wool on his jacket, felt the tip of his tongue trace the seam of her lips.

Her legs trembled. Her pulse thundered in her ears. Long-dormant hunger drew her closer until she felt the heat of him against her breasts.

He didn't rush, didn't press for more, and because he handled her with exquisite care, as if she were something precious and rare, she was helpless against him. A yearning built within her, spread through her veins like warm honey. It had been too long since she'd been kissed . . . and never this way.

Reason returned when she ran out of air. "M-Mr. Whitmeyer . . ."

"Richard." His lips left hers, moved up to her cheek.

"This is unseemly. What if someone—"

"Shh." His mouth came back to hers, trailed gentle kisses from one corner to the other.

Why was it suddenly so hard to breathe?

Those long fingers slid into her hair. "Ask me inside."

"Inside?"

She felt his smile against her lips. "Your room. For starters."

"Oh. Oh!" She jerked back, but the warmth of his big body still surrounded her, fueling desires she hadn't felt in too long.

He straightened. His hand fell away. "Rachel," he chided softly.

A tempest of conflicting emotions raged through her. She shouldn't be doing this. She shouldn't feel this way. He was a stranger to her. Possibly an enemy.

"Good night, Richard—Mr. Whitmeyer." And before he weakened her further, she opened the door and slipped inside.

Good heavens. Heart drumming, she sagged against the door as his footfalls faded down the hall. What had come over her? She was a thirty-year-old widow, not some simpering schoolgirl overcome by her first kiss.

She lifted trembling fingertips to her lips, her senses still reeling with the scent of him, the taste of him. Of Mr. Whitmeyer. Richard.

Who was he? And why was he pursuing her? On impulse, she flung open the door—maybe to ask him that—or maybe to kiss him again—or even to ask him inside. But the hall was empty. Both relieved and disappointed, she shut the door.

Now, more than ever, she needed to know everything about him—why he was here, who he was looking for, and who his employers were, assuming he truly had employers.

A day and a half. That was as long as she'd known him, yet in that short span of time he had awakened urges and thoughts she'd put aside four years earlier when she'd laid Charlie to rest. Even now, her knees felt weak and desire pulsed through her, liquid and low.

And if he got in her way? She pressed a palm over her

racing heart. She had no choice. She would do what she had to do.

A T nine o'clock the next morning, Richard was sitting at the table he had shared with Rachel the previous night, nursing regrets and his first cup of coffee.

He hadn't slept well. Thoughts of Rachel had plagued him through the night. Had he truly pushed her up against the wall like the prostitute he'd once thought her to be? It was humiliating. An indication of how far he had drifted from his purpose. But when he'd come across her outside her door and she'd lied about where she'd been— the water closet was at the opposite end of the hall from where she had been coming—he had been angry and confused. And disappointed.

Still, there was no excuse for it. This wasn't his first time around a pretty woman. Even one as mysterious and alluring as the widow James.

Beyond the window, morning sunlight made the icicles hanging off the depot roof sparkle like cut glass and turned the snow piled alongside the tracks into glistening mounds. The glare off all that snow and ice was a stab in his eyes.

The dining room slowly filled. He recognized several fellow travelers. The elderly couple from the train sat in a dark corner, the old man hunched over his plate, his wife slipping food under her heavy mourning veil. The farm boy sat alone, hiding toast in his pocket, probably to take back to the chicken. Two other tables were occupied by people he didn't recognize, but he surmised by their famil-iarity with the servers that they were Laramie residents.

Movement drew his eye and he looked out the window

to see Rachel daintily picking her way across the slushy
street between the depot and hotel. Today, she wore a blue
dress under her cape, and a jaunty bonnet with trailing
ribbons that caught in the morning breeze and were probably a perfect match to her beautiful blue eyes.

What had she been doing at the depot?

And not alone.

A man moved from the rear of the depot, walked
quickly past the siding where their disabled passenger
cars sat while the locomotive was in the machine shop
awaiting repairs, and disappeared into the Western Union
office next door. Richard could tell by the satchel hanging
from his shoulder it was Muttonchops.

A terrible certainty gripped him. After seeing King
come out of her room yesterday, then learning the latest
news from Omaha City last night, and now seeing them
both leaving the depot at the same time this morning, he
could no longer discount what was obvious. Rachel and
King were working together.

Damn.

"Am I late?"

He looked up to see Rachel approaching. Cold had
turned her cheeks pink. Her eyes sparkled, and her smile
was as dazzling as the snow. She was so beautiful it made
his chest hurt.

Rising, he pulled out her chair. "No, I'm early." Returning to his place across from her, he studied her while she
gave her breakfast order to the server. The pale purple
smudges beneath her eyes told him she hadn't slept well,
either. Not surprising, considering the way he had forced
himself on her in the hall, and the dangerous game she
was playing with King.

"I saw you coming out of the depot," he said after the
server left.

"Yes, I wanted to see if they'd had any more word on how the repairs were going."

"In a hurry, are you?"

She gave him a smile that didn't quite reach her lovely eyes. "Actually, I'm enjoying the respite from the constant jarring."

While she filled the silence with idle chatter, he contemplated the best way to broach the subject of his boorish behavior. If he was ever to learn what she and Harvey King were up to, he had to keep her trust. Besides, he owed her an apology. "Rachel," he said when she paused for breath, "about last night . . ."

"Don't mention it."

"But I—"

"No, truly. Don't mention it. It was simply a regrettable incident that is best forgotten."

Forgotten? He doubted he would ever forget the feel of those soft, plump lips moving against his. "I wouldn't say 'regrettable.' Forward, perhaps. But I have no regrets that I kissed you, Rachel." In fact, even as he sat here offering excuses for his poor behavior, the base part of his mind was devising scenarios where he could do it again. "But I shouldn't have pushed you so hard. You deserve better. I apologize for frightening you."

"You didn't frighten me. I don't scare that easily."

Bravado? Or an invitation to try again? Hope soared.

Breakfast arrived. While he waited for the server to set their plates before them—one poached egg, toast, and tea for her; three eggs, beefsteak, potatoes, toast, and coffee for him—he tried to pull his errant thoughts back on track. "I wonder what Muttonchops was doing at the depot," he asked after the server left.

"Muttonchops? Are you referring to the man with the bushy sideburns?"

He nodded. "Harvey King."

She took a sip of tea and returned the cup to its saucer without a sound. "I don't know why he was there."

She was smooth. No doubt about it.

While they ate, Richard went back over the information he'd received in answer to his wire the previous night. No identity on the bank robber yet, but they suspected the culprit hadn't been acting alone. A witness mentioned a man with heavy sideburns and a bushy mustache who had been in the bank around the time of the robbery in the company of an attractive, dark-haired woman . . . although the witness wasn't sure if they had been in before the robbery, or after.

An apt description of Harvey King and the woman Richard couldn't stop thinking about. A feeling of melancholy moved through him. *Ah, Rachel. If only you were the woman I wished you were.*

R ACHEL was relieved when breakfast was over and she was no longer subjected to Richard Whitmeyer's intense scrutiny.

Something had changed since that unfortunate scene in the hallway. Unfortunate in the sense that it had kept her awake half the night. And that Richard Whitmeyer was the last person with whom she should be contemplating a dalliance. And if Harvey King found out, he could end her chance to build an independent life. If she had any true remorse about the events of the last few days, it was that she hadn't said no when she'd first been approached about taking part in this wretched undertaking.

"Shall we take that walk now?" Mr. Whitmeyer asked her.

Looking up, she met his eyes and wondered, as she had a dozen times since the night before, what might have happened between them had she not chosen the path she was on or had he been less secretive or had she been more willing to act on the feelings he had triggered with that amazing kiss.

Would anyone ever know or care if she took him to her bed? It wasn't as if she was an untried virgin. Was she expected to go the rest of her life without the touch of a man?

The day was fine, if cold, and the stroll through town didn't take long. They met the sheriff, visited a couple of shops, stopped by the newspaper office for the latest edition. Despite its progressive attitudes—Laramie was the first city in the country to seat females on a jury or allow women to vote—the town wasn't an especially thriving community. Most of the businesses catered to the railroad: rolling mills, a tie treatment plant, various rail yards and machine shops. But the setting was lovely—lofty mountain ranges on either side of a broad, high plain with a river running through it. Far different from the farmland of Nebraska where she and Charlie had struggled to carve out a life.

"How long will you be staying with your sister in California?" Richard Whitmeyer asked, jarring her back to the present.

"I haven't decided." Hopefully, if things went well, she wouldn't be going to California at all. "Have you ever been there?"

"I have. Several times. An interesting place." He shot her a speculative look. "Since I have no set plans, perhaps I'll accompany you there."

She stumbled to a stop and peered up at him. "Why would you do that?"

"Why not?" Reaching out, he brushed a trailing ribbon from her shoulder, then stroked the tips of his fingers up to that dip where her jaw joined her neck.

She shivered.

He saw, and smiled. "A woman as beautiful as you shouldn't be traveling alone." Dropping the newspaper onto a nearby bench, he took her hand, placed it in the crook of his arm and started them walking again. "Then, too, I'm hoping if I stick around a little longer, you might change your mind."

"About what?"

"Me. I'm not your enemy, you know." He gave a crooked smile that brought a catch to her throat. "And I'm not giving up on you."

Addled, she followed where he led, Harvey's words echoing through her mind: *Until we know who he is and why he's trailing after you like a hound on a scent, be careful. If he gets too close, you know what to do. We've come too far to go back empty-handed.*

"Why would you be my enemy?" she asked once she was sure she could keep her voice steady.

He was slow to respond, and when he did, he looked straight ahead, rather than meeting her gaze. "Sometimes people get themselves into trouble. Do things they oughtn't or find themselves caught up in something from which they see no escape."

Rachel frowned up at him. "And you think I've done that?"

"If so, I can be your way out."

Way out of what? "I don't understand."

He stopped and faced her, his expression grim. "I know about you and Harvey King."

She stiffened. How had he found out? And what did he think he knew?

"I don't understand the hold he has over you," he went on, "or what you've done. But I can help you."

"Help me? How?"

A sad note came into his voice. "I can let you walk away."

"From what?"

"Harvey King. Whatever the two of you are mixed up in." He made a restless motion with one big hand. "With your quick mind and physical assets you could start over anywhere, doing whatever you wanted."

Rachel pressed her free hand to her forehead, so confused she didn't know what to think or what he was talking about or how he knew the things he did. "But I am doing what I want. I chose this."

When she saw his face harden, understanding dawned. With it came relief that he had reached the wrong conclusions, then hurt that the conclusions he *had* reached were so insulting. She snatched her hand from his arm. "First you accuse me of being a—a—prostitute! Now of being in some sordid relationship with Harvey King. What have I done to make you think me so lacking in character?" When he opened his mouth, she held up a hand. "No, don't answer. I don't want to know. Nor do I want your concern. I don't need saving by you or any other man!" Whirling, she charged down the boardwalk.

She had thought he was different, that he admired an independent spirit. But it seemed Richard Whitmeyer was like every other male, preferring women to be meek and biddable and content to live in the shadows of the men who ruled their lives. Well, she had done that. She had put her life in the hands of a kind, gentle, well-meaning man and had nearly starved because of it. No more. From now on, she would order her own future, Richard Whitmeyer be damned.

Fine words. Then why did they bring so much pain?

Oh, Richard. Why couldn't you be the man I thought you were?

"Rachel," he said, coming up behind her.

She continued walking.

"Rachel, wait." He touched her arm.

Horrified that she might burst into tears, she jerked away. "I have nothing more to say to you, sir. Do not approach me again."

This time when she walked on, he didn't follow. But she could feel his gaze boring into her back as she crossed the street and went into the hotel.

RICHARD slumped onto the bench in front of the mercantile. *Hell.*

Lifting a hand, he pinched the bridge of his nose. What was it about the confounding woman that kept him so off balance he lost all reason? He hadn't meant to accuse her of a liaison with King, only to let her know he suspected them of working together, then gauge her reaction. Instead, he'd blundered again. Now, if she truly was in some dishonest scheme with Muttonchops, they were forewarned. If she wasn't, he'd ruined any feelings she might have had for him. And what if she was being led into some nefarious scheme by Harvey King? How could he help her when she wouldn't even talk to him?

He wasn't usually so inept. Another unsettling indication of how easily he lost focus when he was around her. *Hell.*

He spent the rest of the morning on the bench, watching passersby and pondering what he should do. Then it came to him. The perfect plan that would ensure his success and still keep Rachel safe.

Rising from the bench, he walked quickly down the boardwalk.

J UST after noon, Richard Whitmeyer came into the hotel dining room, walked directly to Rachel's table, and asked if he could join her.

"No."

He sat down across from her. "I'm sorry."

She looked up, tried to mask a sudden rush of . . . something. "Sorry for what? Being high-handed? Irritating? Wrong? An utter buffoon?"

"Yes."

She took a bite of potato and slowly chewed. "You don't look sorry," she observed after she swallowed. "In fact, you look rather pleased with yourself."

"I have a plan."

"Oh. A plan. Well, that excuses everything."

He gave a long, labored sigh. "It excuses nothing. I'm all those things you said I was. But I'm not *totally* at fault," he added with that engaging smile. "If you weren't so damned beautiful I would be able to think more clearly."

Refusing to smile back, she cut a sliver of stewed carrot. "What about my vast intellect and confidence?"

"That, too."

She popped the carrot into her mouth and studied him as she chewed and swallowed. "It's not your ability—or inability—to think that should be of concern to you, Mr. Whitmeyer. It's the foolish words that come out of your mouth."

"I know. I'm as dismayed about it as you are. And I'm really, really sorry."

How could he sound so contrite while his eyes danced

with laughter? And why couldn't she stay as angry with him as she should? "I tire of hearing your weak excuses," she said, pushing her plate aside.

"Then I'll not tire you further by offering more." He frowned at the remains of her luncheon. "Is that all you're going to eat? I could order you a grape for dessert, if you thought that wouldn't be too filling."

"What do you want?"

Amusement changed to hard resolve. "To keep you safe."

"Then leave, and I shall be both safe *and* content. Or better yet, since I've quite lost my appetite, I'll leave."

"You were finished anyway. An entire carrot. You must be stuffed."

Before he could come around to pull out her chair, she rose. "Good day."

"Rachel . . ."

Head high, she swept dramatically from the room and into the lobby, then realized the last place she wanted to go was upstairs to her room. She had spent most of the morning there, after her last confrontation with Whitmeyer, pacing and wondering why she let the man upset her so. Refusing to be chased up there again, she stepped through the open doors onto the boardwalk. The glare was so bright it blinded her. By the time her eyes adjusted, he was beside her.

"Are you crying?"

"Of course not, you big dolt. It's the sun."

"I thought perhaps you were upset by our little run-in."

"Upset? I'll show you upset." She reached for her over-and-under derringer, then realized she'd left her reticule in the dining room.

"Looking for this?" He held up her bag by the wrist strap.

She snatched it away.

"And just so you know, I paid your tab."

She groped inside the purse.

"You shouldn't carry a gun if you're not going to load it."

He looked in her purse? "It is loaded."

"Not now." That smile again. "I may be smitten, but I'm not foolish."

Smitten?

He laughed. "Surely you're not that surprised. Especially after last night."

Horrified that he was about to further entertain the people already staring at them, she plopped onto the bench in front of the hotel and dug in her reticule for the bullets he'd taken from her gun.

"May I join you?"

"No."

He sat down beside her. "How long does it take to load one of those things?"

"You'll know shortly."

"Are they very accurate?"

"At this distance, I pray so." She slipped the bullet into the lower chamber, but before she could snap it closed, he reached over and rested his hand over hers. It was big and warm, the back of it lightly dusted with dark hair. The masculinity of it made her feel feminine and delicate—except for the pistol in her grip.

"I hate when we quarrel, sweetheart."

"Then cease speaking. And I'm not your sweetheart."

"You could be."

"When pigs sprout wings." A trite response, but she was too rattled to think up a better one. Shoving his hand away, she finished loading the pistol and slipped it back into her reticule.

He was smitten?

"I can't believe you pawed through my purse," she said.

"Only out of concern for you." He gave her an indulgent smile. "When I picked it up, I heard the clank of metal and wanted to make certain you hadn't accidentally slipped the hotel silverware inside."

"Had they been a finer grade of tin, I might have. Especially the knife." Narrowing her eyes in warning, she added, "In case someone steals the bullets from my pistol."

"Who would do such a thing?" he said and laughed. A wondrous sound that filled her heart.

You ninny. Determined not to weaken in her resolve to keep this man at arm's length, she abruptly rose. "I have to go."

"Where?"

Away from you. "My room. I'm tired."

"Will you join me later for dinner?"

Of course not. "When?" *God.* Did she really say that?

"Six o'clock. Our usual table by the fire."

"Perhaps," she said and fled before she did something foolish—like shoot him or simper like a schoolgirl, she wasn't sure which.

RICHARD watched her race away, taking part of his heart with her. How had that happened? When had he become so besotted that he no longer cared what her hidden purpose might be, who she was in league with, or what her past was?

He had to get control of himself. Finish the task at hand. And maybe then . . .

He spent the afternoon walking through the town

again, sent a wire back to Omaha City—still no news on the bank robbers—then stopped for a talk with the sheriff.

He wasn't the only one out and about; the old couple visited several of the abandoned shacks along the tracks, the farm boy took his chicken for an outing, and Harvey King sat in the lobby of the hotel, perusing a newspaper that was almost a month old. A slow reader, it seemed.

After a trip to the washroom and a change of clothes, Richard returned to the dining room. Taking the chair facing the lobby, he watched for Rachel.

She didn't come, and by six thirty, he figured she wasn't going to. It should have been a relief. Now he could put aside this obsession and attend to his business.

Instead, he rose and left the dining room. But as he started up the stairs, he saw her coming down and stopped to watch her, his elbow resting on the newel post. She wore a pinkish dress that matched the guilty flush on her cheeks, and her dark, glossy hair was done up in curls that set off her beautiful turquoise eyes.

When she reached the bottom step, he offered his arm and escorted her to their table. "I thought you weren't coming," he said, holding out her chair.

"I wasn't." She sent a saucy smile over her shoulder that turned his thoughts into gibberish. "But then I changed my mind."

"Thank God for prerogatives."

The dining room filled quickly, the drone of so many voices lending a sense of privacy by making it harder for their conversation to be overheard. That pleased Richard. He wanted to focus on her, rather than worrying about what was going on around them.

Their server came to take their order: buffalo steak for him, baked chicken for her, the vegetables of the day, which were the same as yesterday—green beans, carrots, and roasted potato wedges—and hot rolls with creamy butter.

"Why didn't you want to join me?" he asked after the server left.

"It's not that I didn't *want* to." She sighed. "But I'm not sure it's wise for us to pursue this."

"This? Meaning my attraction to you?" There. He'd admitted it. Now he awaited her reaction.

"Yes." Color flooded her cheeks. She didn't look at him. "And mine to you."

That stopped him dead. It was a moment before he could gather his wits to respond. "What's worrying you, Rachel?"

Finally, she looked up and met his gaze. "We just met. We scarcely know each other. Within a few days, we'll part and never see each other again."

"It doesn't have to be that way."

"Doesn't it?" She studied him for a long time, a small furrow between her dark brows. "Who are you, Richard? What do you do?" She spread her hands in a helpless gesture. "How can I trust a man of whom I know so little?"

A dozen glib answers rose in his mind. But he sensed honesty would get him a lot further with this woman, and he respected that. "I'm Richard Whitmeyer and I investigate insurance claims." He saw her surprise and gave a wry smile. "You were hoping for something more exotic, I suppose."

"Not at all. But I am surprised. You seem rather . . . flamboyant. I've always thought of insurance investigators as somewhat stodgy."

He had to laugh. "I usually am. Driven, in fact. But you've brought out a lighter side in me." A happier side, he realized. He couldn't remember when he'd smiled or laughed as much as he had with Rachel James. "Your turn."

"I'm Rachel James. Widow of four years. And I'm . . . ready to make some changes in my life."

An odd thing to say. From his perspective, her life seemed to be going well. She had money, beauty, intelligence, the instant admiration of any man in sight. What more could she want? "You said earlier you wanted to run your own business someday. What kind of business?"

"I haven't decided."

"You'd make an excellent headmistress at a finishing school," he offered. "Or if that wasn't exciting enough, you could put your vast experience with firearms to use by becoming a prison matron."

And there it was—that breathy laugh that made him want to keep teasing her just to hear it again.

Their food came. He managed to eat it all even though he didn't remember the taste of any of it. Around Rachel, he forgot everything—even why he was here in Laramie and what he had been sent to do. Just being with her opened his mind to other possibilities, other wants and desires. New ways of looking at his life. He had been alone too long, And the more time he spent in Rachel's company, the more time with her he wanted.

Soon—if his plan worked out the way he hoped—he might be free to offer her all the time in the world.

WHEN Richard looked at her like that, Rachel felt almost giddy. Nervous, shivery, and daring. What would it be like to feel those strong arms around her? Those lips on hers again? His hands—

Her thoughts scattered when she saw Harvey watching them from a corner table. He gave her a sly wink, a crude reminder that she wasn't here on holiday or at liberty to enjoy the attentions of a handsome man. She had a task to finish.

Was he truly an insurance investigator? Or was that simply a ploy to discourage further questions?

Appetite gone, she pushed her half-finished meal away.

"Not hungry?" Richard studied her with concern. "Would you care to order something else?"

"It was all delicious. I couldn't eat another bite."

"Not even a raisin?"

"Not even."

As he turned to signal their waiter, she wondered what she would do if Richard turned out to be their target. How could she watch such a strong, vibrant man brought low?

Beyond the window, a light snow began to fall. She almost hoped it would develop into a blizzard that would keep them stranded here for a month. By then, Harvey would give up and move on, and perhaps she and Richard . . .

"Shall we go into the lobby for a friendly game of draw poker?" he suggested. "I'm sure with the snow starting again, there will be others unwilling to go out who might want to join us."

She leaped at the suggestion, not wanting to spend the rest of the evening stuck in her room. "A fine idea. But this time, you really must try."

"I'm always trying."

She laughed. "I'll not argue with you about that."

They found three more players—a married couple, who were visiting from Nevada, and Harvey King, who immediately jumped in when he heard Richard asking around in the lobby.

Rachel hadn't told Harvey that Richard suspected them of working together. She wasn't sure why. But as she watched the two of them spar across the card table, she realized she was pulling for her dinner companion, rather than her partner. An indication of how far her loyalties had shifted in the few days she'd known Richard Whitmeyer.

She also noted that this time Richard played in earnest, that intense focus on beating Harvey, rather than enjoying a friendly game. Even though they were only playing for chips, it seemed neither man could tolerate losing, although Richard hid his irritation better than Harvey. The tension built as Harvey's losses mounted, until finally, the Nevada couple had had enough and excused themselves. Other players took their places and, seeing still more players waiting to step in, Rachel begged off, too. Richard immediately gave his chair to the old man in mourning—apparently his wife had already retired—and offered to walk Rachel to her room.

She was aware of Harvey's watchful gaze tracking them up the stairs, but by the time they reached the landing, he was once again engrossed in the game.

Would Richard kiss her again? If he asked to come inside, should she let him? Thoughts muddled in her mind. Resolve warred with desire. She was beginning to suspect she was the brazen hussy he had once accused her of being.

"Not a very friendly game," she said, desperate to fill the silence as they walked down the hallway.

"You can thank your friend for that."

"You were no better than him," she chided, stopping beside her door. "And he's not my friend."

"Then what is he?"

"An acquaintance. Like you."

That intense look came over his face. "That's all I am?"

An unreasoning panic gripped her. She wasn't ready for this. For him. With a trembling hand, she turned the knob. "Good night, Richard. Thank you for another lovely dinner." And before she could change her mind, she opened the door and stepped inside.

She stood in the dark silence of her room, her heart thudding against her ribs. What was she doing? What was she afraid of? That sense of panic came again, but for an entirely different reason.

"Richard," she called and flung open the door.

He stood where she'd left him.

"You didn't kiss me good night," she blurted out.

"You didn't give me a chance to."

They stared at each other. Five seconds. Ten. "Well?" she prodded.

He stepped closer. Taking her face in his hands, he stared hard into her eyes. "I'm more than an acquaintance, Rachel, and you know it."

"Y-yes."

"Say it."

"You're more."

A fierce expression swept his face, then he lowered his mouth to hers.

It wasn't a gentle exploration this time. This kiss was more of an openmouthed demand, filled with such need and emotion it left her weak yet yearning for more. When he finally lifted his head, she was up on tiptoes, leaning into him, and his hands were on her breasts.

Breathing hard, he rested his forehead against hers. "Breakfast. Nine o'clock." Releasing her, he gave her one last short kiss, then turned and walked away.

WHEN Rachel came downstairs the next morning after a restless night of lurid dreams and erotic imaginings, she found the lobby filled with milling people. Because Richard was so tall, his head rose well above most of the others, and when he spotted her on the stairs, he pushed through the crowd toward her.

"What's happening?" she asked when he stopped beside her.

"We're about to find out."

"Listen up, folks," a voice called.

Rachel expected it to be the conductor announcing that the repairs to the locomotive were complete. Instead, she saw the sheriff she and Richard had met on their earlier stroll through town standing in the dining room archway. Speaking loudly enough to be heard by those in the lobby as well as those at the tables, he said, "Seems we have a thief." He waited for the murmurs to die down before continuing. "Several guest rooms have been robbed, and Deputy Beemis"—he motioned to the man beside him—"will be searching your quarters for the missing items. Won't take long." At his nod, the deputy headed up the stairs.

"Before you ask," Rachel murmured to Richard, "I didn't do it."

"That's a relief. Glad you brought your wrap. Let's go outside while they sort this out." She let him help her into her cape, then lead her through the lobby. "It's a beautiful day," he said, pushing opening the door.

It was a freezing day, and the glare was atrocious. But the cold helped chase away the cobwebs in her head, and the sun felt warm on her face. They settled on the bench outside the hotel, nodding politely to other guests wandering out of the lobby to stand, talking, outside.

"This is all highly suspect," she muttered, hunching into her collar. "And illegal. But I suppose a little thing like the Bill of Rights doesn't matter out here."

"Actually, it's the Fourth Amendment," he said, idly

watching the elderly couple from the train wander down the boardwalk. "And if they do find anything, it won't be admissible at trial."

She squinted up at him. "How do you know that?"

He shrugged. "Who do you think the thief is?"

"You?"

He flashed that dazzling smile. "Cranky, are we? Have a restless night?"

She didn't answer, hoping he would attribute the red in her cheeks to the ungodly cold.

"What about those two?" He nodded toward the mourners. "Ever notice anything odd about them?"

"The old folks?" Rachel watched them pause outside one of the abandoned railroad shacks at the end of the street, then disappear inside. A tryst? Sweet, but unlikely. "They seem nice enough. Sad, quiet, obviously devoted to each other. I think she has foot problems."

Richard looked at her in surprise. "Why do you say that?"

"Her shoes are more like brogans. Sensible, but totally unsuitable with a dress."

"Have you ever seen her without that veil?"

"No. Not even when she dines." Rachel had never seen her without gloves, either. But such modesty wasn't unusual in an elderly matron.

They sat in silence for several minutes. Rachel stopped shivering as the sun warmed her. Or maybe that was Richard's nearness. Or her lascivious thoughts about him. She was pathetic.

The old couple came out of the shack and walked back toward the hotel. From a second-floor window overlooking the boardwalk came a woman's high-pitched voice demanding that the deputy stop pawing through her things.

"What about the farm boy with the chicken?" Richard asked. "It would be an ingenious way to hide, say . . . stolen jewels, if he fed them to her."

"Ingenious, but probably fatal. I think he cares too much for her to do that."

"Which leaves Harvey King."

"Does it?" Rachel smoothed a wrinkle from her skirt.

"Where is he?"

"I'm sure I don't know."

"He wasn't in the dining room. Did you see him upstairs?"

"No." Uneasy with his line of questioning, she rose. "If you'll excuse me, I must make certain Deputy Beemis isn't trying on my corset."

Whitmeyer's brows shot up. "Corset?" Surprise gave way to a grin that was positively wicked. "Since when do you wear a corset, Mrs. James? You certainly weren't wearing one the other day when you so kindly warmed my hands."

The heads of several onlookers outside the lobby turned their way.

"You are vile beyond belief. Good day."

"Does that mean no poker later?" he called as she swept inside.

*T*HAT *ought to keep her fretting for a while,* Richard thought, settling back to watch the comings and goings without her distracting him. And she definitely was a distraction. Whenever he looked into those blue-green eyes, he forgot how to think.

Upstairs, the search continued. Several guests came out onto the boardwalk, protesting the intrusion. The farm boy seemed more upset about his chicken than his rights, and one man vowed to write to President Hayes.

The old couple returned. Rachel was right about the footwear. Richard had once owned a pair just like them, only in a larger size.

Still no sign of Muttonchops. Surely, if he held stolen goods in his possession, he would want to get them out of the hotel before they searched his room. So where was he?

Disheartened, Richard rose and went into the dining room for another look around. Seeing only a few late diners, he turned to go, then saw a figure move past a back window.

Rachel. In a hurry. Going where?

Dread and anticipation warring within him, he followed.

HARVEY should be doing this, Rachel fumed as she slipped and slid down the slushy lane behind the hotel. This wasn't her part of the arrangement. She was only to watch and report. But he wasn't in his room or the hotel dining room, so here she was, slogging through half-melted snow, muddying her hem and her new high-heeled lace-up suede walking shoes. If they were ruined, she would make certain he got the bill.

Slipping into the narrow space between the side of the hotel and a millinery shop, she crept toward the main thoroughfare and peeked down the boardwalk.

Richard Whitmeyer wasn't at the bench in front of the hotel. Harvey was nowhere in sight. Relieved at the one and irritated at the other, she took a chance, stepped out into the open, and continued at a brisk pace down the boardwalk.

When she reached the abandoned shack the old couple had gone into, she paused outside the door to pull the derringer from her reticule. She listened for movement, heard none, and pushed open the door. Stepping inside, she looked around.

A broken chair, sagging shelves, and a freestanding rock fireplace that separated this room from the one behind it and was filled with a lacework of cobwebs. Dozens of footprints crisscrossed the dusty floor, all coming to and from the fireplace—too many for just the old folks. Had Harvey been here, too?

She crossed to the hearth. The cobwebs appeared undisturbed, but two stones were out of alignment with the others. On closer study, she saw that they had been sprinkled with loose dirt to disguise the fact that the mortar had been dug away. Clever, that.

Crouching down, she set her reticule and pistol on the hearth within reach, then, using her hanky, brushed away the dirt. The stones were still a tight fit. When she finally worked them free, she saw a bulky oilskin pouch buried beneath them. She carefully lifted it out and set it on the hearth beside her bent knees. Hardly daring to breathe, she untied the closure and peeled back the flap.

And there they were. Safe. Dry. Her chance for a better life.

Tears pricked her eyes. She ran her fingers over the bearer shares, needing to touch them to assure herself they were real. She had worked hard for this moment. Not even Harvey could take it away.

Richard Whitmeyer's image flashed through her mind, damping her elation.

How would he react when he found out how she earned her money? Would he still think her deserving of his protection?

No matter. She could sort all that out later. Right now she wanted to luxuriate in her success. She'd earned it.

With trembling fingers, she undid the smaller pouch beside the shares and tipped it into her hand. Dozens of glittering stones fell out. Thousands of dollars' worth within the palm of her hand.

A feeling of power surged through her. No one could stop her now.

"Rachel."

She bolted to her feet. "R-Richard!" she cried, when she saw him standing in the doorway. "W-what are you doing here?"

"I followed you." His gaze dropped to the bearer shares on the hearth.

She stood frozen, her mind reeling, the stones still in her hand. That sad look in his dark eyes was like a blow to her heart. "Richard, you don't understand."

"No, I don't." He held out his hand. "Give them to me, Rachel."

"No." She clutched the stones tighter, felt the sharp edges dig into her palm. "They don't belong to you."

"They don't belong to you, either." He stepped closer, his hand still outstretched. "This is a dangerous game you're playing. Stop now, before it's too late."

Was he threatening her? She saw a slight tremble in his fingers and wondered what he was thinking, what he intended to do. She glanced down, saw her pistol on the hearth. Even if she could reach it in time, would she have the courage to use it? On Richard? The man she had kissed. The man who thought she was beautiful.

"Hand them over, Rachel." Another step, kicking up a tiny, glittering cyclone of dust to swirl through a beam of morning sunlight. "I'll let you walk away. I promise. But you have to give them to me now."

"No." She stepped back, almost tripped against the hearth. "I'll not let you take them from me."

"We're running out of time! You have to get out of here while you still can."

They stared at each other, the sound of their breathing loud in the small room. Regret mingled with the dust in the stagnant air. She watched his chest rise and fall on a deep breath and remembered the solid strength of it beneath her palm.

"Rachel. Sweetheart. Don't make me do this. Please."

Something shattered inside her. Trust. Her last lingering hope that he was a better man than he was showing himself to be. Bending down, she picked up the derringer with her free hand. "You do what you must, Richard." Blinking hard, she aimed the pistol at his chest. "And I will, too."

He seemed less surprised than sad. "You would really shoot me?"

"If she doesn't, I will."

Rachel gasped as Harvey stepped out from beside the fireplace. Her knees gave way and she plopped down on the hearth, her heart beating so fast she felt light-headed.

Grinning, Harvey pointed his Colt at Richard. "Good work, Rachel. I'll take it from here."

RICHARD looked at King, then back at Rachel. He felt like the floor had given way beneath his feet. "So, it's true. You two are working together."

Rachel wouldn't look at him.

Harvey laughed nastily. "She's a good little piece, isn't she? Had you drooling like a dog in a butcher shop."

At a small sound of distress, Richard glanced back at Rachel, saw her trying to manage the gun and pour the jewels into a pouch at the same time, but her hands shook so badly she spilled most of the stones in her lap.

King noticed, too. "Be careful, woman! I want every one of those accounted for."

Not sure why he would still want to protect her, Richard tried to direct King's anger back to himself. "Using a woman to do your dirty work, Harvey?"

"Shut up, Whitmeyer. Whether you're armed or not, I could shoot you now and get a citation for it."

Citation? From whom?

A footstep outside alerted Richard to a new presence near the door behind him. The sheriff. Finally. To cover the sound of his approach, he raised his voice. "You won't get away with this, King. I'll hound you until you drop."

Harvey laughed. "Hound me how? You'll be in jail."

Jail?

"Actually, he'll be dead," said a voice—not the sheriff's—just as something hard jammed into Richard's back. "You, too, King, if you don't drop that gun."

Rachel lurched to her feet.

Harvey didn't move, his eyes round with surprise in his slack face.

Glancing back, Richard saw the mourning couple behind him, the old man holding the gun to his back, the old lady aiming at Harvey, a big grin on her bearded face.

Hell. He'd been wrong about them, too. His mind racing, he tried to figure out what was going on.

Rachel looked as shocked as he was, which meant she probably wasn't in league with the old couple. Nor was Harvey, judging by his stunned expression.

So it had been the old folks all along. How could he have missed that?

Their disguise was perfect. Who would look too

closely at an elderly couple in mourning? Or question an old lady's footwear? Only Rachel.

But if the old people were the Omaha City bank robbers, what role did Rachel and Harvey play in all this? Had they been running a confidence scheme, stumbled across these two, and decided to abscond with the spoils themselves? Or were they bounty hunters after all?

Brother and sister? Lovers? Was she even a widow?

What the hell was going on?

He doubted the robbers intended to let them leave here alive. No one would know he and Rachel and King were missing until it was time to board tomorrow, and the conductor wouldn't further delay departure just because a few passengers missed the train. The thieves could get off at the next stop, change their disguises, buy new tickets to throw trackers off their scent, then continue on with no one the wiser.

Unless the sheriff arrived in time to stop them. Damn it, where was he?

"You heard him, King," the man in the dress said in a gravelly voice. "Drop it, or I start shooting."

Richard thought quickly. His gun was still in the shoulder holster—a big error on his part. He couldn't tell if Rachel still held hers—both of her arms were straight at her sides, her hands hidden in her skirts. Harvey was the wild card. So far, he hadn't relinquished his weapon, but if he planned to use it, he had better do so soon. If not, Richard would have to act on his own if he hoped to get out of this alive. But how could he protect Rachel if the thieves behind him started shooting? She was directly in their line of fire.

And where the hell was Sheriff Bowman?

"You heard him, King," the one disguised as the old man warned. "Drop it."

With reluctance, Harvey set his Colt on the floor. Hopefully, he still had the pistol in his ankle holster.

Knowing it was up to him now, Richard raised his hands and slowly turned to face the gunmen behind him. "Look, fellows," he said amicably, shifting his weight so his body was partially in front of Rachel. "You start firing, half the town will come running. Then nobody gets anything. But I might have a way where we all can benefit without anybody getting hurt."

"Benefit from our hard work, you mean."

Richard shrugged and moved a few more inches to the side. "Better half the loaf than none of it, right?"

"Better *all* of it." The man posing as the woman thumbed back the hammer.

Richard braced himself. Then saw a familiar figure move into the doorway.

"Put your guns down!" the sheriff shouted, stepping up behind the two gunmen. "Real slow. You, too, King," he added when he saw Muttonchops reach down for his pistol.

"But I'm—"

"One more inch and I'll fire, swear to God."

Muttering, King straightened.

The two gunmen didn't move.

Neither did Richard, since their guns were still pointed at him . . . and at Rachel, standing somewhere behind him next to the hearth. He waited, his heart bouncing against his ribs, watching to see what the men facing him would do.

One wavered. The other held fast. When the old lady's finger tightened on the trigger, Richard whirled and threw himself toward Rachel.

Noise exploded.

Something slammed into his chest.

He flew backward. Heard someone scream. Smelled blood and spent powder. Then he landed hard, the back of his head cracking against the floor. A moment of terror as he fought to drag air into his lungs. Then darkness descended.

H E awoke confused and disoriented. Pain hammered at his head. His chest hurt so bad he was afraid to take a full breath. He had no idea how he had gotten back to his hotel room, or what had happened to cause him so much pain, until he lifted the sheet and saw the thick bandage on the left side of his chest.

It all came rushing back. The gunmen. The deafening noise of several guns firing at once. Rachel standing at the hearth, the smoking derringer in her hand.

Rachel!

Lifting his head, he looked frantically around, saw her familiar figure silhouetted in the window, looking out. Relief pounded through him.

Alive. Whole. Safe.

He slumped back as sudden emotion clogged his throat. It shocked him . . . the intensity of it. He didn't know where it came from or what he was supposed to do with it or what it meant. All this over a woman he scarcely knew?

A woman he desperately wanted.

Turning his head, he watched her as he struggled to come to grips with the realization that this quirky, sassy, fearless woman had almost cost him his life, yet his first thought had been gratitude that she had survived the gunfight unscathed.

The tears filling his eyes made no sense.

"Rachel."

She turned, her look of worry giving way to a brittle smile. "You're awake. We were getting worried. It's been several hours. How do you feel?"

"You shot me."

She made an airy gesture with one shaking hand. "It was bound to happen at some point. You are easily the most aggravating man I've ever met."

"You're saying it's my fault?" *Unbelievable.*

"If you hadn't lied to me, none of this would have happened."

"When did I lie to you?"

"You never told me you were an investigator for Kingston Allied Insurance, the firm that insured the stolen jewels."

"*Lead* investigator. And that's no reason to shoot a man."

"I was aiming at the old woman behind you but then you jumped in the way. Why would you do such a foolish thing?"

Now he was foolish as well as guilty. Lifting his left arm, since it hurt too much to move his right, he pressed the heel of his palm against his throbbing temple. "The man in the dress was about to shoot." Had he really said that aloud? "I knew you were in the line of fire and I didn't want you to get hurt." He shot her a look. "I forgot you don't need saving."

"It's unbecoming to pout. And it was obvious he was about to shoot you. Which is why I shot at him. And if you hadn't gotten in the way, I would have gotten him. I think the other man fired, too, but I'm not sure. It was confusing."

"And yet, here you are, all safe and sound, while I'm"—he looked down at his bandaged chest—"not."

"Don't be such a baby. It's hardly a scratch. Two

scratches at most. A little bruising, and less than a dozen stitches in all. The bullet hit the butt of your pistol and broke apart. Two tiny pieces went into you. Another piece went into your shoulder holster. You were lucky I didn't pull both triggers."

"I certainly feel lucky. Thank you for only shooting me once." In truth, now that he knew his wound was minor, he did feel much better. Not that he was going to admit that. The woman could have killed him, for God's sake. She should feel some remorse. "Why does my head hurt so much?"

"It hit the floor when you fell. In fact, when you went flying, I thought . . ." She turned abruptly to the window and cleared her throat. "I thought you might have cracked a board with that hard head of yours."

He saw her shoulders shaking and wondered if she was laughing at him. Then he heard a faint sniff and realized she was crying. Over him. Bless her heart.

"Rachel."

"I didn't mean to shoot you," she said to the window.

"I know. Would you mind stepping over to the bed?"

"You might have died."

"But I didn't. Please. Just for a moment."

She turned, tears streaming. "I'm so sorry, Richard. I would never hurt you. You must know that."

"I do, sweetheart. Now stop crying and come over here or I won't allow you to kiss me."

She blinked sodden blue eyes. "Kiss you?"

"A kiss of peace. Nothing more." He motioned to his chest. "I am, after all, injured." But not incapacitated, he happily noted as his body stirred.

She came to him, docile as a lamb, unaware that once he had her in his arms, he wouldn't let her go. Not for a while, anyway. As soon as she came within reach, he wrapped his good arm around her, pulled her down onto the bed beside him, and kissed her soundly.

He tasted the salt of her tears, felt the quiver of her lips beneath his, and knew there were more tears to come. "Sweetheart," he whispered, brushing his hand over her damp cheek, "it's all right. I'm okay."

"I was so afraid."

"Me, too." But for an entirely different reason.

She rested against him for a long time while the events in that dusty shack circled in his mind. Whenever he came to that moment when he knew the man in the dress was going to fire, fear gripped him anew. What if he'd hit her?

"We were lucky the sheriff got there in time," she said after a while.

"He'd better have gotten there. That was the plan. Anyone else hit? And what about the thieves?"

"They're in custody. No one else was hurt." She sat up.

Her tears had dried. Rosy lips still bore the mark of his kisses. Curls had slipped free to tumble about her shoulders, and he envisioned them spread across his pillow like ebony wings.

"What plan?" she asked, jerking him from his pleasant musings.

He told her how he had convinced the sheriff to search the hotel rooms on the ruse of hunting for pilfered items, hoping that would flush the Omaha City bank robbers into the open. "And apparently it worked. Fearing the deputy would find the stolen shares and jewels when he searched their room, the old couple must have hidden them in the abandoned shack. They might have gotten away with it if you hadn't become suspicious of her—his—footwear." He rewarded her with a kiss. "Clever girl."

She rose and went back to the window. Pushing aside

the curtain, she looked out. "And when I went to see what they had been up to, you followed me."

"And Muttonchops followed both of us." Richard frowned as a troubling thought arose. "Where is Harvey, by the way?"

"Packing, I presume."

"He's leaving?" Did that mean she would be leaving, too? That notion disturbed him in so many ways Richard didn't want to think about it. "And the stolen shares and jewels?"

She turned from the window and wandered restlessly about the small room, idly touching this and that. "He's taking them back to Omaha City."

"Harvey?" Richard started to sit up, then changed his mind when he realized it hurt too much and he was only wearing his undershorts beneath the sheet.

A whistle in the distance drew her back to the window. Apparently the trains were running again. "You mustn't worry about Harvey," she said, peering across the street toward the tracks. "He's completely trustworthy, if somewhat coarse."

"I hope he's not thinking to get the reward Kingston offered. I already promised it to Sheriff Bowman."

She glanced back at him. "Why did you do that?"

"To entice him to do an illegal search."

"To bribe him, you mean. I thought lawmen weren't allowed to take rewards."

"Not personally. But their offices can."

She considered that for a moment, then resumed pacing. "No matter. Harvey couldn't have accepted any money anyway. Pinkertons aren't allowed to take reward money, either."

Richard reared back in surprise. "Harvey's a Pinkerton detective?"

"We both are."

"What?" This time he bolted upright, despite the pain. "You're a detective? But that's—why didn't you—you're a *Pinkerton*? I can't believe it."

"Indeed?" She stalked over to glare down at him, arms crossed under those soft, round breasts he'd so enjoyed when she'd rested against him. "You were quite prepared to believe I was a prostitute or a confidence schemer or even a thief. Why not a Pinkerton?"

Blue fire flashed in her eyes. But he was too rattled to heed the warning. "Since when do they allow women to be Pinkertons?"

"Since Kate Warne started sleeping with Allan Pinkerton back in the fifties. Even though she's been dead for a decade, they still recruit women occasionally for their Female Detective Bureau." She smiled nastily. "Since we're so good at undercover work and luring foolish men into traps."

Another whistle. She went back to the window and pushed aside the curtain to look out. "The train's here."

Even from his bed, Richard could hear the *chuff* of the locomotive as it rolled into the depot across the street. Her train? How long before it left? Fifteen minutes? A sense of urgency gripped him. "Is that the one headed back to Omaha City?"

"Yes." Letting the curtain fall, she went to look in the mirror over the bureau. "Your employer sent his private car for you. If you're well enough, it will take you back to Baltimore this evening."

He watched her reflection as she smoothed a brow and patted a curl back into place. Even from the bed he could see her hand was shaking.

His panic grew.

"It seems Kingston holds you in high regard. But don't

worry," she added, straightening her collar. "The sheriff didn't tell him it was I who unmasked the robbers, and not you."

"I don't want you to go," he blurted out before he'd thought it through. But as soon as the words left his mouth, he knew the decision was right.

She went still. Her eyes met his in the glass, and what he saw in her face awakened a whole new kind of pain.

"Rachel, don't go back with Harvey. Stay, and go back with me. It would only delay you a day."

"And probably cost me my employment." She slowly turned. She looked sad. Resigned. "And when you move on, Richard, what would I do then?" She walked toward the bed, new tears glistening in her beautiful eyes. "Oh, dearest," she said with a soft sigh, "I have never enjoyed a game of poker more than when you worked so hard to lose to me. You're a magnificent man."

He couldn't breathe. Like a hand had reached into his chest to squeeze the air from his lungs. "Stay. Please."

"I—I . . ." Her voice broke. Bending down, she pressed her lips to his—not gently, but punishing, as if provoked by some desperate emotion. Then it changed to something softer, sweeter, like she was savoring every moment of the contact. When she pulled back, she was crying again. "I shall never forget you."

"Rachel."

But she was already walking away.

Richard stared in disbelief as the door closed behind her. He willed it to open again. Prayed that it would. When it didn't, fury engulfed him. With a curse, he rose up and swept his good arm across his bedside table, sending everything on it crashing to the floor. Then he grabbed his pillow and sent it sailing across the room. How could she leave him?

He wanted to howl. Break things. Find her and demand that she return.

Then weakness overcame him and he flopped back, his body trembling, the ache in his head pulsing like a second heart.

Damn you, Rachel.

Silence and the reek of spilled lamp oil settled around him as he stared up at the ceiling and waited for the departing whistle to blow.

R ACHEL wept as she threw the last of her belongings into her valise.

She had worked too hard to give up her independence now. She had tried marriage. It hadn't worked. Even though she had loved Charlie, she hadn't loved their life together. Never again would she be content to stand at the window and wait for her man to come home to her.

She needed excitement, challenge. A rowdy game of poker now and again.

Pain rolled through her. She bent over, arms clasped to her waist, tears dripping onto the coverlet.

How can I leave him?

Outside, the all-aboard whistle sounded, reminding her time was slipping away. Straightening, she swiped the tears from her eyes and snapped the valise closed then took a last look around.

Everything looked exactly as it had when she'd first arrived. As if she had never slept within these walls. As if none of it had ever happened and he hadn't burst into her life, spinning her around with his outrageous banter and laughing brown eyes and that crooked smile with the tiny chip in his tooth.

She didn't even know how he'd gotten that chip. Or if

he had ever been in love. Or what his dreams were. She hardly knew him at all.

I don't want you to go, he'd said. Just that. No promises. No proposals. No declarations. Six simple words from a man who thought she was beautiful.

How can I leave him?

Yet how could she give up four years of hard work and stay?

Feeling herself waver, she quickly rummaged through her valise until she found her small writing case. Taking out a piece of stationery, she went to the bureau and scribbled a note. After sealing it in the envelope, she wrote the name across the front, then slipped the envelope into her reticule.

Maybe she would give it to Harvey. Maybe she wouldn't. But until she decided, it was always wise to keep one's options open.

Resolved, she picked up her valise and left the room.

IT was late afternoon when Richard left the hotel. On the siding behind the depot, the westbound Union Pacific locomotive sat like a huge slumbering beast, exhaling gentle breaths of steam into the frosty air. Coupled at the end of the short train of boxcars was Ben Kingston's private railcar, the fringed, velvet curtains drawn back to show the luxury within.

Despite lingering regrets over the telegrams he had just exchanged with his employer, Richard was mostly relieved to have the decision made. Ben was sorry that he was leaving Kingston Allied, but was happy to give him use of his private car to Salt Lake City.

So now Richard was on his own. With no idea what to do next.

Still, if there was one thing his short time with Rachel had taught him, it was that there had to be more in his life than work. If he had died in that shack, what legacy would he have left behind?

"Evening, Mr. Whitmeyer."

Richard looked up to see an elderly Negro man in a red jacket standing on the rear platform of the Kingston car.

"My name is Jonas," the man said as Richard came up the steps. "I'll be your steward throughout the trip. If there's anything you need, you let me know." With a flourish, Jonas opened the door. "Welcome aboard, sir."

The president of Kingston Allied Insurance certainly traveled in style, Richard noted as he stepped inside. Paneled walls, thick woolen carpets, upholstered swivel chairs bolted beside overlarge windows that showed hardly any soot at all. There was even a desk and bookcase at the end of the room and a long damask couch on the wall opposite the swivel chairs. Expensive bordello, with a touch of Mississippi riverboat for flash.

Richard headed directly to the couch. With a sigh, he sank down into the soft cushions, trying to jar his head as little as possible. Looking around at the brass and crystal appointments, inlaid tables, ornate coal stove, and tasseled footrests, he felt no regrets about the exorbitant bonus he would earn for recovery of the stolen jewels insured by Kingston Allied. Apparently Ben could well afford it.

"Is there anything I could get you?" Jonas motioned toward the narrow hallway at the forward end of the room. "We have a fully stocked galley up front, in addition to the master bedroom and lavatory next to this parlor."

"Where do you sleep?"

"There's a nice, cozy steward's nook by the front platform. A drink, perhaps? Mr. Kingston keeps a fine bar."

Richard bet he did. Ben was quite a drinker. "Bourbon, if you have it."

"Right away, sir."

As Jonas disappeared toward the galley, Richard slumped down until his head rested on the back of the couch. Rachel's image rose in his mind. She was past Sherman Hill now, probably nearing the water stop at Buford. Was she sitting with King? There hadn't seemed to be much rapport between the two of them.

Pinkertons. He still couldn't believe it, even though all the clues were there.

Was she thinking about him as much as he was thinking about her?

He could feel himself sliding toward melancholy again and was glad when Jonas arrived with his drink. After downing it in two gulps, he gave the empty glass to the steward, along with instructions to wake him when they left for Salt Lake, then he settled deeper into the cushions and closed his eyes.

It was done. There was no turning back now.

Sometime later, Jonas awoke him from a lusty dream starring Rachel and her corset to say they would be departing in five minutes. Oh, and he had a visitor.

Yawning, he rubbed the sleep from his eyes and wondered who would be coming by this late, when the woman of his dreams swept through the doorway in a rush of cold air, trailing scarves and gloves and the scent of roses in her wake.

He bolted upright on the couch. "Rachel?"

"I've been thinking," she said, pausing to unpin her hat and give it, along with her cape and gloves and a smile of gratitude, to Jonas. "With your flair for deductive reasoning, and my rare beauty and intelligence, we would make an excellent team."

"You didn't leave."

"See? You make my point exactly. Nothing escapes that analytical mind."

Now that he was fully awake and able to observe her more carefully, he could see that despite the glib chatter, there was a slight tremble in her voice. Nerves? Rachel? The most self-assured women he'd ever met? Or was this another of her games? "Thank you, Jonas. That'll be all for tonight."

"Yes, sir."

As the steward left, the car jerked. Rachel grabbed for one of the swivel chairs and sat down across from his couch. "I guess we're on our way."

Richard watched her, not sure what to say and half afraid he was dreaming again.

The train picked up speed, settling into a smooth rhythm that was more of a gentle rocking than the jerk and jostle of the older passenger cars. Equipped with the latest design of leaf springs, no doubt.

"Why are you here, Rachel?"

She crossed one knee over the other and began unlacing her elegant, heeled walking boot. "There's no place I would rather be."

"What about the Pinkertons?"

"I'm no longer with them."

"You quit?"

"I did." Pulling off the right boot, she set it aside, then started on the left. "I sent a note back with Harvey. I'm sure Allan will understand."

Allan? She was on a first-name basis with Allan Pinkerton?

The second boot came off.

His pulse quickened. "What are you going to do?"

She mistakenly thought he was referring to her employment options.

"I'm hoping to convince you to leave Kingston and come work for me."

His jaw dropped. *Work for her?* Addled as much by what she was doing as what she was saying, he struggled to stay focused. "Doing what?"

"Detective work." Sliding the hem of her dress above her knees, she rolled down her stockings one by one, shook them out, then draped them over the arm of her chair. With a sigh, she sat back and wiggled her toes in the thick pile of the carpet. "Oh, that feels so good."

And was fun to watch. He shifted and crossed his legs. "I've already left Kingston Allied."

She looked up, her blue eyes round with surprise. "Have you? Why?"

"I'm thinking of opening my own detective agency."

She chuckled in that breathy way that played havoc with the fit of his trousers. "See? We think alike. How could we not make a wonderful team?" Rising, she began to loosen the buttons down the front of her dress.

His mouth went dry. The pulsing in his head moved elsewhere. "Rachel, what are you doing? You know I don't enjoy games."

"But you play them so well." She let the dress slide down to the floor, then her petticoats, one after the other, until she stood in a knee-high pile of fabric, clad only in her corset and chemise. The corset was black, laced up the front, barely reaching from the top of her hips to just below her delightfully plump breasts. Had she not been wearing a silk chemise beneath it, he would have seen all the treasures he had been imagining ever since he saw her standing on the platform in Omaha City.

He lifted his good arm. "Come here."

One dark brow rose. "It's your side that's injured. Not your legs. You'll have to meet me halfway."

"I'm afraid if I stand, I might appear too . . . eager."

"Are you eager?"

"Beyond measure." He uncrossed his legs. "Come see for yourself."

"Don't be crude." Yet she moved toward him, her steps slightly off balance because of the swaying of the railcar. When finally she came within reach, he put his good arm around her waist and pulled her between his bent knees.

He looked up at the silk-clad breasts quivering and jiggling in front of his face and imagined what other delights the motion of a train might enhance. "You are so very beautiful," he said, reaching up with his right hand to stroke the pale skin above the edge of her chemise.

"Don't forget intelligent and confident," she said in a voice that sounded strained. "Although at the moment, I'm feeling rather timid."

"You shouldn't. Not with me." With trembling fingers, he loosened the satin laces. The corset fell away. He reached for the hem of her chemise, but she got there first. Hiking it up to her hips, she climbed into his lap and straddled him.

Sweet Mary. He gritted his teeth, afraid he might embarrass himself while she squirmed around, making herself comfortable. "That's enough," he finally ground out. "Just sit still for a moment."

"We could call it the Rachel James Detective Agency," she said, sliding her hands up his chest to push his coat aside. "Can you take this off without hurting your stitches?"

What stitches? He had it off and tossed aside in a heartbeat. "How about the Richard Whitmeyer Detective

Agency? That has a more manly ring to it, don't you think?"

"I do. But as a full partner, I feel I should be named, too." Her fingers worked at the buttons on his shirt. He fought the urge to bat her hands aside and tear the damn thing off. Instead, he contented himself with testing the weight of her lovely breasts.

"Richard."

"What?" They fit so perfectly in his hands.

"Stop that for a moment and look at me."

He forced his gaze up to hers and saw by the serious look in her eyes that he had reached that critical point in this negotiation when he would either win the day or make a misstep and lose everything. "Yes, sweetheart?"

"You will let me be a full partner, won't you?"

He pretended to give it some thought as he stroked her breasts. "Only if you take shooting lessons."

She punched his chest, narrowly missing his stitches. "I'm not jesting!"

"I'm not, either," he said, once he caught his breath. "I have to know you can take care of yourself, Rachel, or I won't be able to do my job. If we're going into dangerous situations, we must be able to trust each other."

"So that's a yes? You'll be my partner?"

"I would rather you be mine." To distract her, he pulled down the edge of her chemise to admire her nipples. They were so pert. Rosy as new grapes. Inspired, he leaned in to taste one. "You can handle the office duties," he murmured between nibbles, "while I go into the field."

She pulled back. The nipple popped free. "No."

"No?"

"Better if we hire someone to run the office, and we both go into the field."

"Whatever you say, sweetheart." He would never be able to leave her behind anyway. He needed her, not just for this, but in every way that mattered.

"Truly?"

"Truly."

"Oh, Richard." Throwing herself against him, she covered his face with kisses.

He had to end this before he lost reason. "Sweetheart."

She paused in her exploration of his earlobe to sit back, her blue eyes dark with desire, her mouth swollen from his kisses. "What?"

Her impatience fed his hunger. If she was beautiful to him before, in passion she was irresistible. Lust incarnate. The one person in the world who had the ability to destroy him, or lift him to the heights.

"If we married, we could simply call it the Whitmeyer Detective Agency."

Even though she didn't move, he felt her resistance. "I tried marriage once and didn't like it."

He'd expected that answer, but still had to ask. "You're sure?"

"I am. Unless I change my mind."

"Then we'll wait until you do." With regret, he pulled her chemise back over her breasts. "I'll propose to you then, rather than have you refuse me now." He started to lift her aside, wincing at the pull in his stitches.

"Richard, stop before you hurt yourself!"

He sat back. Looking up into her beautiful face, he realized this was no longer a game. This was his life. His future. His heart he was putting at her feet. It was important that she know how deeply he cared for her, and understand the power he was putting into her hands. "Only you can hurt me, Rachel. If you walk away from me again, it'll break me. You need to know that."

Tears filled her beautiful eyes, dripped down onto his chest. "Oh, dearest."

More determined than ever to win her, he slid his hand between them and touched her where she straddled his lap.

She gasped, her eyes going wide.

"Change your mind yet about marrying me?"

"I—I—" Another gasp had her arching. "I think . . ."

He stopped stroking. "You 'think'?"

"Yes!" That breathless laugh swept his face. "Yes, you rogue. I'll marry you. But I won't be left behind while you go off chasing robbers and such."

"No, you won't." Rolling her onto her back atop the soft cushions, he framed her face with his trembling hands. "I love you, Rachel James. Do you love me?"

"I'd be a fool not to. And I'm no fool."

"Say it."

"I love you, Richard. And I always will."

A rush of emotion filled his chest, so intense he laughed with the joy of it. He kissed her. Kissed her again, and as she pulled him closer and moved impatiently beneath him, he knew that finally the lonely years were over and the best part of his life had just begun.

Kaki Warner is a RITA Award–winning author and longtime resident of the Pacific Northwest. Although she now lives on the eastern slopes of the Cascade Mountains in Washington, Kaki grew up in the Southwest and is a proud graduate of the University of Texas. She spends her time gardening, reading, writing, and making lists of stuff for her husband to do while soaking in the view from the deck of her hilltop cabin. For book excerpts and more information, visit Kaki's website at kakiwarner.com

Don't miss her next Heroes of Heartbreak Creek novel, *Where the Horses Run*, coming July 2014 from Berkley Sensation. Turn to the back of this book for a sneak preview.

THE HIRED
GUN'S HEIRESS

Alison Kent

Chapter 1

San Antonio, Texas, 1895

I T wasn't any of Maeve Daugherty's business how Miss
Porter paid her girls, but these disbursement amounts
hardly seemed fair. Annie received half as much for
entertaining the odious Mr. Reed as Etta received for her
time spent with Mr. Jackson, who was young and spry
and smelled delightfully of lavender and bergamot.

Not that Maeve sought out the particulars of what
occurred upstairs; she rarely ventured beyond her room
into the grand parlor, and only then on her way to the
kitchen for breakfast or midmorning tea (when the girls
still slept and few visitors lingered), but the set of ciphers
Miss Porter used had been easy enough to discern.

Never had Maeve been so thankful to her father's
accountant for indulging her fascination with numbers.
Her father hadn't known; he refused to have his daughter

involved in the unseemly pursuit of sums. And only the
charity work her mother approved, not that which called
to Maeve's sense of compassion, was permitted to be done
under the auspices of the Daugherty name.

Of course, should Mr. Feagan see exactly *how* she was
putting her instruction in profits and losses to use, he
would no doubt regret having defied his employer. Fannie
Porter's boardinghouse, while highly thought of, and gen-
erous with donations, and current on all licenses and fees,
was still a brothel.

Demure whispers and delicate laughter and skirts swish-
ing like the wings of large hawks filtered through the door
she'd left ajar while she worked. And there was always
work. When she'd applied for the job, she'd had no idea
there would be so much to keep her busy, but was very glad
there was.

There were the payments to the girls to tabulate, as well
as the proceeds from the gentlemen callers. But there were
also charitable contributions, revenue due to the community for taxes, and various amounts paid in dubious fines
to police officers Maeve found equally dubious.

Then there was the recording of the transactions with
the vendors supplying alcohol and the gains made selling
the drinks by the glass. Miss Porter stocked some of the
best liquor Maeve had ever seen. Until arriving in San
Antonio, she'd never imagined such comforts had found
their way to Texas. After all, Uncle Mick had made the
trip sound like a Grand Adventure into the Wild, Wild
West where savages and buffalo roamed the plains.

Plush carpets, fine crystal, silk sheets . . . though only
on the beds upstairs, not the one Maeve herself slept on.
Her room was a far cry from the luxury she'd known at
home. It was no more than serviceable, in fact, she being
the help. But having expected dirt floors, not rooms red-

olent with the smoke of choice cigars and the warm musk of bonded bourbon, she was quite comfortable in her newfound employment.

Fannie Porter's girls certainly had it better than the families living in Manhattan's Mulberry Bend and Bone Alley. And though Maeve's own conditions were plain and austere, she did, too.

More of the girls' hushed chatter reached her ears.

"Who is he?"

"I've never seen him before."

"Look at his eyes."

"Look at his hands. I would like very much to meet those hands."

Feeling a bit warm, Maeve slipped a finger behind the tie at her blouse collar, tugging slightly as she breathed in. What silliness. Meeting a man's hands. Hands were hands were hands, and the fact that a certain pair came to mind, a pair with broad palms and long, well-shaped fingers and clean nails and a dusting of dark hair along the edges, meant nothing. Even if said pair bore frighteningly harsh scars.

The twittering continued, leaving Maeve curious. Miss Porter's girls rarely engaged in gossip about men, and why would they? They saw so many in the course of a day, and there was nothing new under the sun. What about this latest arrival could possibly be of interest?

Then again, Maeve did keep to herself, to the corner of the office where she worked, to the small adjoining storage area converted to a bedroom where she slept. Since the Day of the Disaster with Uncle Mick, she'd rarely done more than cross South San Saba Street to the druggist for Miss Porter's medicinal supplies or visited the butcher and grocer for the steaks and cream and cheeses the boardinghouse chef required.

She would be the last of the women living in the house to understand the appeal of one man over another. Though, to be honest, that wasn't true. She did understand. She'd made a fool of herself because of that understanding. She preferred not to be reminded of that foolishness, or of the one man who had witnessed her lapse in propriety.

"There's company in the parlor, girls."

Miss Porter's words tumbled through the room down the hall from Maeve's open door, and the piano notes of Charles K. Harris's "After the Ball" followed. It was fairly early in the afternoon, but she had learned that men's needs were not confined to the hours after dark. Or perhaps such was only the case here in the Wild, Wild West, where she recognized very little of the respectability she'd grown up with.

Whoever had arrived, the girls were certainly keen to gain his favor. The hushed chatter and twittering had been replaced by much boisterous laughter. She picked out Annie's and Etta's—if those were the girls' names, any more than Mr. Reed and Mr. Jackson were who they claimed to be. Maeve had no right to presume. She'd been going by the name Mae Hill since the Day of the Disaster with Uncle Mick.

"I'm looking for a young woman," said the company in the parlor, the deep voice a resonant bass that was easily heard above the din.

Maeve's head came up; her hands stilled; her heart nearly stilled, too, before it began beating in her chest like the drums in the Sousa Band.

"I have several young women whose companionship I'm sure you would enjoy."

"No, ma'am, I mean, I'm looking for a particular young woman. Her name is Maeve Daugherty. She stands close to your height and has bright green eyes. Her hair's like that of a chestnut horse. Last I saw her, it was about to her waist. I was told someone of her description was in your employ."

"And when did you last see her?"

"Several weeks ago. A month or more," he was saying, and Maeve pictured him pulling off his hat, using his large hand to rake back his too-long hair. "I work for her father. She left New York with her uncle and hasn't been heard from. Her family's worried."

Maeve closed her eyes, shook her head. Why would her parents not leave her to her life? She was twenty-two years old. She knew her own mind. And why in the world, if they'd had to send somebody to fetch her home, did it have to be Zebulon Crow?

"I don't believe I know a Maeve Daugherty," Miss Porter was saying, but her words were hesitant.

Maeve imagined her frowning and casting a glance toward the hallway that led to the rear of the first floor and to the office. Zeb would follow the direction of her gaze, because nothing slipped his notice, and almost as the thought entered her mind, heavy footsteps thudded closer, leaving her no time to hide.

She pushed back her chair and stood, smoothing her blouse and her skirt, doing the same to her coiffure. She'd had no idea Zeb had ever noticed the color of her hair, though of course she wasn't seeing to her appearance for him. She only wanted him to realize she was in good health and good spirits and not homesick at all.

Yes, that was it. That was all the time she had. The door opened, and there he stood. Tall and broad shouldered, his dark hair hanging to his collar, his dark beard emphasizing the strength of his jaw, his blue eyes like sapphires shining from the bottom of a flute of champagne. The dusting of dark hair along the edges of his hands making her knees inexplicably weak.

"Hello, Miss Daugherty." His voice was deep, almost rough, and nearly angry, as if he resented her actions causing him the inconvenience of this very long trip.

"Good afternoon, Mr. Crow." The formalities. How absolutely ridiculous they were. How banal. "What are you doing here?"

"The night I found you in your father's library drunk on his brandy you asked me a question." He pushed the door almost all the way closed, though Miss Porter would certainly be able to hear her should she cry out, then he moved toward her. "I came to give you my answer."

ZEBULON Crow had seen enough darkness in his day that little was left to surprise him, but the picture of Sean Daugherty's only child working in a whorehouse did.

He took some consolation in the fact that she stood in front of a desk and wasn't sprawled across a bed upstairs. That she was dressed much as when he'd last seen her, looking no worse for the toll of traveling west with Mick, and not . . . well, undressed . . . went a long way toward easing what could've been an awkward confrontation.

Especially since the last time they'd been in the same room she'd asked him if he'd like to see her out of her clothes.

"I don't believe for a moment you came all this way to answer my question," she said, glancing at the book work she'd been doing when he arrived, her cheeks pink stained, her knuckles, where she gripped the back of her chair, bone white. "And it wasn't a real question, so it did not require an answer. You told me that at the time."

She was chattering on, and he understood a proper young woman like Maeve Daugherty wouldn't want to be reminded of a lapse in judgment that had her falling prey to her father's liquor. But she appeared to be *living* a lapse in judgment now, so he wasn't going to worry about reminding her of the other.

"It's time to go home, Maeve," he said, jamming his hat onto his head.

"I don't want to go home. I mean, I am home. This is my home. This is where I live now." She raised her chin, shook off whatever affliction had her tongue rambling, then more calmly said, "Leave me alone, Zebulon."

He waited to see if she was going to put the word "home" into another sentence or ramble some more, but all she did was take her seat at her desk, pick up her pencil, and run a finger down a column in the ledger in front of her. He didn't know if she was seeing what was written there or if she thought he would leave if she looked away.

He wasn't going to leave, and he didn't care what she was seeing. He was here to do a job, not cajole. Once he had her belongings strapped to the packhorse with his, and had her comfortably saddled up on her mount, he could get on with the rest of the reason for his trip to the West.

He took one step forward and reached for her ledger, closing it and taking the pencil from her hand. "You're coming with me, Maeve. You may not want to go back to New York, but I ain't leaving you in a whorehouse."

"Zebulon!"

"You know that's what this place is, don't you? You can't be thinking this is the same type of boardinghouse as the ones that got you riled up enough to drown yourself in your father's drink."

"I know about the services Miss Porter provides," she

said, color rising even higher on her cheekbones as if painted there by one of the girls hovering outside the door. "And I was not attempting to drown myself. Though if you had seen what I saw that day in Bone Alley, you would understand my wish to obliterate such images from my mind."

He knew the things she'd seen. He knew, too, there were worse living conditions that she hadn't. But none of those equaled the images of death he carried with him, which no amount of alcohol would ever erase. "You can't change the world, Maeve. No matter how much reading Jacob Riis makes you want to."

This time when she turned toward him she paled. "You know about 'How the Other Half Lives'?"

Nodding, he crossed his arms and leaned a shoulder against the wall where her desk sat. "You told me that night in the library that you'd read it."

She looked down, defeated, her hands laced primly in her lap. "Then you should know I'm not trying to change the world. I only want to make a difference where I can. But to do that, I need my mother and my father to stay out of my way. And I need you to leave me alone."

"Fine, but I'm not leaving you here," he said, hearing the whispers outside the door growing louder. The last thing he wanted was the sort of trouble that would bring the law into Fannie Porter's house. "And I don't want to know what Mick was thinking, doing just that." Though Mick's trouble was so much bigger than his disrespect for Maeve. "Your father will have his head—"

Maeve's eyes widened. Her voice dropped to a whisper. "You can't tell Father."

Huh. That sounded like a bargaining chip. "About you working in a whorehouse? Or about his brother thinking this was any sort of place to leave you?"

"That's not exactly how it happened," she said and looked away.

"Which part, Maeve?"

"Mick doesn't know I'm working here."

"That so? What does Mick think you're doing?"

"I wouldn't know. I haven't seen him to ask."

He pushed away from the wall, anger working its way through his veins. "How long, Maeve? Since you've seen him?" But he'd barely got the words out before the door behind him opened and the woman responsible for Maeve's room and board walked through.

"Is everything all right, Miss Hill?" Fannie Porter's gaze traveled from Maeve to Zeb and back. "Or should I say, Miss Daugherty?"

Maeve nodded meekly, a meekness that Zeb doubted the other woman believed any more than he did. One thing was certain. Maeve Daugherty, for all her proper gentility, had never been meek.

She gestured toward him. "Miss Porter, this is Zebulon Crow. He provides security for my father."

"Yes, he mentioned that," Miss Porter said, her arms crossed as she turned to face Maeve. "He also mentioned your family is looking for you and is worried about you."

"I came west with my family. Well, with my uncle," Maeve said and waved a hand. "But apparently my mother and father fear I am not being properly supervised and will therefore bring scandal or shame to the Daugherty name."

Miss Porter pursed her lips a moment, then asked, "Is this something you're in the habit of doing?"

"Shaming my family? Of course not," she said, though Zeb caught a flash of guilt in her eyes, as if she recognized the shame in her current situation. "Or did you mean bringing scandal?" When Miss Porter gave an encompassing nod, Maeve shrugged. "I can't recall an instance of doing so, though my mother fears that's what will happen should I pursue the charity work I most want to do."

As if she wasn't sure what to think, Miss Porter lifted a brow and turned to Zeb. "Is this true, Mr. Crow?"

"I wouldn't know, ma'am," he answered, pulling off his hat again to worry the brim. "Mrs. Daugherty does quite a lot of charity work herself. I don't know why Miss Daugherty's causes would be of such concern."

Maeve came up out of her chair, sputtering. "You do know why. I told you why. That night in the library."

"Right," he said, waving his hat toward her. "I'd kinda forgotten everything but the question you asked me."

"If you had really wanted to give me an answer, you should've done so that night, not left the room the way you did."

This woman was going to be the death of him. The very death. "You know why I left without answering, though had I known you wanted me to stay—"

Her eyes were snapping now, her words stinging as if delivered by a whip. "I did not want you to stay. Did I say that I wanted you to stay? As Miss Porter is my witness, I said no such thing."

"Mr. Crow," said Miss Porter, stepping between them like a prizefight referee, "why don't you let Etta show you to the drawing room and get you a drink and, if you'd like, a cigar. Give me some time with Miss Daugherty, then she can join you in the dining room for supper."

Zeb looked from Miss Porter to Maeve, imagining the weeks ahead, the two of them on horseback, the days of bickering, the money her father was paying him for a job that had nothing to do with her. It wasn't enough. No amount would be. But at least he would know exactly where she was and that she was safe. Because that was all that mattered.

"As long as she *does* join me for supper . . ." It would be just like the little hellion to run.

"I'm not going anywhere," was her answer, and though the response was supposed to set him at ease, it didn't. He knew Maeve Daugherty, and she wasn't promising not to take advantage of his back being turned.

She was throwing down a gauntlet.

Chapter 2

⌒⌒⌒

WHILE Maeve retrieved her carpetbag from her bedroom's small closet and set it on the bed to pack, Fannie Porter stood at the window, which faced the brothel's back alley, pulling aside the curtain to peer through. Maeve had never minded the lack of a view, even though her room at home had looked out over gardens sculpted into an intricate maze and accented with statues and fountains.

In the evenings, the alley was quiet, and she was able to read, or write in her diary, before going to sleep. Her bed was narrow, and not terribly comfortable, but she slept soundly enough. She had experienced much austerity during her short time living here in a house known for extravagance. Doing so had made her more determined than ever to help those less fortunate than herself.

In the mornings, the alley woke quickly, the noise of wagon wheels and men yelling and clattering horses' hooves waking her for the day. Her room was rarely more than cool, and hurrying through her ablutions usually warmed her sufficiently. If not, by the time she reached the kitchen—where Miss Porter's cook served her coffee with cream and a hearty breakfast—she no longer needed her shawl.

She folded it now and tucked it into the bottom of her bag. She'd brought so little with her from New York, intending to send for her things once she was settled. Uncle Mick had promised her a Grand Adventure, one that would give her a sense of where she was most needed, where she could do the good she'd been unable to accomplish at home. Mick's love for gaming tables and unfortunate choice of companions, however, had put an end to her plans. Or at least brought them to a temporary halt.

Making such an impetuous trip had been foolish, she supposed, but she'd been at her wits' end and unaccountably desperate. She had no interest in the suitors drawn more to her family's name and her father's station than to her viability as a wife. And embracing a cause without getting her hands dirty was not her idea of charity beginning at home, though it seemed to fit her mother's circle well.

The thing of it was, she respected her parents and understood their wanting the best for her. Wanting to keep her safe. Wanting to ensure she stayed within the bounds of propriety, a thought that had her shuddering at the idea of them seeing her now. She was their only child, that was the duty with which they were charged, and she couldn't abide disappointing them.

She loved them dearly. Truly she did. They'd worked hard to secure their position in New York society, their families coming from Ireland before either was born, both fighting their way out of a poverty similar to that which Maeve was determined to see abolished.

But she wished with all of her heart that they understood her desire to make her own life equally meaningful. Unlike them, she'd been born into fortunate circumstances, yet at every turn, and for no reason that made sense, she felt undeserving. Why should she be so privileged when hosts of others were not?

She could hardly enjoy her fine cotton sheets and down pillows, her morning croissants with butter and jam, not to mention the society balls her father insisted she attend, the emeralds he begged her to wear in her upswept hair, the gowns of exquisite satin and silk he ordered for her from seamstresses with impeccable craftsmanship.

Enjoying any of those things had become especially difficult after reading Jacob Riis's essay in the copy of *Scribner's Magazine* she'd found in her father's library. It was several years old, so why he still had it . . . And then seeing the conditions in Mulberry Bend and Bone Alley for herself . . .

Her parents could not fathom her dissatisfaction with her situation in life. Honestly, she found herself baffled by it as well; she was, quite literally, an heiress. But something had happened three years before, when her father had hired Zebulon Crow, and she hated that she could time her malcontent to his arrival.

He unnerved her, the way he walked through the rooms of their home, always on guard, never accepting what he saw at face value, questioning everything, causing her to question things, too, when never before had she been compelled toward suspicion.

He had seen tragedy the likes of which she never would. He hadn't spoken of the events, or acknowledged their existence, but it was impossible not to sense the hardship he carried. It weighed heavily, creasing his temples, darkening his eyes.

She'd wanted to take away his pain, but she didn't know how. Or why she was drawn to do so. They came from different worlds. They led different lives. Because of that, she'd turned to what she did know, helping those she could. Until her parents had put a stop to her endeavors.

Seeing Zeb walk through her office door earlier had actually come as a relief. She would never admit that to him. She didn't like admitting it to herself. But Zeb would never leave her as Mick had done, even if doing so hadn't been of Mick's choosing. Zeb was solid and sure, not swayed by societal whims or opinions. He did the job he'd been given. He let nothing get in his way.

Those were the only reasons she wasn't going to fight his taking her out of Miss Porter's house. And she would accompany him for now. But she'd meant what she'd told him. She was not going back to New York.

"You understand why I can't keep you here."

Returning to the task at hand, Maeve nodded at Miss Porter's words, picking up the riding breeches the other woman had brought her. "Yes. Of course. Your enterprise cannot afford unnecessary attention from the wrong quarter." And Zeb could very well cause that sort of trouble to get what he wanted.

Miss Porter stepped away from the window and sat at an angle on the foot of the bed. "You've done a good job for me, Maeve. I wish circumstances were different from what they are. I'm not sure I'll be able to find anyone else who will be as favorable an employee."

"I've enjoyed working here, and I am ever so grateful to you for taking me in. I don't wish to consider where I could have ended up without your charity."

Frowning, the other woman shook her head. "It wasn't charity. You did honest work for an honest wage."

And if she'd had the chance to work longer, that honest wage would have amounted to more of a savings, leaving her less at Zeb's mercy as they traveled. But at least she wasn't penniless. Or destitute, begging in Bone Alley for food scraps. "Yes, but I'm sure you could've hired a man with more experience."

"I could have. I chose not to. I prefer to take money from the men who come here, not the other way around."

That brought a smile to Maeve's mouth. "You are quite accomplished at handling men."

The other woman waved a hand. "They are simple beings. Their needs are easily met, and very rarely with much ado."

Maeve slowed in the act of folding the unfamiliar garment. "Traveling with Mr. Crow on horseback is going to be much different from using the railroad with my uncle."

"But you've known Mr. Crow long enough to feel safe in his company?"

Safe, yes, though her history of being alone with him would no doubt make the days ahead uncomfortable. "I'll be fine. My father trusts him."

"Your father is not the one accompanying him on this trip."

"I'll be fine," she repeated, but her hands were trembling.

Miss Porter reached for them, held them in her own. "If this Mr. Crow frightens you, I won't let him take you. I can help you find other employment here in San Antonio and see you well settled in a boardinghouse with a more . . . appropriate reputation. Or I can hire someone to act as chaperone and make the trip with you."

The idea of Zeb traveling with two women was almost enough for Maeve to accept. But she shook her head, refusing to closely examine the reason why. "Thank you, but I don't think you would be able to stop him, or get him to agree to increasing the number in our party. Zebulon is very good at getting his way."

"What does your father do that he requires a hired gun for security?" Miss Porter asked, letting her go.

"My father is in banking. Zebulon makes sure our home is secure and that my father is, as well, when he travels for business."

"I'm not sure I would've guessed that. Your Mr. Crow seems much more civilized than the men I know who deal in personal protection."

"I imagine the dangers from which one might need protecting here are a great deal more . . . savage."

"Does Mr. Crow also live in New York?"

"He does now," she said, realizing how little she actually knew about Zeb, including how he had entered her father's employ. "I believe he originally came from South Carolina. His family owned land there and grew tobacco."

"What about this uncle of yours?" Miss Porter asked, smoothing the turquoise satin of her skirt. "When you applied for the position you said he'd been called away on business, but from what you told Mr. Crow, it sounds like that may not be the case."

"It's not, and I apologize for the deception. My uncle's situation could have brought you the same unwanted attention as Mr. Crow's insistence that I accompany him. I thought it best not to mention the trouble he was in."

"Gambling?"

Maeve nodded, shook out the riding breeches, and refolded them. "I'm not sure how it happened. Uncle Mick is not the businessman my father is, but taking such a chance with our fixed amount of traveling money seemed unnecessarily foolhardy, even for him."

At that, Miss Porter smiled. "Here's what I've learned

as a woman in a business catering to men. There are those who work for what they want, those who take it from others, those who hope to have it but do nothing toward that goal, and those who cheat to get it. Until put under pressure, some of these men may not show their true colors. It's very possible your uncle was never a cautious man at all."

Maeve quietly let that sink in, thinking about Zebulon Crow as she did. He was not a cheat. She would swear to that. Neither did he take from others. He worked fairly for what he had, and in that way was much like her father. Except . . . he wasn't like her father at all. He seemed to be his complete opposite—reserved where her father was effusive, wary where her father appeared to have no care for the things he said, to whom he said them.

Perhaps those differences were the reason her father depended so completely on Zeb. Or why Zeb watched over their family as if their lives depended on his sticking close.

"I have one more thing I'd like to give you." Miss Porter's words broke into Maeve's musings. She held Maeve's gaze as she reached into a pocket in her skirt. Maeve glanced down to see a tiny derringer in the palm of the other woman's hand. "Take this," she said, then lifted her skirt and removed a band from around her thigh that held additional ammunition. "And this," she added, forcing both items into Maeve's grasp.

"I can't—"

"You can. I insist. Even if you trust Mr. Crow, you don't know who or what you'll come across during your travels. And no smart woman puts her safety at the mercy of a man. Even a man she knows. Or loves."

A burst of heat sucked away her breath, and she gasped when she said, "I don't love Mr. Crow."

A corner of Miss Porter's mouth lifted. "I wasn't referring to you necessarily."

Maeve nodded and swallowed, then packed the gun beneath the riding breeches.

"Before you leave in the morning, you put that in your pocket. I'll show you then how to load it. It won't do you any good if you come upon a band of outlaws and it's tucked away in the bottom of your bag."

"I suppose you're right."

"I'm always right," she said with a twist of her mouth. "And, Maeve: If you ever need anything, anything at all, you come to me, or send a telegraph. Don't forget I'm here."

"Miss Porter—"

"Fannie."

"Thank you, Fannie." Maeve squeezed the other woman's hands. "I'm quite certain you saved my life. Literally."

Chapter 3

I T seemed strange to be sharing a meal with a man in
Miss Porter's dining room. Her girls did so often,
engaging in private tête-à-têtes with their callers, or their
callers gathering in groups around a table with their
steaks and bourbon and cigars as if the boardinghouse
were a gentlemen's club, offering an escape from work
too cumbersome to speak of to their families but not for
like-minded men.

Maeve felt as if she were eavesdropping on the very
world in which her father circulated, the very world about
which she was supposed to hold no opinions or thoughts.
And she didn't, except insomuch as these men set rules
that governed the lives of others, rules by which they
themselves never had to abide. Rules that made it impossible for women and children living in poverty to find
their way out.

"You're not eating."

She sighed heavily. "I'm not particularly hungry."

"You should eat anyway," Zeb said and gestured with his fork. "It'll be a long time before you get another meal like this one."

The quality of the meals in her immediate future was not what concerned her, but she picked up her fork to appease him. "First you kidnap me, then you starve me?"

"I'm not kidnapping you," he said, bracing his wrists against the table, a fork in one hand, a knife in the other, the glint of his eyes causing her to drop her gaze. "And I'm not going to starve you. We'll have plenty to eat, and I'm sure it will be just as edible as what Mick fed you. It just won't be baked chicken and creamed peas and corn bread and apple pie."

She didn't want to talk about Mick. She didn't want to think about Mick. Why she'd ever believed anything with him would be an adventure instead of the disaster it was . . . She looked back up so Zeb would know she was unaffected by his words—or his expression. "How are my parents?"

A vein ticked at his temple. "Worried about you, but otherwise fine."

"Worried about me?" She set down her fork, broke off the corner of her corn bread square. "Are you sure they're not more worried about what their friends are whispering behind their backs?"

"Your father told me they were worried," he said, though he frowned down at his plate as he did so. "That's all I know."

"And he asked you to come after me?" she asked. Notes from the piano in the grand parlor drifted into the room.

He shrugged, studying the motion of his fork and his knife as he cut into his chicken. "He knows me. He trusts me. You know me, too. Who better to make the trip?"

"I can't imagine why you would've wanted to." Unless her father was paying him handsomely, which was doubtless the truth of it. "Who is seeing to Father's security while you're away?"

"I arranged for a man I know to be available. As to why I wanted to make the trip . . ." He forked up a bite and held it, along with her gaze, the twitch at the corner of his mouth a fair warning. "I told you. I came to answer your question."

She'd steeled herself in advance of his words, but still they stirred her blood. Was that single moment of indiscretion going to haunt her for the rest of her days? "Can you please not bring up that question? You know I was . . . under the weather."

"Intoxicated, you mean."

"Yes. I was intoxicated. I remember very little of that night actually." Though that was a lie. She remembered all of it. Her father's chair, the table beside it, her legs draped over the chair arm as she held a snifter of brandy, her third . . . or had it been her fourth? Her skirt a tangle of fabric and lace falling around her thighs.

"But you do remember asking me—"

"If you wanted to see me with my clothes off?" she asked, leaning forward, her voice barely a whisper, her chest burning with the same heat rising in a flush up her neck. "Yes. I remember asking you that, but it was the alcohol at fault."

"The alcohol may have loosened your tongue, but that sort of invitation don't come out of nowhere. You'd been thinking about it for a while," he said, reaching for his drink, his gaze boring into hers as he sipped.

There was no hiding the mortification she knew colored her face. "It was not an invitation. And why do you insist on talking as if you have had no education?"

He huffed before looking back down at his food. "Why do you assume I have?"

"I've heard you in conversation with my father. You're well-spoken. You don't resort to the sort of language used by the laboring men in Bone Alley."

He huffed again, giving her observation no mind. "Tell me what happened with Mick. Where is he? Why haven't you seen him?"

Sighing deeply, she returned to her food. "I don't know where he is. I haven't heard from him since he left."

"When was that?"

"He came to my hotel room three weeks ago and told me the accommodations had been paid for another two nights. He gave me what money he had and said I'd need to find someplace less expensive to stay after that. And I'd need to find a position as a housekeeper or a nanny until he returned with the funds we needed to finance our ongoing stay." She pressed her napkin to her mouth before adding, "As far as I knew, we weren't ever supposed to stay."

Zeb mumbled a string of foul words as he scooped up his peas with his corn bread, shaking his head as he shoved the food in his mouth. At least he waited until he had swallowed to ask, "Did he tell you how he lost his money?"

"My best guess is he gambled it away. He went out most evenings after we dined at the hotel." She thought back to those meals, how Mick had never seemed present, but anxious, his mind elsewhere. "I followed him once and saw him take a seat at a gaming table in one of the saloons. He greeted the other men as if they were old friends."

"Or new enemies."

"What do you mean?"

"Never mind," he said, reaching for his plate of pie.

"So your uncle told you to find a position as a housekeeper or nanny, and you found one in a whorehouse instead."

"I found a position where I could use my accounting skills." When he shook his head disparagingly, she said, "I have no experience with children or with keeping house, so when I saw the advertisement for a bookkeeper, I applied."

"I'm surprised you didn't find a way to do the charity work that got you into this mess."

So he, too, thought what she did was worthless? "Charity work does not provide room and board or an income. I was lucky Miss Porter had advertised for help. But I had every intention of devoting my free time to a local cause. Until you showed up."

"I still don't get why you feel the need to be a savior," he said, shaking his head as he ate his way through his pie. "The less fortunate already have a lot of champions."

Perhaps to his naive eye. "Not all the committees and organizations claiming to dedicate their resources to the poor do."

He frowned up at that. "What do you mean?"

"Oh, they have lunches to discuss what they're going to do," she said, waving one hand. "They throw balls to raise funds for charity."

"Where do the funds go?"

"I assume they use them to throw more balls." She shrugged. "Or to pay for the next round of lunches."

He made a snorting sort of sound, chuckling as he chewed.

"I'm not sure what about that is so funny."

"It's not funny."

"Then why are you laughing?" she said, pushing away her plate, then reaching back and pinching off one more bite of corn bread.

"Because I knew you were cynical, but not the extent of your cynicism."

"I am not cynical."

His look said otherwise. "Are you hearing yourself, Maeve?"

Curse him for being right. "Okay. I *am* cynical. But it's hard not to be when the very thing I want to accomplish is the very thing money has been raised for, and yet it's unavailable when I could be putting it to use."

"Being a savior."

"Fixing what's broken." Didn't he understand? "There's so much that's broken. So many rules that make no sense and don't work. So many lives being ruined because those who should be stepping up aren't."

"Again. Why do you have to be the one to fix it?"

Because I don't know how to fix you.

The words surprised her, echoing in her mind, and she shook her head, uncertain how to answer him. Then she reached for her pie. Eating it would keep her from having to talk. Unfortunately, it wouldn't keep her from having to think.

She didn't want to think—not about where her uncle had gone or how she was going to convince Zeb not to take her back to New York or why his being broken bothered her so.

And that was the biggest bother of all.

"WHY must we leave tonight? Why can't we wait until morning? I can't imagine we'll get far enough this evening to make departing now worth all this trouble."

"We'll get far enough," Zeb said, budging Maeve's shoe out of the stirrup so he could adjust the fit of the rise. Her foot swung back and caught his collarbone. He grunted, then said, "And if there's any trouble, it's you making it."

She lifted her chin and knotted the ties of her bonnet beneath it, her pert nose crinkling as if something smelled. "I still don't understand why we can't travel by train. This trip will take forever on horseback."

The answer was simple. He couldn't be confined to a seat in a car on a track and headed in one direction. He had to be free to question anyone who might've heard word of Mick Daugherty.

He weighed his words, regretful that he'd lied when he'd said her father had sent him to bring her home. "It's highly unlikely your uncle's holed up at a railhead somewhere. I don't want to be stuck on a train when it'll be easier to get to him on foot or horseback."

She was frowning as he checked the wear on her horse's bridle, and she asked him, "Why would Mick be holed up anywhere?"

"If he gambled away the money he had, he'd need to avoid any creditors looking to be paid." Though if Sean Daugherty's brother *had* gambled away all that money, Zeb hoped he was having better luck trying to recoup the loss. If that was what he was doing. If he hadn't just hightailed it for good.

"If that's what you meant by his having new enemies, I can't imagine that's the case."

"Start imagining it," he said, earning himself a loud huff as Maeve's foot returned to swinging.

He grabbed her by the ankle, the bones seeming so fragile and tiny, his hand so awkward and large. "You kick me again, Maeve, and so help me God, I will strip off both of your shoes and you'll be riding to New York in your stockings."

"I did not kick you," she said, but she did not pull free from his grasp.

He held her another moment, for no reason that made any sense, then let her go and moved to the packhorse.

Her exasperated breath followed him. "Could you not at least have staged this . . . kidnapping in a wagon?"

A wagon. Might've been a good idea. Slower, sure, but tying her to a wagon would've been a whole lot easier than what he was facing making sure she stayed in the saddle. Which made stealing her shoes sound even better.

"This ain't a kidnapping. You ain't a kid."

"Stop being so literal. You're forcing me to accompany you against my will. That, Zebulon Crow, is exactly what a kidnapping is."

"Take it up with Sean when we get back to New York," he said, walking by her again.

"I do not want to take it up with my father. And I do not want to go back to New York." She leaned close enough to squeeze his shoulder, her fingers like tiny talons holding him as she begged. "Zeb, please. You go back. Tell him you couldn't find me. Or tell him you found me married and living in a home on the range. Or running with the Wild Bunch."

Thinking of Maeve married had Zeb grinding his jaw. Even more so than her making the acquaintance of any Wild Bunch members while working in Fannie Porter's brothel. "I'd rather tell him the truth. That I found you in a whorehouse."

"You can't tell him that," she said, pushing him away with a huff. "It'll kill him. And then he'll kill me."

Zeb felt a hard pull at the corner of his mouth and fought against it. Maeve had never been stupid. Hard-headed and contrary, yes. She knew the trouble she was in. "Maybe you should've thought about that before talking Mick into sneaking you out of New York."

"At least Mick understands," she grumbled, tugging at the fabric caught beneath her knee. "I hate riding horseback."

Of course she did. "I thought you said Miss Porter gave you a pair of breeches so you could sit astride."

"Can you see my mother's face were I to ride up to the door *astride*?" She shuddered as if picturing just that. "I hope by the time we reach the city we can switch to a more suitable means of conveyance."

"Does that mean you're going to stop giving me grief about the trip?"

"I haven't given you any grief about the trip."

She was right. All the grief had been about not wanting to take it, not liking the horse and sidesaddle he'd paid the livery stable handsomely for, and not agreeing to the alternative clothing solution he'd offered. He could hardly wait to hear how many things she found wrong once they got under way.

It was a ride he wasn't looking forward to. He wouldn't be able to sit his horse from dawn to dusk, lost in thought, scanning the horizon for approaching riders, setting up camp free of any care for Maeve's comfort.

Plus, women had to talk. Women had to stop to rest or to see to their personal business. Maeve wasn't as soft as many he'd known and, having come all this way with Mick Daugherty, she was already aware of the difficulties that lay ahead. Still, the next few weeks would be challenging.

"Do we have enough supplies? These packs seem lighter than the ones Mick brought, and he and I had the convenience of scheduled rail and coach stops while you and I will not."

That was because Mick's packs had contained a whole lot more than supplies.

"Stay here," he said. "I need to have a word with Miss Porter."

"Where exactly is it you think I'm going to go?"

He closed his eyes and took a deep breath, then opened them and made his way to the boardinghouse's front door, where Miss Porter had appeared. "Appreciate all you did for Miss Daugherty, keeping her out of trouble, fed, and sheltered."

Miss Porter gave him careful consideration. "I hired her to keep my books. Room and board were part of her pay. She kept herself out of trouble."

"If you say so, ma'am."

"I say so because it's the truth," she said, and Zeb nodded.

He admired an honest woman as much as an honest man, and Fannie Porter's reputation had proved to be true. He handed the brothel's madam a slip of paper he'd carried folded in his vest pocket. "This is my employer's banking contact in Houston. If you hear word of Mick Daugherty, would you telegraph me there?"

She nodded as she gave the information a cursory glance, then, while creasing the paper again, she asked, "Are you going to take care of her?"

"Of course I'm going to take care of her." And why would she think otherwise?

Her expression said she doubted his sincere claim. "Some men wouldn't. Some men would take advantage instead."

"I'm not some men—"

"I know who you are. You work for her father, and you have a vested interest in seeing she gets home safely."

"I do have a vested interest," he said, but it wasn't about getting paid.

What her father had paid him for was to find his brother, find the money his brother had stolen, and get said money to his banker in Houston. Zeb had come after Maeve for another reason.

He'd come after her because no one else would.

Chapter 4

⌒⌒⌒⌒

ZEB may have been surprised to find Sean Daugherty's daughter working in a whorehouse, but he wasn't surprised by how helpful she was in setting up camp for the night. She was driven, whether doing charity work, learning to keep books, running off suitors who asked for her hand, or gathering kindling for their supper's fire.

She didn't let her serviceable skirt get in the way, and she didn't complain about feeling the craggy ground through the soles of her shoes, but picked her way through the brush like she thought nothing of the conditions. She only yelped once, and that he figured was due to a critter of some kind surprising her. He liked that she didn't come running back to where he was unloading their gear from the horses, expecting a rescue or giving up.

Yeah, he knew old Stefan Feagan had been teaching accounting to Maeve. Her mother had been too busy flitting about with her society friends to notice, which was damn sad, to Zeb's way of thinking. Instead of only seeing what her daughter did outside the home and deeming those things improper, Helena Daugherty should've paid attention to how smart Maeve was, how in need of a way to engage her mind.

And Sean was no better. Zeb had considered more than once hiring a couple of Mulberry Bend hooligans to make a true run at the man's carriage. Not because Zeb had any need to prove his worth by stopping an attack Sean himself hadn't staged, but because the other man needed shaking up. How could he be so concerned with his own world that he was blind to the way his daughter spent her time?

Those two were about the least deserving parents he'd run across in his day—

"Is this enough?"

Zeb looked up from where he was securing the horses, allowing them plenty of room to graze. Kindling at her feet, Maeve dusted her hands on her skirt, the ribbons of her bonnet fluttering in the same wind that rustled through the copse of trees at the creek's edge.

It was a wind that was sitting poorly with Zeb, all heavy and sudden and wet. The weather wasn't looking so good, the sky to the west turning the color of the barrel of his Colt, the clouds hanging low, as if aching to give birth to something foul.

They probably should've waited until morning to set out for Houston, meaning it might've been a good idea to listen to Maeve . . . "It'll be enough if we don't get rained on," he said, their bedrolls tucked under his arm.

Her eyes went saucer wide. "Rained on?"

He brushed on by, talking at her as he did. "Ain't you been watching the clouds?"

"No, I *ain't* been watching the clouds," she said, causing him to huff, though his mouth did quirk. "Am I supposed to do that as well as gather kindling?"

"You being the observant sort, I figured you would've noticed how dark it's getting behind us."

"Since we were riding away from that direction, no. I hadn't." She glanced over her shoulder, looked back with less pique in her expression. "But now that you mention it . . . I don't suppose you have any sort of shelter in all your supplies."

The fact that she inquired as to their situation, rather than demanding he return her to San Antonio or see to her comfort right then and there, went a long way to setting his mind at ease. He gave a nod as he snapped the blanket he held by two corners. "Knapsacks. Old army issue. Two beneath your bedroll, two beneath mine. Button all four together, pitch 'em on a rope strung between two trees, and you got yourself a tent."

She looked toward the thicket of trees and brush hugging the banks of the nearby creek. "Should we do that? Get them . . . pitched?"

He preferred not to take the time and gave the sky consideration as he returned to his horse. "Storm looks like it's going to slide by to the north. We should be okay."

"And if it doesn't?"

"Then we'll grab 'em off the ground and wrap up best we can," he said, rustling in his pack for a hand shovel and frowning at what sounded like the wailing of a violin coming from down by the water.

As he set about digging a pit for the fire, Maeve asked, "How did you even find me?"

"There ain't so many rail lines headed west that asking the right questions didn't get me the answers I needed," he said with a shrug. "Besides, Mick had been telling everyone for weeks that he wanted to see Texas before he died. And since you took off at the same time, it weren't hard to figure out where you'd gone."

When she didn't respond, he looked up, only to catch her smiling. "What?"

The smile widened, dimples slicing into her cheeks, her eyes twinkling. "Until this trip, I don't think I've ever heard you speak so many words at one time."

He grunted. "I don't usually have much to say."

"Why is that?" she asked as he began laying out the makings for the fire. "You're obviously well educated. You come from good stock, as my father would say. But you never seem inclined to engage in conversation."

"With you, you mean."

"Well, yes. I wouldn't know if you converse with others when I'm not there."

Wiping his hands on his thighs, he got to his feet. "What do you want to talk about?"

She gave a little lift of her shoulders. "I didn't really have a subject in mind. I was just commenting that you've been less taciturn today than you usually are when we're together. But, since you asked, I wouldn't mind learning more about you."

That wasn't going to happen. "Nothing about me worth saying."

"Oh, I don't know," she said, smoothing her skirt behind her before dropping down to sit on a fallen log. "You work for my father. You have complete access to our home. You hover at the edge of the room during the balls my mother insists we attend, but you never dance."

"Why would I dance? I'm there to keep an eye on your family." Though most of that was for show. "Can't do that if I'm dancing."

"Please. I can't imagine how sharing a single dance with one of the many young women who are curious about you would put my family in danger."

He looked at her, unspeaking, trying to make sense out of what she'd just said, but she laughed before he managed.

And her eyes were twinkling again. "You didn't know, did you?"

"Didn't know what?" he asked, moving past her into the copse of trees to gather items for tinder.

She got up and followed, giving him no privacy. "You are the subject of much gossip, Zebulon Crow."

He didn't need to know that. "Fine. Next time I'll dance."

"There won't be a next time," she said, her steps slowing. "At least not in New York. I'm not going back, remember?"

He grabbed for some dried moss and dead leaves, packing the detritus while he looked at her. "And what exactly are you going to do?"

"Well, when we find Mick—"

"We may never find Mick," he cut in to say as he turned back for their camp. "We don't know what trouble he got into or who he got into it with. And it's very possible that, wherever he is, he doesn't want to be found. He could be in danger. He could be on his way to California. He could've made his way to Galveston and hired on to sail to Ireland."

"He would never go to Ireland," she said.

"Were you just as sure that he'd never leave you stranded in San Antonio?" he asked, squatting in front of the fire pit.

She was silent after that, watching as he struck his flint, blew on the tinder as it sparked. Or at least she was silent until she found a change of subject she liked.

"Miss Porter made an observation I'd like to ask you about."

"What kind of observation?" he asked, the teepee of kindling catching the flames and igniting.

"That the dangers you faced before coming to New York were what made you suitable for my father's employ."

"Hmph." In the three years Zeb had worked for Sean Daugherty, he'd yet to see the man face a threat worse than a pothole in front of his carriage. At least a threat of any legitimacy.

"What's that supposed to mean?"

He stared at the wisps of rising smoke, at the moss as it crackled and turned black, orange sparks leaping into the dried leaves and devouring them. "I'm still trying to work out why your father feels he needs security."

"Men in his position do."

"He's never had a threat made against him since I've been working for him, and he never made mention of having any before I arrived." Then again, those doing Sean's dirty work would be the ones at risk. All Sean had to do was reap the rewards.

She said nothing, as if weighing what he'd said with what she knew about her father. "That was rather convenient. You arriving when you did. It makes me wonder—"

"Why don't you wonder about where you're going to spread out your bedroll for the night?" he asked. He had no intention of discussing with her the things that had driven him to New York.

"Does that mean you're done talking?"

"That depends." He sat back on his haunches, met her gaze from beneath the brim of his hat. "Are you done asking questions?"

She pressed her lips together and glared at him, holding back—he was quite sure—all manner of queries.

They had a long trip ahead of them. Best she parcel

them out slowly, he mused, lest he use one of the shoes he'd threatened to take to gag her.

T HE night had not been as bad as Maeve had feared, though she'd only slept in snatches and was feeling the lack of rest today as they rode. Zeb, on the other hand, had slept soundly, snoring softly into his hat where he'd used it to cover his face. She didn't know why, unless it was to block out the light of the fire she was certain had been visible for miles. Once the storm had moved on, as Zeb had predicted, the air had been utterly clear.

Staring up at the vast night sky had left her breathless. Even through the branches of the trees she could see stars, and what might even be planets, though she knew so little of astronomy. She did know enough to identify several of the stars and had picked out the Big Dipper and the Great Bear, giddy that she'd had not only a cloudless sky to enjoy, but the knowledge of what the endless expanse held in the cradle of its outstretched arms.

She also knew enough to understand that if they continued on this morning's present course, they would eventually find themselves on the Gulf Coast rather than in New York. And though she was certain he was aware of their position, she would be plagued with disquiet if she didn't point it out.

"I don't wish to doubt your navigational skills," she said, the stride of her horse a steady and rhythmic *clop, clop, clop* beneath her, Zeb's mount keeping a similar pace to her right, "but judging by the location of the sun, it would appear we are traveling in an easterly direction, rather than toward the north."

"I know which way we are headed."

It was all he said, and his voice was gruff. Still . . . "Then I am correct."

"I know which way we are headed."

She urged her animal forward until it was even with his. "Then do you mind telling me *why* we are headed east instead of north?"

He seemed to give her question more thought than it needed before saying, "Your father asked me to deliver something to a colleague in Houston."

"I had no idea my father had business associates in Texas," she said, and he barked out a sharp sort of laugh, prompting her to ask, "What was that for?"

He glanced over, his eyes a flash of blue beneath the shadow of his big black hat. "I imagine there's a whole lot about your father you don't know."

An indubitable observation. And yet . . . "Why would you say that?"

"Because it's the truth," he said dismissively.

She hated being dismissed. "And I suppose you know everything about *your* father."

"I knew most of it," he said, looking forward again and adding, "until he died."

Maeve felt as if she'd taken a blow to the chest, and struggled to draw breath to speak. "Oh. I'm so sorry, Zeb. I shouldn't have said—"

"No, you shouldn't have." But he left it at that.

And of course his doing so had her wondering . . . "Was he ill? Was it an accident? I hope he didn't suffer."

He took a long moment to answer, and though he rode slightly in front of her, his eyes trained forward and out of her view, his dark beard hiding the set of his jaw, the way he held his shoulders told her of the tension binding him, and she wished again she was better at letting things go. That she didn't have this compelling need to fix what was broken, to solve problems that weren't even hers.

"He wasn't ill, no," he finally said, his voice devoid of emotion. "As for suffering . . . I wouldn't know." He stopped, lifting his gaze to take in the sun before reining his horse to the right. "I wasn't there. When I got home, both of my parents and my grandfather were already dead."

Thankfully, her horse followed his because she couldn't think past Zeb's revelation to guide the beast beneath her. Her hands in her gloves were so cold, she feared dropping her reins. "What happened?"

"They were murdered." He said it as if the act were nothing, as if he'd grown so used to the ugly truth that it was as much a part of him as the vest he always wore, the pocket watch he was never without. The hat that he rarely removed, and which threw crude shadows.

Maeve wasn't used to murder at all, and she gasped, feeling the unfamiliar, yet hummingbird-light, weight of the derringer in her skirt pocket. "What?"

He nodded. "Three brothers. Blamed my grandfather for not being able to save their old man during the war. Gunshot wounds."

"Your grandfather was a doctor?" she asked, blinking the dampness from her eyes. *Of all the things to ask . . .*

"In the war. My father, too, but later."

"But these men . . . they came after your grandfather? Your family?"

He nodded again. "Held that grudge a long time. And then it seems they had nothing better to do with their time than destroy everyone in my family."

Everyone. Including him. Though he remained alive.

"Do you have siblings?" she asked, but all he did was

tug the brim of his hat lower, a signal that he was done with the conversation.

She fell silent after that, riding to his left and allowing her mount to fall back slightly, though she couldn't imagine he was aware of her presence, or anything but his own grief. She'd stirred that in him. How stupid of her. How incredibly thoughtless. And all because she'd allowed his words about her father to goad her.

She thought back to what he had said. He worked with her father daily. He had access to her father's inner circle, his comings and goings. He knew with whom her father met and, most likely, much of what was accomplished behind closed doors at his office or his club or within the confines of his carriage.

Maeve knew nothing but what her father let slip when unaware she was listening, or what he told her to placate her curiosity, which he abhorred. Of course there would be much about her father's business she didn't know. But it had been truly unconscionable of her to use Zeb as a target for her frustrations. Doing so went against the very core of her desire to make him whole.

She wanted to recall her biting words, even as she recognized all that she'd learned because of her heedless outburst. She'd long sensed he carried a grief-filled burden, but the extent of what he'd suffered . . . she could hardly bear knowing the truth. How had he borne the weight alone all this time?

Unlike the past night, when they'd stopped early, that night they rode until she found herself growing drowsy. Even when Zeb gave in to her plea to stop, he seemed frustrated by the halt to their progress, as if she were keeping him from an important engagement. As if she was a bother, her tagging along, her depending on his skills to survive.

While he gathered firewood, she spread out their bedrolls using only the light of the moon. They ate without speaking, some bread and dried beef and strong coffee, the meal creating a painful longing for the food she'd taken for granted when they'd dined at Miss Porter's the night they'd left. And that even more than the sumptuous meals she'd eaten in her parents' home.

How strange that she missed what she'd known all her life less than that which she'd just discovered. Perhaps she *had* needed Mick to abandon her to find the adventure she'd been seeking. The thought brought a smile to her face, and she looked up to find Zeb watching her, his eyes reflecting the fire's dancing flames.

"The answer is yes, you know."

She leaned forward, stirred the coals with a stick she then tossed into the pit. Her fingers were warm, and she curled them into her palms as she asked, "What answer?"

He waited for her to look up, to meet his gaze, and he held hers as his voice dropped. "To the question you asked me that night in your father's library."

Heat flushed the skin of her throat, heat having nothing to do with the fire's warmth, and she was happy for the blanket of darkness covering them. It hid her physical response, and gave her time to compose her verbal one. Was his yes the answer she wanted?

He lay stretched out on his side, propped on one elbow, the wrist of the other arm draped over his one raised knee. The word "reprobate" came to mind. Then the word "debauchery."

She knew about the intimacies that occurred between men and women. She'd learned the most rudimentary long ago, and had suitors damply speak into her ear of their appetites, as if such liberties might attract her. They had not. Neither had the accompaniment of fumbling hands and thick, pressing lips.

But during her time in San Antonio, Miss Porter's girls had spoken openly of the men they entertained, their preferences and proclivities, and had whispered more circumspectly about their own appreciation of certain acts.

Maeve had never heard some of the words the girls used, but had no trouble determining their meaning in context. The thought that *this* was that context . . .

She swallowed, her heart thumping as if trying to escape her chest, and she recalled Miss Porter asking if she felt safe traveling with this man. "I was not of a mind to disrobe the night I asked the question. My tongue had simply been loosened by the liquor. And I'm not of a mind to do so now, if that's what you are expecting."

"I'm pretty sure you are." He yawned then, as if she bored him. "But I'm even surer the thought will still be there tomorrow."

The very gall . . . "What's that supposed to mean?"

He sat up to add more wood to the fire, and the flames jumped, licking at his face with wicked, lingering tongues. "Tell me, Maeve. What exactly did you learn during the weeks you spent working in Fannie Porter's brothel?"

"If you're implying . . ." She couldn't even bring herself to say the words, yet her restraint was not one of embarrassment. Instead, the idea of Zeb knowing intimately what occurred upstairs at a place like Miss Porter's, and her own knowledge being limited to her imagination coupled with oft-told tales, served to leave her thoroughly frustrated.

"I'm not implying anything, Miss Daugherty. I'm not implying anything at all." Then he laughed, and it was far easier to believe the indecency of the sound than any of the words he'd spoken.

Chapter 5

~~~

AN hour later, all Maeve could think about as she readied herself for sleep was Zebulon Crow's skill as a lover. How he would look undressed. How he would move in bed. How he would touch her. All the things he knew about carnal liaisons that she'd only heard whispered about.

He sat cross-legged on his side of the fire, using a long stick to stir the coals. As she smoothed her bedroll, which didn't need smoothing at all—it was little more than a blanket atop the protective knapsack, and too thin to protect her from the hard ground beneath—she sneaked glimpses of him.

He'd removed his hat, which left her able to see his face clearly rather than having to peer beneath the shadow of the brim behind which he hid. She doubted he would admit to hiding. He would think doing so a weakness. And perhaps she had it all wrong. But if he wasn't hiding, he was certainly keeping himself apart. And yet . . .

She thought about the things he'd told her, certain he'd rarely, if ever, shared the same with anyone else. She couldn't imagine him speaking of his life to her father, who was, she knew, egregiously self-centered. Or with her mother, who was also too fond of placing her interests where others would notice.

Why had he shared his tragic past with her? And why now? Surely it hadn't been a case of making conversation. For that, they could've discussed more of Jacob Riis's essay. Or the flora and fauna of Texas, with which she had grown quite enamored. She'd had no idea there was a breed of cattle with a horn span as wide as their lean, rangy, and quite colorful bodies were long.

Looking at Zebulon now, she wondered what he was thinking. If he'd let go the rather disquieting subject matter of earlier or if the murder of his family was always on his mind. It broke her heart to think he was driven by that tragedy and a need for revenge. No one should be so brutally haunted.

"How did you get those scars?" she asked, nodding toward his hand where the light washed over it.

He spread his fingers, turned his palm up then back down. "Most of them working in the fields when I was younger."

Tobacco. She remembered hearing him mention his family's plantation. "Why didn't you follow in your father's and grandfather's footsteps and study medicine?"

He shook his head. "I grew up watching them treat open wounds and bloody coughs and diseases they couldn't even name. For years I was afraid one or the other would contract whatever was ailing their patients and die." He let that settle, then finally added, "Might've been an easier way for them to go."

His previous words returned to haunt her. "I'm really sorry you lost them the way you did."

He leaned back on his elbows, crossing his feet at the ankles and staring into the fire, his mouth tightening, his expression hardening. But he didn't say anything in response.

That left her wondering what line she'd crossed. And how much further she could go, what else she could learn while his guard was down. "Zeb—"

"Go to sleep, Maeve," he said, and his words, so much like an order, a command, so much like her father's dismissals, sent her to her feet.

"I'll go to sleep when I'm ready and not a moment before," she said and only just stopped herself from stomping the ground. What was wrong with her? What was happening to her? This petulant infant was not who she was.

"You just always have to have your way, don't you?"

"Well, since I rarely get it, I wouldn't know," she said, pacing on the far side of her bedroll, filled with a swell of anxiety she could not explain. "Instead, I have a host of concerned . . . others who seem to know what's best for me. As if I have no mind of my own. Because how could I when all that I know of the world is filtered for me as if I am nothing but a child?"

Her outburst had Zeb tossing the stick into the fire and rolling slowly to stand as if doing so was a bother and he was not in the mood to placate her. "I don't think you're a child."

"No," she said, gesturing wildly and adding, "You think I'm a whore."

"I never said that."

"But you obviously think that, from all your questions about what I learned while working at Miss Porter's.

What I thought was going on upstairs in the rooms at Miss Porter's. I know exactly what was going on," she said, waving her hand again. "But that doesn't make me a whore any more than my ideas to change Bone Alley make me a child."

"I never said that, either."

"You don't have to say anything. The way you treat me says it all."

"And how exactly do I treat you?"

He gave her hope, and he didn't judge her, and he was bossy, yes, but he'd come for her, and he was the experienced traveler, and, oh, he treated her like she mattered, like her opinions were worth considering. He treated her like he cared, and his kindness confused her. She didn't know how to process what she didn't understand.

What she did know was that she was wrong. Her assumptions, her accusations, her acting out.

"You know," was what finally came out of her mouth because words failed her, though it was obviously the wrong thing to say.

He started toward her then, and nothing could get her to move. It was as if her feet had sprouted roots, and said roots had made their way deep into the hard-packed earth, growing where so little else seemed to but prairie grass and mesquite brambles and cottonwoods that drank from every stream and creek.

The closer he got, the more determined his steps, the more rapid the rise and fall of his chest, the more fierce his scowl. She wasn't frightened, however, and she was quite sure she should be. He had something on his mind she couldn't discern, something in no way connected to the conversation she'd been trying to have.

Was he angry about her prying? Were his secrets that deep and dark that her mentioning them had set him on this path of intimidation? Was that what he was doing? Intimidating her? Or was his approach fueled by another emotion, one with which she was unfamiliar and therefore unable to anticipate?

His hands gripping her upper arms stalled the rest of her thoughts. He pulled her body in to his, and she caught back a breath, her heart fluttering in her chest as if it had wings.

Up close, his eyes glowed like the blue flames of a Bunsen burner, but they were icy, too, and she was quite certain that if she touched them her fingertips would freeze. That coldness was at odds with the rest of what she felt from him; heat rolled off his body in waves.

"Zeb—"

He reached up one hand and pressed two fingers to her lips, shaking his head as he did. His long black hair brushed against his shoulders, his beard hid most of his face, and only the lines at the corners of his eyes hinted at what he was feeling. She couldn't look at his mouth. She was afraid to look at his mouth.

But the urge to do so pulled and tempted, and she dropped her gaze, a squeak of sound making its way from between her closed lips, because the set of his wasn't icy at all. It was . . . cocky, and expectant, and primal, and he slid his hand to her jaw and around to her nape, holding her there as he lowered his head.

His lips were dry on hers, chapped by their time in the sun and the wind, and he was warm. He was also hard, his body, his hold, his insistence. His head slanted, and he rubbed against her, pushing until her lips parted of their own accord. His parted as well, then his tongue slid between.

This time when she squeaked, he laughed, but he did it into her mouth and the sound filled her, causing her to rise on her toes, to dig her fingers into his shoulders to keep from falling. That was what she felt like: falling, drifting, losing her balance and her footing and every bit of the grounding she'd prided herself on.

She had sneaked kisses before, of course; what school-girl hadn't? And she'd been kissed by men she'd decried as unsuitable mates. But this was nothing like those sweet, fumbling pecks, those harmless, innocent experiments with attraction. Before, there had been no attraction. None worth speaking of. But this . . .

The indelicate whispers she'd heard from Miss Porter's girls suddenly made such terrible, beautiful sense. Because if they had been giggling about experiencing the sensations pouring through her limbs like warm honey . . . Except she couldn't imagine feeling this liquid desire at the hands of any other man. Or even wanting to have another man touching her.

Oh, my, how naive she had been when she'd asked Zebulon if he wanted to see her out of her clothes. What a horrible child, what an incredibly inappropriate tease. These feelings were not to be trifled with. They were consuming, and genuine, and they left little of her sense in place.

She wanted to climb into his skin. She wanted to take off her own clothes, to take off his, to feel him against her, and this from no more than a kiss. How could she be so swept away by what was only a kiss?

His tongue found hers and tangled with it, and though he kept one hand at her nape, he ran the other down her spine to the small of her back to push, then lower, to her bottom, cupping it, squeezing. Tingles of sensation burst between her legs, and she made more noise, not gasps, not squeaks, but what she could only call moans.

They were full of longing, just as she was full of longing, just as the hard press of Zeb's manliness to her thigh was filled with longing, too. The whispers came again, the giggled appreciation, and she wondered what it said about her that she wanted to know everything Miss Porter's girls did about the pleasures to be found with a man.

The idea sobered her. She was not loose with her affections, or loose at all, and she didn't need this man especially to think any such thing. She pushed against his shoulders and against the pressure of his hands, separating her mouth from his and missing him at once.

He didn't move except to set his hands at his hips, and she crossed her arms tightly in front of her and dropped her gaze to the ground. "I don't know why you felt you had the right—"

"Shut up, Maeve."

Her head came up; her chin, too. "What did you say?"

"You heard me. Don't start in denying you enjoyed every bit of that as much as I did. And don't place blame where no blame belongs."

"I wasn't placing blame—"

"Yes. You were. You wanted to be absolved of your part in starting that fire in your loins."

If her face hadn't already been colored like the brightest lobster tail ever . . . "I am quite accepting of my . . . fire."

"Good," he said, turning to go, then stopping and adding, "Because I'm going to be busy awhile putting out my own flame. I sure as hell don't have time to be dealing with yours."

ANOTHER night behind her and Maeve was ready to be done with this trip. She would go back to New York. She would surrender to her parents' demands. She would be the dutiful daughter, marry well, provide her husband an heir.

She would stay out of Bone Alley and Mulberry Bend and instead host luncheons to raise awareness of the conditions in the city—if only she could be done with this trip.

Her bottom hurt and her thighs ached, and her face stung and no doubt resembled a beet, and the gloves Zeb had given her to wear were next to worthless because his hands were so large. But none of those complaints held a candle to the one responsible for her change of heart.

She was ready for this trip to be done because he had kissed her.

"It's okay to grumble. You don't have to be all proper and stoic. No one is going to know."

She would know. And he would know, she mused, looking over to where he moved with his horse as if the two of them were a single beast. A centaur of sorts, though she much preferred the picture of Zeb in his hat and his boots and his vest, a gun belt strapped to his hip and thigh, his hand on the reins in the most deceptively careless manner.

Her words to Miss Porter returned then to haunt her: *I don't love Mr. Crow.* She didn't, of course. And she hadn't once wondered what doing so would be like.

"I don't grumble. And I don't complain." Or at least she only did in her own mind.

"Maybe you should," he said, then huffed to himself. "Work out some of whatever is keeping you so . . . tight."

Tight? "And what's wrong with being . . . tight?" She wasn't even sure she knew what he was implying.

"Nothing, I suppose, though the opposite makes for a much more comfortable seat on a horse."

Ah. He was probably right about that. "Our journey will only last a few weeks. I can endure the temporary discomfort and inconvenience." *But only if you don't kiss me again. Please, please don't kiss me again.*

Her lips still tingled, and the rest of her body ached in ways that had nothing to do with the gait of her horse and her being . . . tight. Why had she let him kiss her? Why had she so feverishly kissed him back?

"Is that some sort of statement about conditions that ain't temporary?"

Oh, good. A distraction. "Are you even aware of how the other half does live? The filth and the sickness and the very acts the destitute are forced into in order to survive?"

"I'm aware," he said, though his words held little conviction.

"I'm not sure you are," she said, frustrated that he would take her no more seriously than anyone else. "I believe you are, like my mother, simply giving lip service to—"

"Stop it, Maeve," he said, but her passion drove her on.

"I've volunteered my time and my efforts in those places. I know the struggles those people suffer through daily. How their lives hang by a tenuous thread. How their very survival—"

He reined his horse around in front of hers. The sudden movement had the beast rearing back and snorting, then pawing at the ground. Zeb leaned forward, rubbed the animal's neck, his words for the horse soothing. His words to her were not. "Do you want me to tell you about survival? About true survival? About going on day after day when the easiest thing to do would be biting down on a gun barrel and pulling the trigger?"

"Zeb—" It was all she got out before he looked beyond her, bit off a sharp curse, and turned again, muttering, "Let's go," before she could object.

But something told her to glance in the direction he had, and she cried out at seeing what had caused Zeb's harsh words.

"Damn it, Maeve. I said let's go."

But she was rooted to the spot, watching the body swing from the branch of a tree they'd just ridden past. Shivers stole up her spine to raise the hair at her nape. "You can't just leave him hanging there."

"Yeah. I can."

"Zeb—"

"We don't know who he was or what he done—"

"It doesn't matter—"

"And we don't know who's watching and waiting for someone to take an interest."

"Why would—"

"Stop asking *why* all the time, Maeve," he said, riding behind her to smack her horse's rump and set her moving again. "This ain't New York. This ain't polite society. There ain't rhyme or reason for some of the things that go on. And you're questioning everything ain't going to change any of that, any more than you poking your nose into what happens in Bone Alley and Mulberry Street is going to fix the wrongs happening there."

Heat raced over her chest and up her neck, a rush of humiliation and anger, and it took all of her resolve not to bite back at his hurtful words. And they were hurtful. So terribly so. They were also insulting. How dare he insinuate that her interest in the suffering she'd seen would yield no change?

It would. She knew so with all of her heart and her soul and her being. She had worked too hard for her efforts to fail. Because of that, she would not dignify his barb with a defensive response . . . and then realization struck.

He was goading her to get her mind off the man in the tree. "You're slipping again. Your language. It happens when you're upset."

"I ain't— I'm not upset."

"But you corrected yourself anyway."

"Just so as you'd leave me alone."

And there he went, slipping again. "I'm sorry if I upset you."

"It wasn't you so much . . ."

"As the hanged man."

He stayed silent as they rode, the breeze lifting the ends of his hair, dropping them back to his shoulders. They were tight again, his spine stiff. She imagined his jaw beneath his beard was equally taut, and she thought back to what he'd told her about coming home to find his family murdered.

And what he'd just said about biting down on a gun barrel. "Zeb?"

"Hmm?"

"Was your family hanged?"

He continued to ride without speaking, and she remained mute as well. She knew he'd heard her, but she also knew he would not appreciate being provoked. Her asking such a question had been unnecessarily forward.

She was being too presumptuous. It was not her business what had gone on in his past to turn him so harsh and bitter. She thought again of the scars on his hands, some of which she knew were burns.

Then she realized he had rarely, in all of the three years she'd known him, been harsh or bitter with her.

For the rest of the afternoon, they rode with little said between them. She asked him to stop once so she could relieve herself, a request that no longer embarrassed her. He asked before they started up again if she'd like to rest or if she was hungry.

Neither spoke of the man they'd seen, though the picture of the body in the tree never left her mind, or her

many, many questions, and certainly not her inappropriate inquiry into his loss. Why did she think she had to
know everything or that her knowing would allow her to
fix things? And why was she consumed by such a desire?

Why did she need so badly to have her calling taken
seriously?

"Maeve? Are you listening to me?"

She looked over to where Zeb was leaning forward to
take the reins of her horse from beneath the animal's
head. But rather than answering him, and in an effort to
distance her thoughts from the haunting images of the
hanged man, she said, "I think I'm an inconvenience to
my parents."

"What brought on that thinking?"

"They don't understand my curious nature. Or how
that curiosity pushes me into situations of which they
disapprove. I don't share their concerns with social status.
Quite frankly," she said, her throat growing tight, "I think
I embarrass them."

"If you do, that's on them."

He reached up to help her down, but she stepped away,
needing distance between them.

"I don't know why I told you that. Or why I ask you
so many questions—"

"I don't mind you asking me questions, Maeve," he
said, but he dragged a weary hand down his face as he
did. "Some are more painful than others, and some I
might not want to answer. But don't ever stop being curious. Your nature's a sight more honest than that of most
folks I've known since leaving South Carolina. And that's
a refreshment I find that I very often need."

Chapter 6

~~~~~

DIGGING a shallow grave with nothing to use but a hand shovel was not how Zeb had wished to spend this night, but he had to get the hanged man down from the tree and into the ground while Maeve slept—and before she realized it was her uncle Mick swinging.

Once the sun had set, Zeb had taken a circuitous route back to the copse of trees where Mick hung and made camp at the farthest edge. The distance between their small fire and the spot he'd chosen to put Mick in the ground allowed for Zeb to hear her, should Maeve cry out, and get to her quickly if riders approached.

And that was his biggest fear. That whoever had strung Mick up remained nearby. He hoped that by riding on earlier, they hadn't attracted attention. That anyone on the lookout wouldn't be staring too intently into the dark. And that Maeve, should she wake, wouldn't peer beyond the fire's low flames.

Zeb had recognized Mick earlier but had hurried on

without making mention to Maeve. He'd have to tell her, of course, but later, once her uncle had been laid to rest and they'd put too much time between now and then for her to demand a proper burial.

He'd known as they set up camp that she was ready for sleep. Coming across a body hanging by the neck took an emotional toll, as he, having coming across three, well knew. But she was also exhausted from the realizations about her parents, and that angered him in ways far different from his own situation.

Maeve was a beautiful woman, not a child, and her short temper of late he attributed to their long days on horseback. She was quick-witted, with a good head on her shoulders, not flighty as were so many of her society peers. She cared more about things that mattered than she did about herself, and that told Zeb everything he needed to know.

What he knew was that he wanted her for himself. And the realization had come as a surprise.

The body was not overly far from the ground, those who'd passed sentence not much for judging the strength of tree branches. Zeb was able to stand on a log he dragged close, one arm around the stiff torso as he sliced through the rope above Mick's head.

He lowered the deadweight, then looked down at the face of the man who'd been as different from his brother as Maeve was from New York society's other young women of her age. Though maybe he hadn't been that different after all, considering both men had turned out to be thieves.

Before shrouding the body in one of his blankets, Zeb did a quick search of the man's pockets, coming up with a watch and a scrawled note. He waited until Mick was in the ground and properly covered before looking at either, which at least kept Maeve from seeing her uncle, since she walked up just as Zeb was using the light of the moon to read the inscription on the back.

"Where did you get that?"

Her voice was small, her arms wrapped tightly around her middle as she made her way slowly to where he stood at the head of the grave. She stopped opposite, looked down at the mound of newly turned earth, the full moon casting crooked shadows of tree branches across it, looked up again.

"Where did you get that?" she repeated, her gaze falling to the watch.

"I heard you the first time," he said, closing it and circling the fresh-packed dirt. He took her by the arm to lead her back to their camp, but she shook him off.

"Answer me, Zeb."

"I'll answer you as soon as we're away from here and back with the horses," he said, reaching out once more.

But Maeve wouldn't be budged and wrenched away, her eyes wild. "That watch belongs to Mick. Did that man steal it from him?"

Zeb kept walking. He wasn't saying another word until he'd seen to their supplies and left Mick Daugherty behind.

"Who did you cut down and bury, Zeb? Was it Uncle Mick?"

She was yelling now, loud enough in the clear air to be heard for miles. He wheeled around and came for her, grabbing her, shaking her. "Are you trying to let all of Texas know where we are?"

"Did you just put my uncle in the ground?"

He thought about lying, then about saying nothing. But in the end he nodded.

She swayed, her hands coming up to cover her mouth,

her knees buckling before he could reach her. She wailed once, then broke into sobs.

"Why? Why would anyone do this to him?"

Zeb was tired of keeping things from her. As ugly as the truth was, she deserved it. "Your uncle had something with him belonging to your father and, by association, to some very bad men."

"You're saying my father had this association? Not Mick?"

More truths. "Has, Maeve. Has. To this day."

"Aren't you supposed to keep him safe from unsavory elements?" she asked, reaching up to rub at her temples.

"I do keep him safe." Not that the other man deserved it. "That doesn't mean he doesn't have dealings with them."

"He would never—"

He hunkered down in front of her, wanting to know she heard him. "He does. He has for years. More years than I've been in his employ," he said, reaching for a stick and dragging it across the ground. "It's how I came to *be* in his employ."

"What do you mean?"

"I'd only been in the city a week," he said, not even sure why he was telling her this. "I saw a group of thugs roughing up his carriage. I had nothing else to do, and pretty much no care if I lived or died, so I intervened."

"In a group of thugs."

He shrugged. "Turned out, the roughing up was for show. The men were in cahoots with your father."

She stared at him wordlessly.

"He knows a lot of wealthy men. Their habits. Their assets. The contents of their safes." He jabbed the stick at the dirt. The tip broke, but he kept jabbing. "Sometimes the combinations. Knows, too, the best time for a robbery to take place and go undetected for hours. Days, even. He's made a lot of money this way. So have the thugs."

"How can that be possible?" she asked, twisting her hands in the fabric of her skirt. "My father is a respectable member of society. A trusted member of society. He's a *banker*."

All of which enabled him to get away with his crimes. "It's not unheard-of, rich men having their way at the expense of others."

"I don't believe this. I won't. Not of my father," she said, surging back to her feet. "I don't care what you or Fannie Porter say. There are honest men in this world. And my father is one of them. Are you an honest man, Zeb? Do you steal or lie or cheat to get what you want?"

"Which part of that do you want me to answer?"

"Never mind," she said and turned.

He reached out and grabbed her, spun her around. "Listen to me, Maeve. Yes, I've been known to lie." He tossed away the stick he still held. "I'm sure you have, too. But I wouldn't say that makes me a dishonest man any more than it makes you a dishonest woman. Lying's not something I make a habit of. I don't steal and I do my best not to cheat, though I suppose at some time in my life I may have committed both sins. But I think a man deserves to be judged on the bulk of his deeds, not taken to task on one or two that may have occurred under extraordinary circumstances. So, yes. I'd say I'm an honest man."

"But you would say that my father is not, and my uncle . . ."

"Your uncle may very well have been trying to right your father's wrong." He doubted such was the case, but he'd tell the lie a thousand times if it gave Maeve some peace. "We'll never know that now."

As she let that sink in, she nodded toward the paper now wadded in his hand. "What does the note say?"

He held her gaze as he unfolded it, then glanced down, ready to choke on the words even before he spoke them. "'You need to keep her safe. Promise me you'll keep her safe.'"

And when he promised her he would, Maeve cried.

H E wanted to hold her, to wrap his arms around her and take all the grief she had to shed. Instead, he left her to her tears while he did his best to remove all traces of their having been near the grave. It was bad enough that he couldn't bury Mick properly, but Maeve was going to have to accept that that was the way of it.

Returning to do what he could for her uncle had been a risk. Now they needed to go.

And even as he had the thought, he realized she was no longer crying. He turned around to see her standing still, hugging herself and staring at the long ragged patch of disturbed earth. The full moon lit up her cheekbones, damp from her tears, and her eyes, which were as bright as they were terrified.

"If my father is the type of man you say, why would he send you after me?" she asked, looking up as he approached. "Wouldn't the risk of his enterprise's discovery be lessened with his curious daughter out of the way?"

He held her gaze for a very long moment, long enough for her to realize things were about to get worse. He couldn't deceive her any longer. "He didn't."

"What?" Her voice scraped up her throat, a desperate, ragged sound.

He hated himself for having to tell her the truth. But

not as much as he hated those responsible. "Your father didn't send me to fetch you home. He sent me after Mick."

"Right," she said, confusion causing her to frown. "He sent you after both of us."

But he had to shake his head. "The day we left San Antonio, you mentioned that Mick had carried more supplies than we did. That's because Mick's packs were loaded down with money he'd stolen from your father. He wasn't carrying supplies at all."

She was silent for so long he wasn't sure she had heard him, but then, with a cold and level voice, she asked, "Mick stole from my father? Was it money he and his band of thugs illegally gained?" When he nodded, she asked more. "Was that the money he gambled away? It wasn't our traveling money he lost?"

Another nod, and more appreciation for her very sharp mind as she painted the picture of what had happened for herself. "The amount was enough that losing it would've earned him some unwanted attention."

"By the men he lost it to?"

"Or by anyone who saw him lose it and thought there might be more where that came from." Which was what he feared had happened.

She closed her eyes again, the remains of her tears seeping from the corners. "I can't believe he's gone. I can't believe *this* is where he lost his life. I can't believe he stole from my father, or that my father would even know the type of men that do what you've suggested."

For a long moment he said nothing. Then he yanked off his hat, plowed his fingers through his hair. "Have you ever wondered why your father isn't interested in reforming Bone Alley?"

"He thinks it's a waste of my time," she said, scuffing

her toe at the loose dirt. "That it's too dangerous for me to be in that part of the city."

"It's not about you. It's about your proposed changes getting in his way."

"I'm sorry, Zeb," she said, her exhaustion evident in the crease of her frown. "I really don't understand."

Seeing her so close to broken should've had him softening his words. But he couldn't. She had to know. "There are a lot of folks down there desperate for money. They'll do most anything to get it. Men like your father know that. And they don't want that source of willing manpower drying up."

"This is where he found the men, the thieves, the . . . thugs you say work for him?"

He nodded as he returned his hat to his head. She took a moment to let that sink in, and he wished the moon was brighter so he could better see the play of expressions on her face. But a rack of clouds had scudded in front of it to block out the light, and the distance between them was greater than he wished.

It was a distance of doubt and uncertainty, and he wanted those things out of the way of the long weeks ahead. He wanted her to know that, no matter his own crimes, he was not her father. He would not treat her so callously. And he was, if not honest, the best man he knew how to be.

"Then why," she finally asked, "if you're here for Mick and the money, did you come after me?"

He dropped his gaze to the ground, took a deep breath, then looked up. "Because I couldn't do either of those things until I found you."

"But you had no reason to find me. You have no stake in what happens to me," she said, bringing her fingers in a rush to her mouth. "Oh, Zeb. Without you, I would never have known what had happened to Mick. I would still be working for Miss Porter." She swallowed, her lips trembling. "If you hadn't come after me, I would never have seen you again."

Oh, that was where she was so very wrong. But he was stopped from saying so by the crack of twigs off to the side, and before he could reach for his gun, two men with theirs cocked and drawn came into view.

Chapter 7

MAEVE spun in the same direction as Zeb, her hands going to her mouth to muffle her cry, but the effort was too late and in vain. The man she assumed was in charge waved his gun in her direction, eyeing her rather than Zeb. He and his companion were both filthy, as if they'd been riding for days, stirring up dust, using the coating as some sort of disguise.

Or perhaps they were simply as uncouth as they were dangerous, because not for a moment did she think either man incapable of pulling the trigger. The mottled moonlight shining down through the trees showed her that in their eyes. They glinted with a hard and violent purpose, not unlike the look of the rats in Bone Alley as they scurried about with bold disregard.

"Miss Daugherty, I presume?" the nearest man asked. "Your uncle said a lot of nice things about you, but damn, the man could *not* hold his drink or his cards, I'm sorry to say. Sorry for you, that is."

"What do you want?" Zeb asked, having moved to guard her with his body in front of hers.

The other man came closer to Mick's grave and looked down. "I want what's owed me. And since I won't be getting it from him"—he kicked the toe of his boot into the pile of loose dirt—"I'll just have to get it from his kin. In whatever way I can."

Maeve looked up at Zeb in time to see his gaze harden and glint like railroad steel. "I don't know who you are, but you won't be laying a finger on Miss Daugherty and living to tell the tale."

"Lewis Brady's who I am," he said, "and this is my friend Sharp. Sharp here's got a thing for redheads, and my holding the note on Mick's debt means I'll get to see if he's right about how sweet—"

Zeb stepped forward and swung, connecting with air as Brady feinted away. But Zeb wasn't deterred. He spun and charged at the man like a bull, his boot heels stirring a cloud from the freshly turned earth.

Maeve cried out.

She needed Zeb. Oh, she needed him. For so many reasons. In so many ways. Losing him now . . . The thought choked her, crushing her chest as his protective efforts seemed close to costing him his life. If only he weren't outnumbered. If only the derringer in her pocket were more powerful. But if she got it to him, because she'd never fired a gun in her life and feared making things worse, at least he'd have—

Two guns cocking brought Zeb up short, and put an end to her thoughts. Brady dug his gun barrel into the hollow of Zeb's throat, and Sharp pressed his to Zeb's ear. Brady laughed. Sharp, a ragged skinny frame and silent thus far, laughed, too. Maeve rushed to Zeb's side, holding tightly to his arm as they were forced from the site of Mick's hanging through the copse of trees and back to their camp.

They settled side by side on his bedroll and watched as Brady searched their belongings, taking Zeb's weapons and tools, and most of their food, before leading their horses away. Sharpe kept his gaze—and his gun—trained in their direction the entire time, preventing Maeve from slipping the derringer to Zeb.

They were two full days' ride from San Antonio. Walking back would take them longer, but they were both strong and healthy, with a will to survive. They'd be fine. She had to believe that. They'd have nothing, but they'd be together. If the men didn't separate them. If the men left them alive.

"I should've waited for you," she whispered, frightened by the course of her thoughts. "The horses were still here when I woke, so I knew you hadn't gone far. This is all my fault."

He wrapped an arm around her and brought her close. His body was firm and solid and she wanted to soak in his strength. "I don't even want to think about what might've happened if Brady had found you alone."

She breathed deeply, his leather and musk and woodsy fragrance a comfort. "Would it have mattered if something had? Truly? There's no one at home to miss me any more than anyone will miss Mick."

"Don't say that—"

"It's true." And how sad that they had that in common. "Mick was the only one in my corner. He was the only one who understood what I hoped to accomplish . . . And now, with what you've told me about my father, it seems that nothing in my life was even real."

He lowered his head, pressed his lips to her brow, warmed her and calmed her. "You are the most real person I know. You don't hide behind causes the way your mother does. And I've seen you show more than one weak-chinned boy to the door once he starts calculating your father's true worth."

"I can't believe you've noticed those things." The very things she had most recently resented.

"I notice everything."

For a very simple reason. "Because you're paid to do so."

"Not those things," he said, shaking his head.

"Then why?"

He used a crooked finger to lift her chin, forcing her gaze up to his. "Because you deserve to be noticed."

She waited a minute, let his caring for her settle, let the flutter of joy in her chest come to a rest, then said, "Oh, Zeb. I think you're going to break my heart."

"Then I'll be here to put it back together," he told her, and her flutter spread its wings and soared.

"Enough with all the whispering over there. Shut up and go to sleep."

Maeve tucked her skirt around her legs and laid her head on Zeb's thigh. She couldn't imagine either of them would sleep, but soon enough the sun was rising, her eyes coming open to bright rays slicing through the treetops— and to the picture of Zeb with his hands laced on top of his head, Brady's gun waving in front of his face.

"Back away, Crow. You keep your distance or I'll make sure you hang from the same tree as ol' Mick did. In fact," he said, cocking the hammer on his gun and stepping over the remains of the fire to where Maeve had pushed up to sit, "why don't I send you to meet your Maker now and be done with it?"

"You can't," she said, jumping to her feet and ignoring the burning in her stomach as she shoved past Brady to where Zeb stood, and faced the outlaw head-on.

"And why's that?" he asked, Zeb cursing ruthlessly behind her.

She thought fast and didn't blink even once as she told the lie. "Because I know where Mick hid the money. And if you harm a hair on Zebulon's head, I will go to my grave without telling you."

*Y*OU *need to keep her safe. Promise me you'll keep her safe.*

Mick's hastily scrawled words churned in Zeb's gut. He knew the type of man Brady was. He knew what he was capable of. Maeve holding the carrot of Mick's money in front of the outlaw's nose was the only reason Zeb was still thinking straight. She'd done what he'd been unable to—bought them both time. But he had to get to her before Brady bit. Once he realized Maeve was bluffing . . .

Zeb refused to entertain thoughts of what might happen to her then. It was bad enough she was out there alone in his company.

The two had left at sunup. Neither Zeb nor Maeve had slept much, though she'd dozed against his thigh in fits and starts. He didn't imagine Brady would stop long for the night, if at all, and unless Maeve cleverly thought of a way to delay them, the pace he'd set as they left would put them in San Antonio the next day.

Zeb could move faster, and ride straight through, arriving at Fannie Porter's not long after. Because that was where he knew Maeve would take the other man.

It was where she had allies. It was where she had the best chance at being safe. It was the most logical place for her to have hidden the money Mick had left her.

Except he hadn't left her anything. There wasn't any money to hide.

He looked over at Brady's man Sharp where he sat staring at the sun, as if watching it set would make time pass faster. "You going to cut me loose?"

"Brady said sundown. It ain't sundown."

"It's close enough."

"It ain't sundown," the man reiterated with enough meanness to have Zeb's own stirring.

"You're taking my horse, leaving me on foot. What can another half hour matter? Give me that so I can gather what I need for the night while I've still got light to see by."

Sharp pushed up to his feet and hawked up a big wad he spat to the ground. Zeb was doing his best not to rile the other man, and instead to reinforce Sharp's false belief that he held all the cards. The man seemed to believe the lie was true, because he made his cocky way to where Zeb was tied to the trunk of a tree, leaning down to loosen the knot of the rope as if doing so was a big favor Zeb would owe him for.

Zeb turned his head, as much to avoid the stench of horse shit that clung to the man as to give himself the advantage of body weight. He freed his hand and swung his arm, his fist landing solidly against his captor's neck. The other man stumbled, reaching for the Colt at his hip, but Zeb was there, his finger slipping through to the trigger and pulling as he forced the barrel down.

The shot sent the other man stumbling backward, screaming and writhing as he fell. Zeb yanked the gun from the holster and stood, watching Brady's man cradle his foot and wail. "It could've been worse, you know. I could've aimed for your nuts."

"Fuck you, Crow. Fuck you."

"Yeah, I figured you might be thinking that, but here's the thing." He set about gathering up his and Maeve's belongings and redistributing the weight between his two horses. "I'm going to leave you your horse. As long as you can boost your way onto his back, you can get out of here and find yourself a doc to see to that wound."

"If I don't bleed to death first."

"You won't bleed to death. And you won't even have to walk on that foot. But you might keep it bound up in your saddle so you don't drip a trail that might bring a pack of wild critters after you." That said, he swung onto the back of his horse, tipping his hat to the man on the ground still cursing and crying and now no threat at all.

Zeb held his horse's reins in one hand, those of the packhorse in the other. Not the most efficient or comfortable way to ride, but he'd make better time without the second animal tied to the first. And time was critical. He had to get to Maeve before it was too late.

He couldn't lose everything that mattered to him again.

Chapter 8

───∾∾∾──────

"I NEED to stop now. Not in another few miles." Stopping to relieve herself would require Lewis Brady to untie her hands, and Maeve needed her hands free. She had no doubt Zeb would be coming after her, but that didn't mean she could wait to be rescued. The outlaw guarding Zeb could very well foil any plans he made to get away. Could kill him even, and leave him tied to the tree where she'd last seen him—a thought that brought fear to stab at her heart.

"You can sit another hour," Brady said, plodding on. "Then once I have what's mine—"

"It's not yours. I have more rights to it than you do."

He glanced over, his expression as foul as the stench rising from his person and his clothes. "You think so, huh?"

"Yes. After all, my uncle took it from my father," she said, hoping this game of pretend would save her life and Zeb's.

"Well, now it belongs to me. Every bit of it." He gave

a scoffing sort of laugh. "Guess losing all those games to ol' Mick didn't turn out so bad after all."

If only, if only, *if only* her hands were untied . . . "You didn't have to kill him."

"Sure I did. He left without settling his debt." His tone was careless. And callous. "That's what they call an eye for an eye."

"You took his life," she said. "How is that at all equal to the loss of a few dollars?"

He waved a dirty hand at her. "Oh, stop with the bellyaching."

She waited until she felt able to speak without spewing all her stored hatred. "If you will stop for my aching belly," she said, too desperate to give sway to embarrassment, "I won't say another word until we reach San Antonio."

"You do and you'll only have yourself to blame for what happens," he said as he reached for her reins and brought both horses to a halt, holding her gaze while he untied her. She dismounted as slowly as possible, then circled behind a small thicket of brush, taking her time there, too.

She wished she had figured out what Uncle Mick had been up to, she mused, staring at the parched ground and the industrious ants scurrying from crack to crack. She'd been curious enough about his comings and goings to follow him, but she hadn't confronted him with what she'd seen, and she regretted that now more than she could put into words.

If she had, perhaps he would have confessed the truth of the trouble he was in, or even how he'd come to have money to gamble away in the first place. They could easily have settled his debts before they grew too large, and returned to New York.

No, Mick would not have wanted to face her father, and she certainly would not have wished to go back to the life she'd left there, but at least Mick would be alive. She would have endured anything, and would even now, to have him with her again, the thought bringing her pent-up tears to flow.

"You'd better be hurrying it up now, Miss Daugherty," Lewis Brady called, a snarl in his voice, "before I'm of a mind to come see for myself what the holdup is."

The idea of his doing so had Maeve returning to her horse, wiping her eyes with her blouse's filthy cuffs, then wiping her nose. Still, she took her time walking and took even more mounting her horse unassisted, doing her best to create a delay.

Seated again, her pocketed derringer resting against her thigh, she prayed that Zeb wasn't far behind. She didn't want to be forced to use the gun before she and Brady reached their destination. Having an outlaw for company was still better than riding alone through this barely tamed land would be.

By the time they arrived in San Antonio, Maeve's stomach was tight with nerves and dread. Brady had left her hands untied, allowing her to rub at the red marks on her wrists as they made their way through the wildly bustling city to Fannie Porter's boardinghouse.

Her captor dismounted first, secured both of their horses, then reached up to lift her from her saddle. He held tight to her upper arm, guiding her while using her body as a shield, and giving her no chance to reach for the derringer.

Once through the front door, Brady leaned close to her ear. "Say nothin' to nobody, you got it? Get the damn bag and hand it over. We walk out the way we walked in. You ride with me as far as the edge of town, then I don't give a shit what you do."

What had he just said? "You're leaving me behind?"

"I sure as hell ain't taking you with me."

"But, Zeb—"

"Hope you said your proper good-byes last night because that was it for you two lovebirds."

Maeve gasped, her knees buckling. Brady's grip tightened as the whispers from the girls in the parlor began, but she didn't need his warning as he dragged her along. What she needed was a plan, because at the moment she couldn't think beyond what Zeb might already be suffering at the hands of Brady's man.

The derringer was in her pocket, and though she'd had no time to learn its workings, she slid her hand around it, hugging the grip with her palm and resting her finger on the trigger mechanism. As soon as he released her to step toward the closet, she'd turn, she'd fire—*damn the layers of her skirt in the way!*—and she'd pray.

They were almost clear of the grand parlor when Miss Porter met them at the hallway leading to Maeve's old room, her brows arched, her lips pursed as she looked from Maeve to Brady and back. Maeve wasn't sure whether to panic or breathe a sigh of relief.

"Miss Daugherty. I'm surprised to see you again so soon."

Maeve held the other woman's gaze, pleading silently for her to hold her questions. "I wasn't planning to return, but when Mr. Crow and I ran into Mr. Brady, I was reminded that I left something in my room. I hope you haven't let it out again already. And that I can still access the closet."

"The closet?" Miss Porter had been in the room looking on when Maeve had emptied the small storage space and the bureau drawers.

Maeve nodded. "I had a second carpetbag. I was holding on to it for my uncle. It slipped my mind that it was still in the top."

"I see. And, yes. You're most welcome to fetch anything you left in the room." She turned then to Maeve's captor. "Mr. Brady, is it? Could I have one of the girls get you a bourbon or a brandy while you wait?"

"No need," Brady said, his fingers gouging Maeve's upper arm. "I'll be accompanying Miss Daugherty here."

"I'm sorry. I can't allow that." Miss Porter stepped to block the hallway, her right hand slipping into the pocket of her bronze skirt. "No one but the girls who work for me are permitted into my private rooms."

"Miss Daugherty don't work for you, ma'am."

"No, but she did," she said, her pocketed hand coming up with a soft click. "That makes her one of mine. And I always take care of mine."

Brady bit off a curse, releasing Maeve and sidling away as Miss Porter gestured. Before he could make another move, or Maeve could flee, a commotion sounded behind them in the front room . . . a clattering of furniture and doors slamming and voices raised in shouted warnings. Male voices, deep and full of demands.

Resignation pulled angrily at the corners of Brady's mouth, while a smile spread over Miss Porter's. Maeve took her cue from the other woman, breathing deeply as she turned back for the parlor, the other two directly behind.

The scene the group walked into stopped Maeve in her tracks. Brady slammed to a halt as well. Miss Porter pressed her fingers to her mouth to hold back what sounded to Maeve like laughter. Brady wasn't laughing at all, and no wonder.

Zeb stood behind the parlor's center settee, his hands curled over the frame near the shoulders of the two men who sat there. Both were scruffy and dusty and in extreme need of a bath. Such was often the case with those of their ilk who used Miss Porter's brothel as a stop-off when on the run from the law.

"Desperate" had always been the word to come to mind when Maeve had heard tales of Robert LeRoy Parker, the leader of the Wild Bunch. She'd thought the same of his accomplice, Harry Alonzo Longabaugh, whose girlfriend, Etta Place, was one of Fannie Porter's girls. And, desperate or not, the tableau made for the most perfect greeting.

Robert sat on the right, one ankle squared over the opposite knee, a gun balanced on his calf and pointed at Brady. Harry sat forward, his elbows on his thighs, his gun held with both hands and aimed in the same direction. Maeve could only surmise, based on the men's expressions, that Lewis Brady was not a friend of either Butch Cassidy or the Sundance Kid.

She was relishing the scene when Brady suddenly spun away from Miss Porter, backing into the nearest wall and pulling Maeve to his chest. With his free hand he reached for the gun at his hip. But he was slow getting it out of the holster, and Maeve still had her hand in her pocket.

She palmed the derringer, shoved the barrel into Brady's abdomen, and looked up as she cocked it. Brady froze and looked down—not into her face but at the hard piece of metal wrapped in her skirt's fabric that was easily distinguishable as the weapon it was.

He released her arm, cursing beneath his breath, and raised both his hands. Zeb came purposefully around the settee, grabbed Brady's gun, and took her aside, reaching into her pocket for the derringer. He shook his head with disbelief, asking, "You had a gun?"

Before she could speak, however, he put her behind him and backed them across the room, where she held his arm and peered from around his side. Robert and Harry pushed up from the settee as one, neither holstering his weapon, both giving Brady a look that had Maeve trembling. Things after that happened quickly.

Miss Porter herded her girls from the parlor toward the kitchen at the same time that the two Wild Bunch members escorted Lewis Brady from the room and out the front door. Only after it closed did anyone speak, though Maeve ignored the shrill chatter, having only one question for Zeb.

She looked up into his blue eyes and thought she might drown. "Are you okay? Did the man he left you with hurt you?"

His arm tightened around her waist. "As long as you're fine, I'm fine."

"I thought you—"

"Stop thinking, Maeve. You need food and sleep and a hot bath. The hotel down the street—"

"You're not taking her anywhere," Miss Porter said, obviously having heard part of their conversation. "And if you don't think a woman can stop you, let me remind you of what happened not ten minutes ago." Her tone was firm, her jaw set.

And still Zeb laughed before saying, "Yes, ma'am."

When the other woman bit off some choice words, Maeve wanted to laugh, too, but held her tongue.

Once again composed, Miss Porter said to Zeb, "She needs a bath. She needs clean clothes. She needs a night's sleep in a decent bed. Upstairs. If she doesn't wish for you to join her," she added, and Maeve felt her whole body flush, "you can sleep in the room she was using while in my employ. But she is staying the night. And that's that."

"THIS seems so . . . scandalous," Maeve said, perched on the foot of the plush bed, bouncing in agitation as she watched Zeb rid himself of his gun belt and boots.

Her throat was tight. Her chest was tight. Even her fingers were tight where she curled them into the quilt. It felt as if it were filled with feathers and clouds and air. "So totally inappropriate. So indecent. Are you sure—"

He turned to her with a gaze that burned, his deft fingers making quick work of his vest buttons and his shirt, stripping both garments away until his torso was left beautifully bare. "I couldn't give less of a damn what anyone thinks is proper or seemly or anything close to appropriate. All I care about is you being safe."

"I don't know why," she said, scooting away from him to the center of the bed, her heart in her throat, an ache blooming in her breasts and in her limbs, in her belly, and below.

He followed her, crawled over her, his weight on one elbow as he looked down. His beard was dark, his hair, falling forward, was dark, and his chest was shadowed with a pelt that was equally so. All that darkness and yet she felt no fear, only anticipation and hunger and nervousness at the unknown.

"The last three years in New York, you made it bearable. You were like a light, always burning, always there. My life . . ." He brushed her hair from her face, drawing his fingers against her scalp until her body wanted to burst from the lightning-bolt shivers. "Everything in it had been dark for so long."

She didn't want to think about her father's criminal dealings. She didn't want to think about her father at all. It confused and angered her. The idea that she was important to Zebulon, this man who had rescued her and protected her when no one else would, that was all that mattered right now. . . .

She reached up and brushed a fall of hair from his

brow, following the strands with her fingers and tucking them behind his ear. His eyes were so very bright, so very blue. She wondered what he saw when he looked at her, because she saw her entire life when she looked at him.

His gaze softened, the lines at the corners of his eyes deepening as he smiled, and bringing to mind tiny footprints, as if happiness had stepped there and stayed. "You are my world and my life. I love you, Maeve Daugherty."

"Then you don't hold that night in my father's library against me?"

He dropped his forehead to hers, breathed heavily before asking her, "Do you know how hard it was for me not to undress you then and there?"

The very idea left her breathless, as if her heart had swelled to squeeze the air from her lungs. "And what would you have done if you had?"

"Do you want me to tell you? Or do you want me to show you?"

Instead of answering, she smiled and lay back in the deliciously decadent bed on the second floor of Fannie Porter's brothel. "I want to ask you something first."

He nuzzled his cheek to her neck. "What's that?"

"Are we going back to New York?" When he shook his head, hope blossomed within her. "Are we going to stay here?"

He leaned his head to the side and considered her like he might a valuable gem. "In Texas? Yeah. I think so. But in San Antonio only long enough to get married." When she didn't respond right away—how could she when his words wouldn't settle long enough for her to grab them?— he asked, "What's wrong?"

She was frowning when she came back with, "Did you just ask me to marry you?"

The grin that broke across his face had her toes curling in her stockings. "I believe that was exactly what I was asking you. Unless that's not what you want."

"It's everything I want," she said and kissed him. "Oh, Zeb. I love you."

"Good. Because I love you, too."

"So now that we've settled that, are you going to show me?"

"If that's what you want," he said, arching a brow in question.

She pushed at his shoulder and tumbled him back, rolling over him and climbing up to straddle his thighs. He moved his hands to her waist, spanning her as if she were the tiniest thing in the world. He held her gaze for a long, tender moment before bringing his hands to her shoulders, then quickly to her face, pulling her mouth down to his.

But before she kissed him, she told him, "What I want is you." And truer words had never been spoken.

Alison Kent is the bestselling author of nearly fifty novels, novellas, and short stories written across multiple subgenres: contemporary, action-adventure, romantic suspense, and erotic romance. She is very active online in the reading and writing community, and lives in Houston with her petroleum geologist husband and three rescue dogs, one a Hurricane Katrina survivor. Visit her website at alisonkent.com.

Don't miss her latest Dalton Gang novel, *Unforgettable*, available now from Berkley Heat. Turn to the back of this book for a sneak preview.

BETTING THE RAINBOW

by Jodi Thomas

Available April 2014 from Berkley

New York Times bestselling author Jodi Thomas returns
to the town of Harmony, Texas, where life has a way of
making better plans than anyone ever imagined . . .

Sisters Abby and Dusti Delaney have spent their entire
lives on Rainbow Lane, but they dream of something
bigger. So when a poker tournament comes to town, Dusti
is determined to win enough money to pay for Abby to
finish school. Enlisting expert Kieran O'Toole to teach
her the game, Dusti feels the sparks fly as they play their
hands. But Kieran refuses to stand in the way of her
dream, even if it means losing her forever . . .

After a year of traveling, Ronny Logan is settling into
a home on Rainbow Lane, but that's all the settling she'll
be doing. Ronny refuses to fall for anyone, regardless of
the chemistry she has with her neighbor Austin Hawk.
Still, something undeniable begins to grow between the
two loners—if only they can let their barriers fall and
open their hearts . . .

In Want of a Wife

by Jo Goodman

Coming May 2014 from Berkley Sensation

She has nowhere left to turn . . .

Jane Middlebourne needs a way out. In 1891, life in New York is unforgiving for a young woman with no prospects, especially when her family wants nothing to do with her. So when Jane discovers an ad for a mail-order bride needed in Bitter Springs, Wyoming, she responds with a hopeful heart.

He has everything to lose . . .

Rancher Morgan Longstreet is in want of a wife who will be his partner at Morning Star, someone who will work beside him and stand by him. His first impression of the fair and fragile Jane is that she is not that woman. But when she sets out to prove him wrong, the secrets he cannot share put into jeopardy every happiness they hope to find . . .

WHERE THE HORSES RUN

by Kaki Warner

Coming July 2014 from Berkley Sensation

"A truly original new voice,"* award-winning author
Kaki Warner returns to the characters of Heartbreak
Creek, Colorado, as a troubled cowboy and a desperate
Englishwoman come together to mend their mistakes
from the past and create an exciting new future . . .

Wounded in body and spirit after a shootout, Rayford
Jessup leaves his career as a lawman and uses his gift
with damaged horses to bring meaning to his solitary life.
Hired by a Scotsman in Heartbreak Creek, Colorado, to
purchase thoroughbreds, he travels to England, unaware
that a traumatized horse and a beautiful Englishwoman
will change his life forever.

Josephine Cathcart loves two things: her illegitimate
son and her injured stallion. Faced with her father's looming bankruptcy, she must choose between a loveless marriage to the man who ruined her, or risk her horse and
her future on a handsome, taciturn Texan and a high-
stakes horse race. But as vengeful forces conspire against
them, will Rafe's love and healing touch be enough to
save her horse and protect her and her son . . .

*Jodi Thomas, *New York Times*

UNFORGETTABLE
by Alison Kent

Available now from Berkley Heat

The Dalton boys take the reigns . . .

The infamous Dalton Gang was once known for riding—
and playing—hard. Now, as owners of the Dalton Ranch
in Crow Hill, Texas, they're working from sunup to sundown. But one look from the right woman can tempt them
back into the saddle . . .

When a walk on the wild side turned into a nightmare
for Everly Grant, she escaped her abusive ex by taking a
job with Crow Hill's small newspaper. Now she's assigned
to write a human interest story on the return of the Dalton
Gang, and she soon discovers that Boone Mitchell could
give her plenty more than a good interview. As much as
she craves safety, she finds herself irresistibly drawn to
Boone's dangerous streak. Before she takes the cowboy to
bed, she lays down the law: There are no strings attached,
and she's the one in charge.

That's fine for Boone. In fact, Everly teaches him
things no other woman ever dared. Soon they find themselves wanting more than their simple arrangement will
allow. But to get there, Everly will have to open up in
ways she thought she never could . . .